Twilight Sleep
(1927)

by

Edith Wharton

The Wildhern Press 2008

Published by

The Wildhern Press

131 High St.
Teddington
Middlesex TW11 8HH

ISBN 978-1-84830-912-8

FAUST. Und du, wer bist du?

SORGE. Bin einmal da.

FAUST. Entferne dich!

SORGE. Ich bin am rechten Ort.

--Faust. Teil II. Akt V.

BOOK I

I

Miss Bruss, the perfect secretary, received Nona Manford at the door of her mother's boudoir ("the office," Mrs. Manford's children called it) with a gesture of the kindliest denial.

"She wants to, you know, dear—your mother always WANTS to see you," pleaded Maisie Bruss, in a voice which seemed to be thinned and sharpened by continuous telephoning. Miss Bruss, attached to Mrs. Manford's service since shortly after the latter's second marriage, had known Nona from her childhood, and was privileged, even now that she was "out," to treat her with a certain benevolent familiarity—benevolence being the note of the Manford household.

"But look at her list—just for this morning!" the secretary continued, handing over a tall morocco-framed tablet, on which was inscribed, in the colourless secretarial hand: "7.30 Mental uplift. 7.45 Breakfast. 8. Psycho-analysis. 8.15 See cook. 8.30 Silent Meditation. 8.45 Facial massage. 9. Man with Persian miniatures. 9.15 Correspondence. 9.30 Manicure. 9.45 Eurythmic exercises. 10. Hair waved. 10.15 Sit for bust. 10.30 Receive Mothers' Day deputation. 11. Dancing lesson. 11.30 Birth Control committee at Mrs.—"

"The manicure is there now, late as usual. That's what martyrizes your mother; everybody's being so unpunctual. This New York life is killing her."

"I'm not unpunctual," said Nona Manford, leaning in the doorway.

"No; and a miracle, too! The way you girls keep up your dancing all night. You and Lita—what times you two do have!" Miss Bruss was becoming almost maternal. "But just run your eye down that list—. You see your mother didn't EXPECT to see you before lunch; now did she?"

Nona shook her head. "No; but you might perhaps squeeze me in."

It was said in a friendly, a reasonable tone; on both sides the matter was being examined with an evident desire for impartiality and good-will. Nona was used to her mother's engagements; used to being squeezed in between faith-healers, art-dealers, social service workers and manicures. When Mrs. Manford did see her children she was perfect to them; but in this killing New York life, with its ever-multiplying duties and responsibilities, if her family had been allowed to tumble in at all hours and devour her time, her nervous system simply couldn't have stood it—and how many duties would have been left undone!

Mrs. Manford's motto had always been: "There's a time for everything." But there were moments when this optimistic view failed her, and she began to think there wasn't. This morning, for instance, as Miss Bruss pointed out, she had had to tell the new French sculptor who had been all the rage in New York for the last month that she wouldn't be able to sit to him for more than fifteen minutes, on account of the Birth Control committee meeting at 11.30 at Mrs.—

Nona seldom assisted at these meetings, her own time being—through force of habit rather than real inclination—so fully taken up with exercise, athletics and the ceaseless rush from thrill to thrill which was supposed to be the happy privilege of youth. But she had had glimpses enough of the scene: of the audience of bright elderly women, with snowy hair, eurythmic movements, and finely-wrinkled over-massaged faces on which a smile of glassy benevolence sat like their rimless pince-nez. They were all inexorably earnest, aimlessly kind and fathomlessly pure; and all rather too well- dressed, except the "prominent woman" of the occasion, who usually wore dowdy clothes, and had steel-rimmed spectacles and straggling wisps of hair. Whatever the question dealt with, these ladies always seemed to be the same, and always advocated with equal zeal Birth Control and unlimited maternity, free love or the return to the traditions of the American home; and neither they nor Mrs. Manford seemed aware that there was anything contradictory in these doctrines. All they knew was that they were determined to force certain persons to do things that those persons preferred not to do. Nona, glancing down the serried list, recalled a saying of her mother's former husband, Arthur Wyant: "Your mother and her friends would like to teach the whole world how to say its prayers and brush its teeth."

The girl had laughed, as she could never help laughing at Wyant's sallies; but in reality she admired her mother's zeal, though she sometimes wondered if it were not a little too promiscuous. Nona was the daughter of Mrs. Manford's second marriage, and her own father, Dexter Manford, who had had to make his way in the world, had taught her to revere activity as a virtue in itself; his tone in speaking of Pauline's zeal was very different from Wyant's. He had been brought up to think there was a virtue in work per se, even if it served no more useful purpose than the revolving of a squirrel in a wheel. "Perhaps your mother tries to cover too much ground; but it's very fine of her, you know—she never spares herself."

"Nor us!" Nona sometimes felt tempted to add; but Manford's admiration was contagious. Yes; Nona did admire her mother's altruistic energy; but she knew well enough that neither she nor her brother's wife Lita would ever follow such an example—she no more than Lita. They belonged to another generation: to the bewildered disenchanted young people who had grown up since the Great War, whose energies were more spasmodic and less definitely directed, and who, above all, wanted a more personal outlet for them. "Bother earthquakes in Bolivia!" Lita had once whispered to Nona, when Mrs. Manford had convoked the bright elderly women to deal with a seismic disaster at the other end of the world, the repetition of which these ladies somehow felt could be avoided if they sent out a commission immediately to teach the Bolivians to do something they didn't want to do—not to BELIEVE in earthquakes, for instance.

The young people certainly felt no corresponding desire to set the houses of others in order. Why shouldn't the Bolivians have earthquakes if they chose to live in Bolivia? And why must Pauline Manford lie awake over it in New York, and have to learn a new set of Mahatma exercises to dispel the resulting wrinkles? "I suppose if we feel like that it's really because we're too lazy to care," Nona reflected, with her incorrigible honesty.

She turned from Miss Bruss with a slight shrug. "Oh, well," she murmured.

"You know, pet," Miss Bruss volunteered, "things always get worse as the season goes on; and the last fortnight in February is the worst of all, especially with Easter coming as early as it does this year. I never COULD see why they picked out such an awkward date for Easter: perhaps those Florida hotel people did it. Why, your poor mother wasn't even able to see your father this morning before he went down town, though she thinks it's ALL WRONG to let him go off to his office like that, without finding time for a quiet little chat first. . . Just a cheery word to put him in the right mood for the day. . . Oh, by the way, my dear, I wonder if you happen to have heard him say if he's dining at home tonight? Because you know he never DOES remember to leave word about his plans, and if he hasn't, I'd better telephone to the office to remind him that it's the night of the big dinner for the Marchesa—"

"Well, I don't think father's dining at home," said the girl indifferently.

"Not—not—not? Oh, my gracious!" clucked Miss Bruss, dashing across the room to the telephone on her own private desk.

The engagement-list had slipped from her hands, and Nona Manford, picking it up, ran her glance over it. She read: "4 P.M. See A.— 4.30 P.M. Musical: Torfried Lobb."

"4 P.M. See A." Nona had been almost sure it was Mrs. Manford's day for going to see her divorced husband, Arthur Wyant, the effaced mysterious person always designated on Mrs. Manford's lists as "A," and hence known to her children as "Exhibit A." It was rather a bore, for Nona had meant to go and see him herself at about that hour, and she always timed her visits so that they should not clash with Mrs. Manford's, not because the latter disapproved of Nona's friendship with Arthur Wyant (she thought it "beautiful" of the girl to show him so much kindness), but because Wyant and Nona were agreed that on these occasions the presence of the former Mrs. Wyant spoilt their fun. But there was nothing to do about it. Mrs. Manford's plans were unchangeable. Even illness and death barely caused a ripple in them. One might as well have tried to bring down one of the Pyramids by poking it with a parasol as attempt to disarrange the close mosaic of Mrs. Manford's engagement-list. Mrs. Manford herself couldn't have done it; not with the best will in the world; and Mrs. Manford's will, as her children and all her household knew, WAS the best in the world.

Nona Manford moved away with a final shrug. She had wanted to speak to her mother about something rather important; something she had caught a startled glimpse of, the evening before, in the queer little half-formed mind of her sister-in-law Lita, the wife of her half-brother Jim Wyant—the Lita with whom, as Miss Bruss remarked, she, Nona, danced away the nights. There was nobody on earth as dear to Nona as that same Jim, her elder by six or seven years, and who had been brother, comrade, guardian, almost father to her—her own father, Dexter Manford, who was so clever, capable and kind, being almost always too busy at the office, or too firmly requisitioned by Mrs. Manford, when he was at home, to be able to spare much time for his daughter.

Jim, bless him, always had time; no doubt that was what his mother meant when she called him lazy—as lazy as his father, she had once added, with one of her rare flashes of impatience. Nothing so conduced to impatience in Mrs. Manford as the thought of anybody's having the least fraction of unapportioned time and not immediately planning to do something with it. If only they could have given it to HER! And Jim, who loved and admired her (as all her family did) was always conscientiously trying to fill his days, or to conceal from her their occasional vacuity. But he had a way of not being in a hurry, and this had been all to the good for little Nona, who could always count on him to ride or walk with her, to slip off with her to a concert or a "movie," or, more pleasantly still, just to BE THERE—idling in the big untenanted library of Cedarledge, the place in the country, or in his untidy study on the third floor of the town house, and ready to answer questions, help her to look up hard words in dictionaries, mend her golf-sticks, or get a thorn out of her Sealyham's paw. Jim was wonderful with his hands: he could repair clocks, start up mechanical toys, make fascinating models of houses or gardens, apply a tourniquet, scramble eggs, mimic his mother's visitors—preferably the "earnest" ones who held forth about "causes" or "messages" in her gilded drawing-rooms—and make delicious coloured maps of imaginary continents, concerning which Nona wrote interminable stories. And of all these gifts he had, alas, made no particular use as yet—except to enchant his little half-sister.

It had been just the same, Nona knew, with his father: poor useless "Exhibit A"! Mrs. Manford said it was their "old New York blood"— she spoke of them with mingled contempt and pride, as if they were the last of the Capetians, exhausted by a thousand years of sovereignty. Her own red corpuscles were tinged with a more plebeian dye. Her progenitors had mined in Pennsylvania and made bicycles at Exploit, and now gave their name to one of the most popular automobiles in the United States. Not that other ingredients were lacking in her hereditary make-up: her mother was said to have contributed southern gentility by being a Pascal of Tallahassee. Mrs. Manford, in certain moods, spoke of "The Pascals of Tallahassee" as if they accounted for all that was noblest in her; but when she was exhorting Jim to action it was her father's blood that she invoked. "After all, in spite of the Pascal tradition, there is no shame in being in trade. My father's father came over from Scotland with two sixpences in his pocket . . ." and Mrs. Manford would glance with pardonable pride at the glorious Gainsborough over the dining-room mantelpiece (which she sometimes almost mistook for an ancestral portrait), and at her healthy handsome family sitting about the dinner-table laden with Georgian silver and orchids from her own hot-houses.

From the threshold, Nona called back to Miss Bruss: "Please tell mother I shall probably be lunching with Jim and Lita—" but Miss Bruss was passionately saying to an unseen interlocutor: "Oh, but Mr. Rigley, but you MUST make Mr. Manford understand that Mrs. Manford counts on him for dinner this evening. . . The dinner- dance for the Marchesa, you know. . ."

The marriage of her half-brother had been Nona Manford's first real sorrow. Not that she had disapproved of his choice: how could any one take that funny irresponsible little Lita Cliffe seriously enough to disapprove of her? The sisters-in-law were soon the best of friends; if Nona had a fault to find with Lita, it was that she didn't worship the incomparable Jim as blindly as his sister did. But then Lita was made to be worshipped, not to worship; that was manifest in the calm gaze of her long narrow nut-coloured eyes, in the hieratic fixity of her lovely smile, in the very shape of her hands, so slim yet dimpled, hands which had never grown up, and which drooped from her wrists as if listlessly waiting to be kissed, or lay like rare shells or upcurved magnolia-petals on the cushions luxuriously piled about her indolent body.

The Jim Wyants had been married for nearly two years now; the baby was six months old; the pair were beginning to be regarded as one of the "old couples" of their set, one of the settled landmarks in the matrimonial quicksands of New York. Nona's love for her brother was too disinterested for her not to rejoice in this: above all things she wanted her old Jim to be happy, and happy she was sure he was—or had been until lately. The mere getting away from Mrs. Manford's iron rule had been a greater relief than he himself perhaps guessed. And then he was still the foremost of Lita's worshippers; still enchanted by the childish whims, the unpunctuality, the irresponsibility, which made life with her such a thrillingly unsettled business after the clock-work routine of his mother's perfect establishment.

All this Nona rejoiced in; but she ached at times with the loneliness of the perfect establishment, now that Jim, its one disturbing element, had left. Jim guessed her loneliness, she was sure: it was he who encouraged the growing intimacy between his wife and his half-sister, and tried to make the latter feel that his house was another home to her.

Lita had always been amiably disposed toward Nona. The two, though so fundamentally different, were nearly of an age, and united by the prevailing passion for every form of sport. Lita, in spite of her soft curled-up attitudes, was not only a tireless dancer but a brilliant if uncertain tennis-player, and an adventurous rider to hounds. Between her hours of lolling, and smoking amber-scented cigarettes, every moment of her life was crammed with dancing, riding or games. During the two or three months before the baby's birth, when Lita had been reduced to partial inactivity, Nona had rather feared that her perpetual craving for new "thrills" might lead to some insidious form of time-killing—some of the drinking or drugging that went on among the young women of their set; but Lita had sunk into a state of smiling animal patience, as if the mysterious work going on in her tender young body had a sacred significance for her, and it was enough to lie still and let it happen. All she asked was that nothing should "hurt" her: she had the blind dread of physical pain common also to most of the young women of her set. But all that was so easily managed nowadays: Mrs. Manford (who took charge of the business, Lita being an orphan) of course knew the most perfect "Twilight Sleep" establishment in the country, installed Lita in its most luxurious suite, and filled her rooms with spring flowers, hot-house fruits, new novels and all the latest picture-papers—and Lita drifted into motherhood as lightly and unperceivingly as if the wax doll which suddenly appeared in the cradle at her bedside had been brought there in one of the big bunches of hot-house roses that she found every morning on her pillow.

"Of course there ought to be no Pain . . . nothing but Beauty. . . It ought to be one of the loveliest, most poetic things in the world to have a baby," Mrs. Manford declared, in that bright efficient voice which made loveliness and poetry sound like the attributes of an advanced industrialism, and babies something to be turned out in series like Fords. And Jim's joy in his son had been unbounded; and Lita really hadn't minded in the least.

II

The Marchesa was something which happened at irregular but inevitable moments in Mrs. Manford's life.

Most people would have regarded the Marchesa as a disturbance; some as a distinct inconvenience; the pessimistic as a misfortune. It was a matter of conscious pride to Mrs. Manford that, while recognizing these elements in the case, she had always contrived to make out of it something not only showy but even enviable.

For, after all, if your husband (even an ex-husband) has a first cousin called Amalasuntha degli Duchi di Lucera, who has married the Marchese Venturino di San Fedele, of one of the great Neapolitan families, it seems stupid and wasteful not to make some use of such a conjunction of names and situations, and to remember only (as the Wyants did) that when Amalasuntha came to New York it was always to get money, or to get her dreadful son out of a new scrape, or to consult the family lawyers as to some new way of guarding the remains of her fortune against Venturino's systematic depredations.

Mrs. Manford knew in advance the hopelessness of these quests—all of them, that is, except that which consisted in borrowing money from herself. She always lent Amalasuntha two or three thousand dollars (and put it down to the profit-and-loss column of her carefully-kept private accounts); she even gave the Marchesa her own last year's clothes, cleverly retouched; and in return she expected Amalasuntha to shed on the Manford entertainments that exotic lustre which the near relative of a Duke who is also a grandee of Spain and a great dignitary of the Papal Court trails with her through the dustiest by-ways, even if her mother has been a mere Mary Wyant of Albany.

Mrs. Manford had been successful. The Marchesa, without taking thought, fell naturally into the part assigned to her. In her stormy and uncertain life, New York, where her rich relations lived, and from which she always came back with a few thousand dollars, and clothes that could be made to last a year, and good advice about putting the screws on Venturino, was like a foretaste of heaven. "Live there? Carina, NO! It is too—too uneventful. As heaven must be. But everybody is celestially kind . . . and Venturino has learnt that there are certain things my American relations will not tolerate. . ." Such was Amalasuntha's version of her visits to New York, when she recounted them in the drawing-rooms of Rome, Naples or St. Moritz; whereas in New York, quite carelessly and unthinkingly—for no one was simpler at heart than Amalasuntha—she pronounced names, and raised suggestions, which cast a romantic glow of unreality over a world bounded by Wall Street on the south and Long Island in most other directions; and in this glow Pauline Manford was always eager to sun her other guests.

"My husband's cousin" (become, since the divorce from Wyant "my son's cousin") was still, after twenty-seven years, a useful social card. The Marchesa di San Fedele, now a woman of fifty, was still, in Pauline's set, a pretext for dinners, a means of paying off social scores, a small but steady luminary in the uncertain New York heavens. Pauline could never see her rather forlorn wisp of a figure, always clothed in careless unnoticeable black (even when she wore Mrs. Manford's old dresses), without a vision of echoing Roman staircases, of the torchlit arrival of Cardinals at the Lucera receptions, of a great fresco-like background of Popes, princes, dilapidated palaces, cypress-guarded villas, scandals, tragedies, and interminable feuds about inheritances.

"It's all so dreadful—the wicked lives those great Roman families lead. After all, poor Amalasuntha has good American blood in her— her mother was a Wyant; yes—Mary Wyant married Prince Ottaviano di Lago Negro, the Duke of Lucera's son, who used to be at the Italian Legation in Washington; but what is Amalasuntha to do, in a country where there's no divorce, and a woman just has to put up with EVERYTHING? The Pope has been most kind; he sides entirely with Amalasuntha. But Venturino's people are very powerful too—a great Neapolitan family—yes, Cardinal Ravello is Venturino's uncle . . . so that altogether it's been dreadful for Amalasuntha . . . and such an oasis to her, coming back to her own people. . ."

Pauline Manford was quite sincere in believing that it was dreadful for Amalasuntha. Pauline herself could conceive of nothing more shocking than a social organization which did not recognize divorce, and let all kinds of domestic evils fester undisturbed, instead of having people's lives disinfected and whitewashed at regular intervals, like the cellar. But while Mrs. Manford thought all this—in fact, in the very act of thinking it—she remembered that Cardinal Ravello, Venturino's uncle, had been mentioned as one of the probable delegates to the Roman Catholic Congress which was to meet at Baltimore that winter, and wondered whether an evening party for his Eminence could not be organized with Amalasuntha's help; even got as far as considering the effect of torch-bearing footmen (in silk stockings) lining the Manford staircase—which was of marble, thank goodness!—and of Dexter Manford and Jim receiving the Prince of the Church on the doorstep, and walking upstairs backward carrying silver candelabra; though Pauline wasn't sure she could persuade them to go as far as that.

Pauline felt no more inconsistency in this double train of thought than she did in shuddering at the crimes of the Roman Church and longing to receive one of its dignitaries with all the proper ceremonial. She was used to such rapid adjustments, and proud of the fact that whole categories of contradictory opinions lay down together in her mind as peacefully as the Happy Families exhibited by strolling circuses. And of course, if the Cardinal DID come to her house, she would show her American independence by inviting also the Bishop of New York—her own Episcopal Bishop—and possibly the Chief Rabbi (also a friend of hers), and certainly that wonderful much-slandered "Mahatma" in whom she still so thoroughly believed. . .

But the word pulled her up short. Yes; certainly she believed in the "Mahatma." She had every reason to. Standing before the tall threefold mirror in her dressing-room, she glanced into the huge bathroom beyond—which looked like a biological laboratory, with its white tiles, polished pipes, weighing machines, mysterious appliances for douches, gymnastics and "physical culture"—and recalled with gratitude that it was certainly those eurythmic exercises of the Mahatma's ("holy ecstasy," he called them) which had reduced her hips after everything else had failed. And this gratitude for the reduction of her hips was exactly on the same plane, in her neat card-catalogued mind, with her enthusiastic faith in his wonderful mystical teachings about Self-Annihilation, Anterior Existence and Astral Affinities . . . all so incomprehensible and so pure. . . Yes; she would certainly ask the Mahatma. It would do the Cardinal good to have a talk with him. She could almost hear his Eminence saying, in a voice shaken by emotion: "Mrs. Manford, I want to thank you for making me know that Wonderful Man. If it hadn't been for you—"

Ah, she did like people who said to her: "If it hadn't been for you—!"

The telephone on her dressing-table rang. Miss Bruss had switched on from the boudoir. Mrs. Manford, as she unhooked the receiver, cast a nervous glance at the clock. She was already seven minutes late for her Marcel-waving, and—

Ah: it was Dexter's voice! Automatically she composed her face to a wifely smile, and her voice to a corresponding intonation. "Yes? Pauline, dear. Oh—about dinner tonight? Why, you know, Amalasuntha. . . You say you're going to the theatre with Jim and Lita? But, Dexter, you can't! They're dining here—Jim and Lita are. But OF COURSE. . . Yes, it must have been a mistake; Lita's so flighty. . . I know. . ." (The smile grew a little pinched; the voice echoed it. Then, patiently): "Yes; what else? . . . OH. . . oh, Dexter. . . what do you mean? . . . The Mahatma? WHAT? I don't understand!"

But she did. She was conscious of turning white under her discreet cosmetics. Somewhere in the depths of her there had lurked for the last weeks an unexpressed fear of this very thing: a fear that the people who were opposed to the teaching of the Hindu sage—New York's great "spiritual uplift" of the last two years—were gaining power and beginning to be a menace. And here was Dexter Manford actually saying something about having been asked to conduct an investigation into the state of things at the Mahatma's "School of Oriental Thought," in which all sorts of unpleasantness might be involved. Of course Dexter never said much about professional matters on the telephone; he did not, to his wife's thinking, say enough about them when he got home. But what little she now gathered made her feel positively ill.

"Oh, Dexter, but I must see you about this! At once! You couldn't come back to lunch, I suppose? Not possibly? No—this evening there'll be no chance. Why, the dinner for Amalasuntha—oh, please don't forget it AGAIN!"

With one hand on the receiver, she reached with the other for her engagement-list (the duplicate of Miss Bruss's), and ran a nervous unseeing eye over it. A scandal—another scandal! It mustn't be. She loathed scandals. And besides, she did believe in the Mahatma. He had "vision." From the moment when she had picked up that word in a magazine article she had felt she had a complete answer about him. . .

"But I must see you before this evening, Dexter. Wait! I'm looking over my engagements." She came to "4 p.m. See A. 4.30 Musical—Torfried Lobb." No; she couldn't give up Torfried Lobb: she was one of the fifty or sixty ladies who had "discovered" him the previous winter, and she knew he counted on her presence at his recital. Well, then—for once "A" must be sacrificed.

"Listen, Dexter; if I were to come to the office at 4? Yes; sharp. Is that right? And don't do anything till I see you—promise!"

She hung up with a sigh of relief. She would try to readjust things so as to see "A" the next day; though readjusting her list in the height of the season was as exhausting as a major operation.

In her momentary irritation she was almost inclined to feel as if it were Arthur's fault for figuring on that day's list, and thus unsettling all her arrangements. Poor Arthur—from the first he had been one of her failures. She had a little cemetery of them—a very small one—planted over with quick-growing things, so that you might have walked all through her life and not noticed there were any graves in it. To the inexperienced Pauline of thirty years ago, fresh from the factory-smoke of Exploit, Arthur Wyant had symbolized the tempting contrast between a city absorbed in making money and a society bent on enjoying it. Such a brilliant figure— and nothing to show for it! She didn't know exactly what she had expected, her own ideal of manly achievement being at that time solely based on the power of getting rich faster than your neighbours—which Arthur would certainly never do. His father-in- law at Exploit had seen at a glance that it was no use taking him into the motor-business, and had remarked philosophically to Pauline: "Better just regard him as a piece of jewellery: I guess we can afford it."

But jewellery must at least be brilliant; and Arthur had somehow— faded. At one time she had hoped he might play a part in state politics—with Washington and its enticing diplomatic society at the end of the vista—but he shrugged that away as contemptuously as what he called "trade." At Cedarledge he farmed a little, fussed over the accounts, and muddled away her money till she replaced him by a trained superintendent; and in town he spent hours playing bridge at his club, took an intermittent interest in racing, and went and sat every afternoon with his mother, old Mrs. Wyant, in the dreary house near Stuyvesant Square which had never been "done over," and was still lit by Carcel lamps.

An obstacle and a disappointment; that was what he had always been. Still, she would have borne with his inadequacy, his resultless planning, dreaming and dawdling, even his growing tendency to drink, as the wives of her generation were taught to bear with such failings, had it not been for the discovery that he was also "immoral." Immorality no high-minded woman could condone; and when, on her return from a rest-cure in California, she found that he had drifted into a furtive love affair with the dependent cousin who lived with his mother, every law of self-respect known to Pauline decreed his repudiation. Old Mrs. Wyant, horror-struck, banished the cousin and pleaded for her son: Pauline was adamant. She addressed herself to the rising divorce-lawyer, Dexter Manford, and in his capable hands the affair was settled rapidly, discreetly, without scandal, wrangling or recrimination. Wyant withdrew to his mother's house, and Pauline went to Europe, a free woman.

In the early days of the new century divorce had not become a social institution in New York, and the blow to Wyant's pride was deeper than Pauline had foreseen. He lived in complete retirement at his mother's, saw his boy at the dates prescribed by the court, and sank into a sort of premature old age which contrasted painfully—even to Pauline herself—with her own recovered youth and elasticity. The contrast caused her a retrospective pang, and gradually, after her second marriage, and old Mrs. Wyant's death, she came to regard poor Arthur not as a grievance but as a responsibility. She prided herself on never neglecting her responsibilities, and therefore felt a not unnatural vexation with Arthur for having figured among her engagements that day, and thus obliged her to postpone him.

Moving back to the dressing-table she caught her reflection in the tall triple glass. Again those fine wrinkles about lids and lips, those vertical lines between the eyes! She would not permit it; no, not for a moment. She commanded herself: "Now, Pauline, STOP WORRYING. You know perfectly well there's no such thing as worry; it's only dyspepsia or want of exercise, and everything's really all right—" in the insincere tone of a mother soothing a bruised baby.

She looked again, and fancied the wrinkles were really fainter, the vertical lines less deep. Once more she saw before her an erect athletic woman, with all her hair and all her teeth, and just a hint of rouge (because "people did it") brightening a still fresh complexion; saw her small symmetrical features, the black brows drawn with a light stroke over handsome directly-gazing gray eyes, the abundant whitening hair which still responded so crisply to the waver's wand, the firmly planted feet with arched insteps rising to slim ankles.

How absurd, how unlike herself, to be upset by that foolish news! She would look in on Dexter and settle the Mahatma business in five minutes. If there was to be a scandal she wasn't going to have Dexter mixed up in it—above all not against the Mahatma. She could never forget that it was the Mahatma who had first told her she was psychic.

The maid opened an inner door an inch or two to say rebukingly: "Madam, the hair-dresser; and Miss Bruss asked me to remind you—"

"Yes, yes, yes," Mrs. Manford responded hastily; repeating below her breath, as she flung herself into her kimono and settled down before her toilet-table: "Now, I forbid you to let yourself feel hurried! You KNOW there's no such thing as hurry."

But her eye again turned anxiously to the little clock among her scent-bottles, and she wondered if she might not save time by dictating to Maisie Bruss while she was being waved and manicured. She envied women who had no sense of responsibility—like Jim's little Lita. As for herself, the only world she knew rested on her shoulders.

III

At a quarter past one, when Nona arrived at her half-brother's house, she was told that Mrs. Wyant was not yet down.

"And Mr. Wyant not yet up, I suppose? From his office, I mean," she added, as the young butler looked his surprise.

Pauline Manford had been very generous at the time of her son's marriage. She was relieved at his settling down, and at his seeming to understand that marriage connoted the choice of a profession, and the adoption of what people called regular habits. Not that Jim's irregularities had ever been such as the phrase habitually suggests. They had chiefly consisted in his not being able to make up his mind what to do with his life (so like his poor father, that!), in his always forgetting what time it was, or what engagements his mother had made for him, in his wanting a chemical laboratory fitted up for him at Cedarledge, and then, when it was all done, using it first as a kennel for breeding fox-terriers and then as a quiet place to practise the violin.

Nona knew how sorely these vacillations had tried her mother, and how reassured Mrs. Manford had been when the young man, in the heat of his infatuation for Lita, had vowed that if she would have him he would turn to and grind in an office like all the other husbands.

LITA HAVE HIM! Lita Cliffe, a portionless orphan, with no one to guide her in the world but a harum-scarum and somewhat blown-upon aunt, the "impossible" Mrs. Percy Landish! Mrs. Manford smiled at her son's modesty while she applauded his good resolutions. "This experience has made a man of dear Jim," she said, mildly triumphing in the latest confirmation of her optimism. "If only it lasts—!" she added, relapsing into human uncertainty.

"Oh, it will, mother; you'll see; as long as Lita doesn't get tired of him," Nona had assured her.

"As long—? But, my dear child, why should Lita ever get tired of him? You seem to forget what a miracle it was that a girl like Lita, with no one but poor Kitty Landish to look after her, should ever have got such a husband!"

Nona held her ground. "Well—just look about you, mother! Don't they almost all get tired of each other? And when they do, will anything ever stop their having another try? Think of your big dinners! Doesn't Maisie always have to make out a list of previous marriages as long as a cross-word puzzle, to prevent your calling people by the wrong names?"

Mrs. Manford waved away the challenge. "Jim and Lita are not like that; and I don't like your way of speaking of divorce, Nona," she had added, rather weakly for her—since, as Nona might have reminded her, her own way of speaking of divorce varied disconcertingly with the time, the place and the divorce.

The young girl had leisure to recall this discussion while she sat and waited for her brother and his wife. In the freshly decorated and studiously empty house there seemed to be no one to welcome her. The baby (whom she had first enquired for) was asleep, his mother hardly awake, and the head of the house still "at the office." Nona looked about the drawing-room and wondered—the habit was growing on her.

The drawing-room (it suddenly occurred to her) was very expressive of the modern marriage state. It looked, for all its studied effects, its rather nervous attention to "values," complementary colours, and the things the modern decorator lies awake over, more like the waiting-room of a glorified railway station than the setting of an established way of life. Nothing in it seemed at home or at ease—from the early kakemono of a bearded sage, on walls of pale buff silk, to the three mourning irises isolated in a white Sung vase in the desert of an otherwise empty table. The only life in the room was contributed by the agitations of the exotic goldfish in a huge spherical aquarium; and they too were but transients, since Lita insisted on having the aquarium illuminated night and day with electric bulbs, and the sleepless fish were always dying off and having to be replaced.

Mrs. Manford had paid for the house and its decoration. It was not what she would have wished for herself—she had not yet quite caught up with the new bareness and selectiveness. But neither would she have wished the young couple to live in the opulent setting of tapestries and "period" furniture which she herself preferred. Above all she wanted them to keep up; to do what the other young couples were doing; she had even digested—in one huge terrified gulp— Lita's black boudoir, with its welter of ebony velvet cushions overlooked by a statue as to which Mrs. Manford could only minimize the indecency by saying that she understood it was Cubist. But she did think it unkind—after all she had done— to have Nona suggest that Lita might get tired of Jim!

The idea had never really troubled Nona—at least not till lately. Even now she had nothing definite in her mind. Nothing beyond the vague question: what would a woman like Lita be likely to do if she suddenly grew tired of the life she was leading? But that question kept coming back so often that she had really wanted, that morning, to consult her mother about it; for who else was there to consult? Arthur Wyant? Why, poor Arthur had never been able to manage his own poor little concerns with any sort of common sense or consistency; and at the suggestion that any one might tire of Jim he would be as indignant as Mrs. Manford, and without her power of controlling her emotions.

Dexter Manford? Well—Dexter Manford's daughter had to admit that it really wasn't his business if his step-son's marriage threatened to be a failure; and besides, Nona knew how overwhelmed with work her father always was, and hesitated to lay this extra burden on him. For it would be a burden. Manford was very fond of Jim (as indeed they all were), and had been extremely kind to him. It was entirely owing to Manford's influence that Jim, who was regarded as vague and unreliable, had got such a good berth in the Amalgamated Trust Co.; and Manford had been much pleased at the way in which the boy had stuck to his job. Just like Jim, Nona thought tenderly— if ever you could induce him to do anything at all, he always did it with such marvellous neatness and persistency. And the incentive of working for Lita and the boy was enough to anchor him to his task for life.

A new scent—unrecognizable but exquisite. In its wake came Lita Wyant, half-dancing, half-drifting, fastening a necklace, humming a tune, her little round head, with the goldfish-coloured hair, the mother-of-pearl complexion and screwed-up auburn eyes, turning sideways like a bird's on her long throat. She was astonished but delighted to see Nona, indifferent to her husband's non-arrival, and utterly unaware that lunch had been waiting for half an hour.

"I had a sandwich and a cocktail after my exercises. I don't suppose it's time for me to be hungry again," she conjectured. "But perhaps you are, you poor child. Have you been waiting long?"

"Not much! I know you too well to be punctual," Nona laughed.

Lita widened her eyes. "Are you suggesting that I'm not? Well, then, how about your ideal brother?"

"He's down town working to keep a roof over your head and your son's."

Lita shrugged. "Oh, a roof—I don't care much for roofs, do you— or is it ROOVES? Not this one, at any rate." She caught Nona by the shoulders, held her at arm's-length, and with tilted head and persuasively narrowed eyes, demanded: "This room is AWFUL, isn't it? Now acknowledge that it is! And Jim won't give me the money to do it over."

"Do it over? But, Lita, you did it exactly as you pleased two years ago!"

"Two years ago? Do you mean to say you like anything that you liked two years ago?"

"Yes—you!" Nona retorted: adding rather helplessly: "And, besides, everybody admires the room so much—." She stopped, feeling that she was talking exactly like her mother.

Lita's little hands dropped in a gesture of despair. "That's just it! EVERYBODY admires it. Even Mrs. Manford does. And when you think what sort of things EVERYBODY admires! What's the use of pretending, Nona? It's the typical cliché drawing-room. Every one of the couples who were married the year we were has one like it. The first time Tommy Ardwin saw it—you know he's the new decorator— he said: 'Gracious, how familiar all this seems!' and began to whistle 'Home, Sweet Home'!"

"But of course he would, you simpleton! When what he wants is to be asked to do it over!"

Lita heaved a sigh. "If he only could! Perhaps he might reconcile me to this house. But I don't believe anybody could do that." She glanced about her with an air of ineffable disgust. "I'd like to throw everything in it into the street. I've been so bored here."

Nona laughed. "You'd be bored anywhere. I wish another Tommy Ardwin would come along and tell you what an old cliché being bored is."

"An old cliché? Why shouldn't it be? When life itself is such a bore? You can't redecorate life!"

"If you could, what would you begin by throwing into the street? The baby?"

Lita's eyes woke to fire. "Don't be an idiot! You know I adore my baby."

"Well—then Jim?"

"You know I adore my Jim!" echoed the young wife, mimicking her own emotion.

"Hullo—that sounds ominous!" Jim Wyant came in, clearing the air with his fresh good-humoured presence. "I fear my bride when she says she adores me," he said, taking Nona into a brotherly embrace.

As he stood there, sturdy and tawny, a trifle undersized, with his bright blue eyes and short blunt-nosed face, in which everything was so handsomely modelled and yet so safe and sober, Nona fell again to her dangerous wondering. Something had gone out of his face—all the wild uncertain things, the violin, model-making, inventing, dreaming, vacillating—everything she had best loved except the twinkle in his sobered eyes. Whatever else was left now was all plain utility. Well, better so, no doubt—when one looked at Lita! Her glance caught her sister-in-law's face in a mirror between two panels, and the reflection of her own beside it; she winced a little at the contrast. At her best she had none of that milky translucence, or of the long lines which made Lita seem in perpetual motion, as a tremor of air lives in certain trees. Though Nona was as tall and nearly as slim, she seemed to herself to be built, while Lita was spun of spray and sunlight. Perhaps it was Nona's general brownness—she had Dexter Manford's brown crinkled hair, his strong black lashes setting her rather usual-looking gray eyes; and the texture of her dusky healthy skin, compared to Lita's, seemed rough and opaque. The comparison added to her general vague sense of discouragement. "It's not one of my beauty days," she thought.

Jim was drawing her arm through his. "Come along, my girl. Is there going to be any lunch?" he queried, turning toward the dining-room.

"Oh, probably. In this house the same things always happen every day," Lita averred with a slight grimace.

"Well, I'm glad lunch does—on the days when I can make a dash up-town for it."

"On others Lita eats goldfish food," Nona laughed.

"Luncheon is served, madam," the butler announced.

The meal, as usual under Lita's roof, was one in which delicacies alternated with delays. Mrs. Manford would have been driven out of her mind by the uncertainties of the service and the incoherence of the menu; but she would have admitted that no one did a pilaff better than Lita's cook. Gastronomic refinements were wasted on Jim, whose indifference to the possession of the Wyant madeira was one of his father's severest trials. ("I shouldn't have been surprised if YOU hadn't cared, Nona; after all, you're a Manford; but that a Wyant shouldn't have a respect for old wine!" Arthur Wyant often lamented to her.) As for Lita, she either nibbled languidly at new health foods, or made ravenous inroads into the most indigestible dish presented to her. To-day she leaned back, dumb and indifferent, while Jim devoured what was put before him as if unaware that it was anything but canned beef; and Nona watched the two under guarded lids.

The telephone tinkled, and the butler announced: "Mr. Manford, madam."

Nona Manford looked up. "For me?"

"No, miss; Mrs. Wyant."

Lita was on her feet, suddenly animated. "Oh, all right. . . Don't wait for me," she flung over her shoulder as she made for the door.

"Have the receiver brought in here," Jim suggested; but she brushed by without heeding.

"That's something new—Lita sprinting for the telephone!" Jim laughed.

"And to talk to father!" For the life of her, Nona could not have told why she stopped short with a vague sense of embarrassment. Dexter Manford had always been very kind to his stepson's wife; but then everybody was kind to Lita.

Jim's head was bent over the pilaff; he took it down in quick undiscerning mouthfuls.

"Well, I hope he's saying something that will amuse her: nothing seems to, nowadays."

It was on the tip of Nona's tongue to rejoin: "Oh, yes; it amuses her to say that nothing amuses her." But she looked at her brother's face, faintly troubled under its surface serenity, and refrained.

Instead, she remarked on the beauty of the two yellow arums in a bronze jar reflected in the mahogany of the dining-table. "Lita has a genius for flowers."

"And for everything else—when she chooses!"

The door opened and Lita sauntered back and dropped into her seat. She shook her head disdainfully at the proffered pilaff. There was a pause.

"Well—what's the news?" Jim asked.

His wife arched her exquisite brows. "News? I expect you to provide that. I'm only just awake."

"I mean—" But he broke off, and signed to the butler to remove his plate. There was another pause; then Lita's little head turned on its long interrogative neck toward Nona. "It seems we're banqueting tonight at the Palazzo Manford. Did you know?"

"Did I know? Why, Lita! I've heard of nothing else for weeks. It's the annual feast for the Marchesa."

"I was never told," said Lita calmly. "I'm afraid I'm engaged."

Jim lifted his head with a jerk. "You were told a fortnight ago."

"Oh, a fortnight! That's too long to remember anything. It's like Nona's telling me that I ought to admire my drawing-room because I admired it two years ago."

Her husband reddened to the roots of his tawny hair. "Don't you admire it?" he asked, with a sort of juvenile dismay.

"There; Lita'll be happy now—she's produced her effect!" Nona laughed a little nervously.

Lita joined in the laugh. "Isn't he like his mother?" she shrugged.

Jim was silent, and his sister guessed that he was afraid to insist on the dinner engagement lest he should increase his wife's determination to ignore it. The same motive kept Nona from saying anything more; and the lunch ended in a clatter of talk about other things. But what puzzled Nona was that her father's communication to Lita should have concerned the fact that she was dining at his house that night. It was unlike Dexter Manford to remember the fact himself (as Miss Bruss's frantic telephoning had testified), and still more unlike him to remind his wife's guests, even if he knew who they were to be—which he seldom did. Nona pondered. "They must have been going somewhere together—he told me he was engaged tonight—and Lita's in a temper because they can't. But then she's in a temper about everything today." Nona tried to make that cover all her perplexities. She wondered if it did as much for Jim.

IV

It would have been hard, Nona Manford thought, to find a greater contrast than between Lita Wyant's house and that at which, two hours later, she descended from Lita Wyant's smart Brewster.

"You won't come, Lita?" The girl paused, her hand on the motor door. "He'd like it awfully."

Lita shook off the suggestion. "I'm not in the humour."

"But he's such fun—he can be better company than anybody."

"Oh, for you he's a fad—for me he's a duty; and I don't happen to feel like duties." Lita waved one of her flower-hands and was off.

Nona mounted the pock-marked brown steps. The house was old Mrs. Wyant's, a faded derelict habitation in a street past which fashion and business had long since flowed. After his mother's death Wyant, from motives of economy, had divided it into small flats. He kept one for himself, and in the one overhead lived his mother's former companion, the dependent cousin who had been the cause of his divorce. Wyant had never married her; he had never deserted her; that, to Nona's mind, gave one a fair notion of his character. When he was ill—and he had developed, rather early, a queer sort of nervous hypochondria—the cousin came downstairs and nursed him; when he was well his visitors never saw her. But she was reported to attend to his mending, keep some sort of order in his accounts, and prevent his falling a prey to the unscrupulous. Pauline Manford said it was probably for the best. She herself would have thought it natural, and in fact proper, that her former husband should have married his cousin; as he had not, she preferred to decide that since the divorce they had been "only friends." The Wyant code was always a puzzle to her. She never met the cousin when she called on her former husband; but Jim, two or three times a year, made it a point to ring the bell of the upper flat, and at Christmas sent its invisible tenant an azalea.

Nona ran up the stairs to Wyant's door. On the threshold a thin gray-haired lady with a shadowy face awaited her.

"Come in, do. He's got the gout, and can't get up to open the door, and I had to send the cook out to get something tempting for his dinner."

"Oh, thank you, cousin Eleanor." The girl looked sympathetically into the other's dimly tragic eyes. "Poor Exhibit A! I'm sorry he's ill again."

"He's been—imprudent. But the worst of it's over. It will brighten him up to see you. Your cousin Stanley's there."

"Is he?" Nona half drew back, feeling herself faintly redden.

"He'll be going soon. Mr. Wyant will be disappointed if you don't go in."

"But of course I'm going in."

The older woman smiled a worn smile, and vanished upstairs while Nona slipped off her furs. The girl knew it would be useless to urge cousin Eleanor to stay. If one wished to see her one had to ring at her own door.

Arthur Wyant's shabby sitting-room was full of February sunshine, illustrated magazines, newspapers and cigar ashes. There were some books on shelves, shabby also: Wyant had apparently once cared for them, and his talk was still coloured by traces of early cultivation, especially when visitors like Nona or Stan Heuston were with him. But the range of his allusions suggested that he must have stopped reading years ago. Even novels were too great a strain on his attention. As far back as Nona could remember he had fared only on the popular magazines, picture-papers and the weekly purveyors of social scandal. He took an intense interest in the private affairs of the world he had ceased to frequent, though he always ridiculed this interest in talking to Nona or Heuston.

While he sat there, deep in his armchair, with bent shoulders, sunk head and clumsy bandaged foot, Nona saw him, as she always did, as taller, slimmer, more handsomely upstanding than any man she had ever known. He stooped now, even when he was on his feet; he was prematurely aged; and the fact perhaps helped to connect him with vanished institutions to which only his first youth could have belonged.

To Nona, at any rate, he would always be the Arthur Wyant of the race-meeting group in the yellowing photograph on his mantelpiece: clad in the gray frock-coat and topper of the early 'eighties, and tallest in a tall line of the similarly garbed, behind ladies with puffed sleeves and little hats tilting forward on elaborate hair. How peaceful, smiling and unhurried they all seemed! Nona never looked at them without a pang of regret that she had not been born in those spacious days of dogcarts, victorias, leisurely tennis and afternoon calls. . .

Wyant's face, even more than his figure, related him to that past: the small shapely head, the crisp hair grown thin on a narrow slanting forehead, the eyes in which a twinkle still lingered, eyes probably blue when the hair was brown, but now faded with the rest, and the slight fair moustache above an uncertain ironic mouth.

A romantic figure; or rather the faded photograph of one. Yes; perhaps Arthur Wyant had always been faded—like a charming reflection in a sallow mirror. And all that length of limb and beauty of port had been meant for some other man, a man to whom the things had really happened which Wyant had only dreamed.

His visitor, though of the same stock, could never have inspired such conjectures. Stanley Heuston was much younger—in the middle thirties—and most things about him were middling: height, complexion, features. But he had a strong forehead, his mouth was curved for power and mockery, and only his small quick eyes betrayed the uncertainty and lassitude inherited from a Wyant mother.

Wyant, at Nona's approach, held out a dry feverish hand. "Well, this is luck! Stan was just getting ready to fly at your mother's approach, and you turn up instead!"

Heuston got to his feet, and greeted Nona somewhat ceremoniously. "Perhaps I'd better fly all the same," he said in a singularly agreeable voice. His eyes were intent on the girl's.

She made a slight gesture, not so much to detain or dismiss as to signify her complete indifference. "Isn't mother coming presently?" she said, addressing the question to Wyant.

"No; I'm moved on till tomorrow. There must have been some big upheaval to make her change her plans at the last minute. Sit down and tell us all about it."

"I don't know of any upheaval. There's only the dinner-dance for Amalasuntha this evening."

"Oh, but that sort of thing is in your mother's stride. You underrate her capacity. Stan has been giving me a hint of something a good deal more volcanic."

Nona felt an inward tremor; was she going to hear Lita's name? She turned her glance on Heuston with a certain hostility.

"Oh, Stan's hints—."

"You see what Nona thinks of my views on cities and men," Heuston shrugged. He had remained on his feet, as though about to take leave; but once again the girl felt his eager eyes beseeching her.

"Are you waiting to walk home with me? You needn't. I'm going to stay for hours," she said, smiling across him at Wyant as she settled down into one of the chintz armchairs.

"Aren't you a little hard on him?" Wyant suggested, when the door had closed on their visitor. "It's not exactly a crime to want to walk home with you."

Nona made an impatient gesture. "Stan bores me."

"Ah, well, I suppose he's not enough of a novelty. Or not up-to- date enough; YOUR dates. Some of his ideas seem to me pretty subversive; but I suppose in your set and Lita's a young man who doesn't jazz all day and drink all night—or vice versa—is a back number."

The girl did not take this up, and after a moment Wyant continued, in his half-mocking half-querulous voice: "Or is it that he isn't 'psychic' enough? That's the latest, isn't it? When you're not high-kicking you're all high-thinking; and that reminds me of Stan's news—"

"Yes?" Nona brought it out between parched lips. Her gaze turned from Wyant to the coals smouldering in the grate. She did not want to face any one just then.

"Well, it seems there's going to be a gigantic muck-raking—one of the worst we've had yet. Into this Mahatma business; you know, the nigger chap your mother's always talking about. There's a hint of it in the last number of the 'Looker-on'; here . . . where is it? Never mind, though. What it says isn't a patch on the real facts, Stan tells me. It seems the goings-on in that School of Oriental Thought—what does he call the place: Dawnside?—have reached such a point that the Grant Lindons, whose girl has been making a 'retreat' there, or whatever they call it, are out to have a thorough probing. They say the police don't want to move because so many people we know are mixed up in it; but Lindon's back is up, and he swears he won't rest till he gets the case before the Grand Jury. . ."

As Wyant talked, the weight lifted from Nona's breast. Much she cared for the Mahatma, or for the Grant Lindons! Stuffy old- fashioned people—she didn't wonder Bee Lindon had broken away from such parents—though she was a silly fool, no doubt. Besides, the Mahatma certainly had reduced Mrs. Manford's hips—and made her less nervous too: for Mrs. Manford sometimes WAS nervous, in spite of her breathless pursuit of repose. Not, of course, in the same querulous uncontrolled way as poor Arthur Wyant, who had never been taught poise, or mental uplift, or being in tune with the Infinite; but rather as one agitated by the incessant effort to be calm. And in that respect the Mahatma's rhythmic exercises had without doubt been helpful. No; Nona didn't care a fig for scandals about the School of Oriental Thought. And the relief of finding that the subject she had dreaded to hear broached had probably never even come to Wyant's ears, gave her a reaction of light-heartedness.

There were moments when Nona felt oppressed by responsibilities and anxieties not of her age, apprehensions that she could not shake off and yet had not enough experience of life to know how to meet. One or two of her girl friends—in the brief intervals between whirls and thrills—had confessed to the same vague disquietude. It was as if, in the beaming determination of the middle-aged, one and all of them, to ignore sorrow and evil, "think them away" as superannuated bogies, survivals of some obsolete European superstition unworthy of enlightened Americans, to whom plumbing and dentistry had given higher standards, and bi-focal glasses a clearer view of the universe—as if the demons the elder generation ignored, baulked of their natural prey, had cast their hungry shadow over the young. After all, somebody in every family had to remember now and then that such things as wickedness, suffering and death had not yet been banished from the earth; and with all those bright-complexioned white-haired mothers mailed in massage and optimism, and behaving as if they had never heard of anything but the Good and the Beautiful, perhaps their children had to serve as vicarious sacrifices. There were hours when Nona Manford, bewildered little Iphigenia, uneasily argued in this way: others when youth and inexperience reasserted themselves, and the load slipped from her, and she wondered why she didn't always believe, like her elders, that one had only to be brisk, benevolent and fond to prevail against the powers of darkness.

She felt this relief now; but a vague restlessness remained with her, and to ease it, and prove to herself that she was not nervous, she mentioned to Wyant that she had just been lunching with Jim and Lita.

Wyant brightened, as he always did at his son's name. "Poor old Jim! He dropped in yesterday, and I thought he looked overworked! I sometimes wonder if that father of yours hasn't put more hustle into him than a Wyant can assimilate." Wyant spoke good- humouredly; his first bitterness against the man who had supplanted him (a sentiment regarded by Pauline as barbarous and mediæval) had gradually been swallowed up in gratitude for Dexter Manford's kindness to Jim. The oddly-assorted trio, Wyant, Pauline and her new husband, had been drawn into a kind of inarticulate understanding by their mutual tenderness for the progeny of the two marriages, and Manford loved Jim almost as much as Wyant loved Nona.

"Oh, well," the girl said, "Jim always does everything with all his might. And now that he's doing it for Lita and the baby, he's got to keep on, whether he wants to or not."

"I suppose so. But why do you say 'whether'?" Wyant questioned with one of his disconcerting flashes. "Doesn't he want to?"

Nona was vexed at her slip. "Of course. I only meant that he used to be rather changeable in his tastes, and that getting married has given him an object."

"How very old-fashioned! You ARE old-fashioned, you know, my child; in spite of the jazz. I suppose that's what I've done for YOU, in exchange for Manford's modernizing Jim. Not much of an exchange, I'm afraid. But how long do you suppose Lita will care about being an object to Jim?"

"Why shouldn't she care? She'd go on caring about the baby, even if . . . not that I mean. . ."

"Oh, I know. That's a great baby. Queer, you know—I can see he's going to have the Wyant nose and forehead. It's about all we've left to give. But look here—haven't you really heard anything more about the Mahatma? I thought that Lindon girl was a pal of yours. Now listen—"

When Nona Manford emerged into the street she was not surprised to meet Stanley Heuston strolling toward her across Stuyvesant Square. Neither surprised, nor altogether sorry; do what she would, she could never quite repress the sense of ease and well-being that his nearness gave. And yet half the time they were together she always spent in being angry with him and wishing him away. If only the relation between them had been as simple as that between herself and Jim! And it might have been—ought to have been—seeing that

Heuston was Jim's cousin, and nearly twice her age; yes, and had been married before she left the schoolroom. Really, her exasperation was justified. Yet no one understood her as well as Stanley; not even Jim, who was so much dearer and more lovable. Life was a confusing business to Nona Manford.

"How absurd! I asked you not to wait. I suppose you think I'm not old enough to be out alone after dark."

"That hadn't occurred to me; and I'm not waiting to walk home with you," Heuston rejoined with some asperity. "But I do want to say two words," he added, his voice breaking into persuasion.

Nona stopped, her heels firmly set on the pavement. "The same old two?"

"No. Besides, there are three of those. You never COULD count." He hesitated: "This time it's only about Arthur—"

"Why; what's the matter?" The sense of apprehension woke in her again. What if Wyant really had begun to suspect that there was something, an imponderable something, wrong between Jim and Lita, and had been too shrewd to let Nona detect his suspicion?

"Haven't you noticed? He looks like the devil. He's been drinking again. Eleanor spoke to me—"

"Oh, dear." There it was—all the responsibilities and worries always closed in on Nona! But this one, after all, was relatively bearable.

"What can I do, Stan? I can't imagine why you come to ME!"

He smiled a little, in his queer derisive way. "Doesn't everybody? The fact is—I didn't want to bother Jim."

She was silent. She understood; but she resented his knowing that she understood.

"Jim has got to be bothered. He's got to look after his father."

"Yes; but I—Oh, look here, Nona; won't you see?"

"See what?"

"Why—that if Jim is worried about his father now—Jim's a queer chap; he's tried his hand at fifty things, and never stuck to one; and if he gets a shock now, on top of everything else—"

Nona felt her lips grow hard: all her pride and tenderness for her brother stiffened into ice about her heart.

"I don't know what you mean. Jim's grown up—he's got to face things."

"Yes; I know. I've been told the same thing about myself. But there are things one doesn't ever have a chance to face in this slippery sliding modern world, because they don't come out into the open. They just lurk and peep and mouth. My case exactly. What on earth is there about Aggie that a fellow can FACE?"

Nona stopped short with a jerk. "We don't happen to be talking about you and Aggie," she said.

"Oh, well; I was merely using myself as an example. But there are plenty of others to choose from."

Her voice broke into anger. "I don't imagine you're comparing your married life to Jim's?"

"Lord, no. God forbid!" He burst into a dry laugh. "When I think of Aggie's life and Lita's—!"

"Never mind about Lita's life. What do you know about it, anyhow? Oh, Stan, why are we quarrelling again?" She felt the tears in her throat. "What you wanted was only to tell me about poor Arthur. And I'd guessed that myself—I know something ought to be done. But WHAT? How on earth can I tell? I'm always being asked by everybody what ought to be done . . . and sometimes I feel too young to be always the one to judge, to decide. . ."

Heuston stood watching her in silence. Suddenly he took her hand and drew it through his arm. She did not resist, and thus linked they walked on slowly and without further speech through the cold deserted streets. As they approached more populous regions she freed her arm from his, and signalled to a taxi.

"May I come?"

"No. I'm going to meet Lita at the Cubist Cabaret. I promised to be there by four."

"Oh, all right." He looked at her irresolutely as the taxi drew up. "I wish to God I could always be on hand to help you when you're bothered!"

She shook her head.

"Never?"

"Not while Aggie—"

"That means never."

"Then never." She held out her hand, but he had turned and was already striding off in the opposite direction. She threw the address to the chauffeur and got in.

"Yes; I suppose it IS never," she said to herself. After all, instead of helping her with the Wyant problem, Stan had only brought her another: his own—and hers. As long as Aggie Heuston, a sort of lay nun, absorbed in High Church practices and the exercise of a bleak but efficient philanthropy, continued to set her face against divorce, Nona would not admit that Heuston had any right to force it upon her. "It's her way of loving him," the girl said to herself for the hundredth time. "She wants to keep him for herself too—though she doesn't know it; but she does above all want to save him. And she thinks that's the way to do it. I rather admire her for thinking that there IS a way to save people. . ." She pushed that problem once more into the back of her mind, and turned her thoughts toward the other and far more pressing one: that of poor Arthur Wyant's growing infirmity. Stanley was probably right in not wanting to speak to Jim about it at that particular moment—though how did Stanley know about Jim's troubles, and what did he know?—and she herself, after all, was perhaps the only person to deal with Arthur Wyant. Another interval of anxious consideration made her decide that the best way would be to seek her father's advice. After an hour's dancing she would feel better, more alive and competent, and there would still be time to dash down to Manford's office, the only place— as she knew by experience—where Manford was ever likely to have time for her.

V

The door of his private office clicked on a withdrawing client, and Dexter Manford, giving his vigorous shoulders a shake, rose from his desk and stood irresolute.

"I must get out to Cedarledge for some golf on Saturday," he thought. He lived among people who regarded golf as a universal panacea, and in a world which believed in panaceas.

As he stood there, his glance lit on the looking-glass above the mantel and he mustered his image impatiently. Queer thing, for a man of his age to gape at himself in a looking-glass like a dago dancing-master! He saw a swarthy straight-nosed face, dark crinkling hair with a dash of gray on the temples, dark eyes under brows that were beginning to beetle across a deep vertical cleft. Complexion turning from ruddy to sallow; eyes heavy—would he put his tongue out next? The matter with him was. . .

He dropped back into his desk-chair and unhooked the telephone receiver.

"Mrs. James Wyant? Yes. . . Oh—OUT? You're sure? And you don't know when she'll be back? Who? Yes; Mr. Manford. I had a message for Mrs. Wyant. No matter."

He hung up and leaned back, stretching his legs under the table and staring moodily at the heap of letters and legal papers in the morocco-lined baskets set out before him.

"I look ten years older than my age," he thought. Yet that last new type-writer, Miss Vollard, or whatever her name was, really behaved as if . . . was always looking at him when she thought he wasn't looking. . . "Oh, what rot!" he exclaimed.

His day had been as all his days were now: a starting in with a great sense of pressure, importance and authority—and a drop at the close into staleness and futility.

The evening before, he had stopped to see his doctor and been told that he was over-working, and needed a nerve-tonic and a change of scene. "Cruise to the West Indies, or something of the sort. Couldn't you get away for three or four weeks? No? Well, more golf then, anyhow."

Getting away from things; the perpetual evasion, moral, mental, physical, which he heard preached, and saw practised, everywhere about him, except where money-making was concerned! He, Dexter Manford, who had been brought up on a Minnesota farm, paid his own way through the State College at Delos, and his subsequent course in the Harvard Law School; and who, ever since, had been working at the top of his pitch with no more sense of strain, no more desire for evasion (shirking, he called it) than a healthy able-bodied man of fifty had a right to feel! If his task had been mere money- getting he might have known—and acknowledged—weariness. But he gloried in his profession, in its labours and difficulties as well as its rewards, it satisfied him intellectually and gave him that calm sense of mastery—mastery over himself and others—known only to those who are doing what they were born to do.

Of course, at every stage of his career—and never more than now, on its slippery pinnacle—he had suffered the thousand irritations inseparable from a hard-working life: the trifles which waste one's time, the fools who consume one's patience, the tricky failure of the best-laid plans, the endless labour of rolling human stupidity up the steep hill of understanding. But until lately these things had been a stimulus: it had amused him to shake off trifles, baffle bores, circumvent failure, and exercise his mental muscles in persuading stupid people to do intelligent things. There was pioneer blood in him: he was used to starting out every morning to hack his way through a fresh growth of prejudices and obstacles; and though he liked his big retaining fees he liked arguing a case even better.

Professionally, he was used to intellectual loneliness, and no longer minded it. Outside of his profession he had a brain above the average, but a general education hardly up to it; and the discrepancy between what he would have been capable of enjoying had his mind been prepared for it, and what it could actually take in, made him modest and almost shy in what he considered cultivated society. He had long believed his wife to be cultivated because she had fits of book-buying and there was an expensively bound library in the New York house. In his raw youth, in the old Delos days, he had got together a little library of his own in which Robert Ingersoll's lectures represented science, the sermons of the Reverend Frank Gunsaulus of Chicago, theology, John Burroughs, natural history, and Jared Sparks and Bancroft almost the whole of history. He had gradually discovered the inadequacy of these guides, but without ever having done much to replace them. Now and then, when he was not too tired, and had the rare chance of a quiet evening, he picked up a book from Pauline's table; but the works she acquired were so heterogeneous, and of such unequal value, that he rarely found one worth reading. Mrs. Tallentyre's "Voltaire" had been a revelation: he discovered, to his surprise, that he had never really known who Voltaire was, or what sort of a world he had lived in, and why his name had survived it. After that, Manford decided to start in on a course of European history, and got as far as taking the first volume of Macaulay up to bed. But he was tired at night, and found Macaulay's periods too long (though their eloquence appealed to his forensic instinct): and there had never been time for that course of history.

In his early wedded days, before he knew much of his wife's world, he had dreamed of quiet evenings at home, when Pauline would read instructive books aloud while he sat by the fire and turned over his briefs in some quiet inner chamber of his mind. But Pauline had never known any one who wanted to be read aloud to except children getting over infantile complaints. She regarded the desire almost as a symptom of illness, and decided that Dexter needed "rousing," and that she must do more to amuse him. As soon as she was able after Nona's birth she girt herself up for this new duty; and from that day Manford's life, out of office hours, had been one of almost incessant social activity. At first the endless going out had bewildered, then for a while amused and flattered him, then gradually grown to be a soothing routine, a sort of mild

28

drug-taking after the high pressure of professional hours; but of late it had become simply a bore, a duty to be persisted in because— as he had at last discovered—Pauline could not live without it. After twenty years of marriage he was only just beginning to exercise his intellectual acumen on his wife.

The thought of Pauline made him glance at his clock: she would be coming in a moment. He unhooked the receiver again, and named, impatiently, the same number as before. "Out, you say? Still?" (The same stupid voice making the same stupid answer!) "Oh, no; no matter. I say IT'S NO MATTER," he almost shouted, replacing the receiver. Of all idiotic servants—!

Miss Vollard, the susceptible type-writer, shot a shingled head around the door, said "ALL right" with an envious sigh to some one outside, and effaced herself before the brisk entrance of her employer's wife. Manford got to his feet.

"Well, my dear—" He pushed an armchair near the fire, solicitous, still a little awed by her presence—the beautiful Mrs. Wyant who had deigned to marry him. Pauline, throwing back her furs, cast a quick house-keeping glance about her. The scent she used always reminded him of a superior disinfectant; and in another moment, he knew, she would find some pretext for assuring herself, by the application of a gloved finger-tip, that there was no dust on desk or mantelpiece. She had very nearly obliged him, when he moved into his new office, to have concave surbases, as in a hospital ward or a hygienic nursery. She had adopted with enthusiasm the idea of the concave tiling fitted to every cove and angle, so that there were no corners anywhere to catch the dust. People's lives ought to be like that: with no corners in them. She wanted to de- microbe life.

But, in the case of his own office, Manford had resisted; and now, he understood, the fad had gone to the scrap-heap—with how many others!

"Not too near the fire." Pauline pushed her armchair back and glanced up to see if the ceiling ventilators were working. "You DO renew the air at regular intervals? I'm sure everything depends on that; that and thought-direction. What the Mahatma calls mental deep-breathing." She smiled persuasively. "You look tired, Dexter . . . tired and drawn."

"Oh, rot!—A cigarette?"

She shook her small resolute head. "You forget that he's cured me of that too—the Mahatma. Dexter," she exclaimed suddenly, "I'm sure it's this silly business of the Grant Lindons' that's worrying you. I want to talk to you about it—to clear it up with you. It's out of the question that you should be mixed up in it."

Manford had gone back to his desk-chair. Habit made him feel more at home there, in fuller possession of himself; Pauline, in the seat facing him, the light full on her, seemed no more than a client to be advised, or an opponent to be talked over. He knew she felt the difference too. So far he had managed to preserve his professional privacy and his professional authority. What he did "at the office" was clouded over, for his family, by the vague word "business," which meant that a man didn't want to be bothered. Pauline had never really distinguished between practising the law and manufacturing motors; nor had

Manford encouraged her to. But today he suspected that she meant her interference to go to the extreme limit which her well-known "tact" would permit.

"You must not be mixed up in this investigation. Why not hand it over to somebody else? Alfred Cosby, or that new Jew who's so clever? The Lindons would accept any one you recommended; unless, of course," she continued, "you could persuade them to drop it, which would be so much better. I'm sure you could, Dexter; you always know what to say—and your opinion carries such weight. Besides, what is it they complain of? Some nonsense of Bee's, I've no doubt—she took a rest-cure at the School. If they'd brought the girl up properly there'd have been no trouble. Look at Nona!"

"Oh—Nona!" Manford gave a laugh of pride. Nona was the one warm rich spot in his life: the corner on which the sun always shone. Fancy comparing that degenerate fool of a Bee Lindon to his Nona, and imagining that "bringing-up" made the difference! Still, he had to admit that Pauline—always admirable—had been especially so as a mother. Yet she too was bitten with this theosophical virus!

He lounged back, hands in pockets, one leg swinging, instinctively seeking an easier attitude as his moral ease diminished.

"My dear, it's always been understood, hasn't it, that what goes on in this office is between me and my clients, and not—"

"Oh, nonsense, Dexter!" She seldom took that tone: he saw that she was losing her self-control. "Look here: I make it a rule never to interfere; you've just said so. Well—if I interfere now, it's because I've a right to—because it's a duty! The Lindons are my son's cousins: Fanny Lindon was a Wyant. Isn't that reason enough?"

"It was one of the Lindons' reasons. They appealed to me on that very ground."

Pauline gave an irritated laugh. "How like Fanny! Always pushing in and claiming things. I wonder such an argument took you in. Do consider, Dexter! I won't for a minute admit that there CAN be anything wrong about the Mahatma; but supposing there were. . ." She drew herself up, her lips tightening. "I hope I know how to respect professional secrecy, and I don't ask you to repeat their nasty insinuations; in fact, as you know, I always take particular pains to avoid hearing anything painful or offensive. But, supposing there were any ground for what they say; do they realize how the publicity is going to affect Bee's reputation? And how shall you feel if you set the police at work and find them publishing the name of a girl who is Jim's cousin, and a friend of your own daughter's?"

Manford moved restlessly in his chair, and in so doing caught his reflexion in the mirror, and saw that his jaw had lost its stern professional cast. He made an attempt to recover it, but unsuccessfully.

"But all this is too absurd," Pauline continued on a smoother note. "The Mahatma and his friends have nothing to fear. Whose judgment would you sooner trust: mine, or poor Fanny's? What really bothers me is your allowing the

Lindons to drag you into an affair which is going to discredit them, and not the Mahatma." She smiled her bright frosty smile. "You know how proud I am of your professional prestige: I should hate to have you associated with a failure." She paused, and he saw that she meant to rest on that.

"This is a pretty bad business. The Lindons have got their proofs all right," he said.

Pauline reddened, and her face lost its look of undaunted serenity. "How can you believe such rubbish, Dexter? If you're going to take Fanny Lindon's word against mine—"

"It's not a question of your word or hers. Lindon is fully documented: he didn't come to me till he was. I'm sorry, Pauline; but you've been deceived. This man has got to be shown up, and the Lindons have had the pluck to do what everybody else has shirked."

Pauline's angry colour had faded. She got up and stood before her husband, distressed and uncertain; then, with a visible effort at self-command, she seated herself again, and locked her hands about her gold-mounted bag.

"Then you'd rather the scandal, if there is one, should be paraded before the world? Who will gain by that except the newspaper reporters, and the people who want to drag down society? And how shall you feel if Nona is called as a witness—or Lita?"

"Oh, nonsense—" He stopped abruptly, and got up too. The discussion was lasting longer than he had intended, and he could not find the word to end it. His mind felt suddenly empty—empty of arguments and formulas. "I don't know why you persist in bringing in Nona—or Lita—"

"I don't; it's you. You will, that is, if you take this case. Bee and Nona have been intimate since they were babies, and Bee is always at Lita's. Don't you suppose the Mahatma's lawyers will make use of that if you OBLIGE him to fight? You may say you're prepared for it; and I admire your courage—but I can't share it. The idea that our children may be involved simply sickens me."

"Neither Nona nor Lita has ever had anything to do with this charlatan and his humbug, as far as I know," said Manford irritably.

"Nona has attended his eurythmic classes at our house, and gone to his lectures with me: at one time they interested her intensely." Pauline paused. "About Lita I don't know: I know so little about Lita's life before her marriage."

"It was presumably that of any of Nona's other girl friends."

"Presumably. Kitty Landish might enlighten us. But of course, if it WAS—" he noted her faintly sceptical emphasis—"I don't admit that that would preclude Lita's having known the Mahatma, or believed in him. And you must remember, Dexter, that I should be the most deeply involved of all! I mean to take a rest-cure at Dawnside in March." She gave the little playful laugh with which she had been used, in old times, to ridicule the naughtiness of her children.

Manford drummed on his blotting-pad. "Look here, suppose we drop this for the present—"

She glanced at her wrist-watch. "If you can spare the time—"

"Spare the time?"

She answered softly: "I'm not going away till you've promised."

Manford could remember the day when that tone—so feminine under its firmness—would have had the power to shake him. Pauline, in her wifely dealings, so seldom invoked the prerogative of her grace, her competence, her persuasiveness, that when she did he had once found it hard to resist. But that day was past. Under his admiration for her brains, and his esteem for her character, he had felt, of late, a stealing boredom. She was too clever, too efficient, too uniformly sagacious and serene. Perhaps his own growing sense of power—professional and social—had secretly undermined his awe of hers, made him feel himself first her equal, then ever so little her superior. He began to detect something obtuse in that unfaltering competence. And as his professional authority grew he had become more jealous of interference with it. His wife ought at least to have understood that! If her famous tact were going to fail her, what would be left, he asked himself?

"Look here, Pauline, you know all this is useless. In professional matters no one else can judge for me. I'm busy this afternoon; I'm sure you are too—"

She settled more deeply into her armchair. "Never too busy for you, Dexter."

"Thank you, dear. But the time I ask you to give me is outside of business hours," he rejoined with a slight smile.

"Then I'm dismissed?" She smiled back. "I understand; you needn't ring!" She rose with recovered serenity and laid a light hand on his shoulder. "Sorry to have bothered you; I don't often, do I? All I ask is that you should think over—"

He lifted the hand to his lips. "Of course, of course." Now that she was going he could say it.

"I'm forgiven?"

He smiled: "You're forgiven;" and from the threshold she called, almost gaily: "Don't forget tonight—Amalasuntha!"

His brow clouded as he returned to his chair; and oddly enough—he was aware of the oddness—it was clouded not by the tiresome scene he had been through, but by his wife's reminder. "Damn that dinner," he swore to himself.

He turned to the telephone, unhooked it for the third time, and called for the same number.

That evening, as he slipped the key into his front-door, Dexter Manford felt the oppression of all that lay behind it. He never entered his house without a slight consciousness of the importance of the act—never completely took for granted the resounding vestibule, the big hall with its marble staircase ascending to all the light and warmth and luxury which skill could devise, money buy, and Pauline's ingenuity combine in a harmonious whole. He had not yet forgotten the day when, after one of his first legal successes, he had installed a bathroom in his mother's house at Delos, and all the neighbours had driven in from miles around to see it.

But luxury, and above all comfort, had never weighed on him; he was too busy to think much about them, and sure enough of himself and his powers to accept them as his right. It was not the splendour of his house that oppressed him but the sense of the corporative bonds it imposed. It seemed part of an elaborate social and domestic structure, put together with the baffling ingenuity of certain bird's-nests of which he had seen the pictures. His own career, Pauline's multiple activities, the problem of poor Arthur Wyant, Nona, Jim, Lita Wyant, the Mahatma, the tiresome Grant Lindons, the perennial and inevitable Amalasuntha, for whom the house was being illuminated tonight—all were strands woven into the very pile of the carpet he trod on his way up the stairs. As he passed the dining-room he saw, through half-open doors, the glitter of glass and silver, a shirt-sleeved man placing bowls of roses down the long table, and Maisie Bruss, wan but undaunted, dealing out dinner cards to Powder, the English butler.

VI

Pauline Manford sent a satisfied glance down the table.

It was on such occasions that she visibly reaped her reward. No one else in New York had so accomplished a cook, such smoothly running service, a dinner-table so softly yet brightly lit, or such skill in grouping about it persons not only eminent in wealth or fashion, but likely to find pleasure in each other's society.

The intimate reunion, of the not-more-than-the-Muses kind, was not Pauline's affair. She was aware of this, and seldom made the attempt—though, when she did, she was never able to discover why it was not a success. But in the organizing and administering of a big dinner she was conscious of mastery. Not the stupid big dinner of old days, when the "crowned heads" used to be treated like a caste apart, and everlastingly invited to meet each other through a whole monotonous season: Pauline was too modern for that. She excelled in a judicious blending of Wall Street and Bohemia, and her particular art lay in her selection of the latter element. Of course there were Bohemians and Bohemians; as she had once remarked to Nona, people weren't always amusing just because they were clever, or dull just because they were rich—though at the last clause Nona had screwed up her nose incredulously. . . Well, even Nona would be satisfied tonight, Pauline thought. It wasn't everybody who would have been bold enough to ask a social reformer like Parker Greg with the very people least disposed to encourage social reform, nor a young composer like Torfried Lobb (a disciple of "The Six") with all those stolid opera-goers, nor that disturbing Tommy Ardwin, the Cubist decorator, with the owners of the most expensive "period houses" in Fifth Avenue.

Pauline was not a bit afraid of such combinations. She knew in advance that at one of her dinners everything would "go"—it always did. And her success amused and exhilarated her so much that, even tonight, though she had come down oppressed with problems, they slipped from her before she even had time to remind herself that they were nonexistent. She had only to look at the faces gathered about that subdued radiance of old silver and scattered flowers to be sure of it. There, at the other end of the table, was her husband's dark head, comely and resolute in its vigorous middle- age; on his right the Marchesa di San Fedele, the famous San Fedele pearls illuminating her inconspicuous black; on his left the handsome Mrs. Herman Toy, magnanimously placed there by Pauline because she knew that Manford was said to be "taken" by her, and she wanted him to be in good-humour that evening. To measure her own competence she had only to take in this group, already settling down to an evening's enjoyment, and then let her glance travel on to the others, the young and handsome women, the well-dressed confident-looking men. Nona, grave yet eager, was talking to Manford's legal rival, the brilliant Alfred Cosby, who was known to have said she was the cleverest girl in New York. Lita, cool and aloof, drooped her head slightly to listen to Torfried Lobb, the composer; Jim gazed across the table at Lita as if his adoration made every intervening obstacle transparent; Aggie Heuston, whose coldness certainly made her look distinguished, though people complained that she was dull, dispensed occasional monosyllables to the ponderous Herman Toy; and Stanley Heuston, leaning back with that faint dry smile which Pauline found irritating because it was so inscrutable, kept his eyes discreetly but steadily on Nona. Dear good Stan, always like a brother to Nona! People who knew him well said he wasn't as sardonic as he looked.

It was a world after Pauline's heart—a world such as she believed its Maker meant it to be. She turned to the Bishop on her right, wondering if he shared her satisfaction, and encountered a glance of understanding.

"So refreshing to be among old friends. . . This is one of the few houses left. . . Always such a pleasure to meet the dear Marchesa; I hope she has better reports of her son? Wretched business, I'm afraid. My dear Mrs. Manford, I wonder if you know how blessed you are in your children? That wise little Nona, who is going to make some man so happy one of these days—not Cosby, no? Too much difference in age? And your steady Jim and his idol . . . yes, I know it doesn't become my cloth to speak indulgently of idolatry. But happy marriages are so rare nowadays: where else could one find such examples as there are about this table? Your Jim and his Lita, and my good friend Heuston with that saint of a wife—" The Bishop paused, as if, even on so privileged an occasion, he was put to it to prolong the list. "Well, you've given them the example. . ." He stopped again, probably remembering that his hostess's matrimonial bliss was built on the ruins of her first husband's. But in divorcing she had invoked a cause which even the Church recognizes; and the Bishop proceeded serenely: "Her children shall rise up and call her blessed—yes, dear friend, you must let me say it."

The words were balm to Pauline. Every syllable carried conviction: all was right with her world and the Bishop's! Why did she ever need any other spiritual guidance than that of her own creed? She felt a twinge of regret at having so involved herself with the Mahatma. Yet what did Episcopal Bishops know of "holy ecstasy"? And could any number of Church services have reduced her hips? After all, there was room for all the creeds in her easy rosy world. And the thought led her straight to her other preoccupation: the reception for the Cardinal. She resolved to secure the Bishop's approval at once. After that, of course the Chief Rabbi would have to come. And what a lesson in tolerance and good-will to the discordant world she was trying to reform!

Nona, half-way down the table, viewed its guests from another angle. She had come back depressed rather than fortified from her flying visit to her father. There were days when Manford liked to be "surprised" at the office; when he and his daughter had their little jokes together over these clandestine visits. But this one had not come off in that spirit. She had found Manford tired and slightly irritable; Nona, before he had time to tell her of her mother's visit, caught a lingering whiff of Pauline's cool hygienic scent, and wondered nervously what could have happened to make Mrs. Manford break through her tightly packed engagements, and dash down to her husband's office. It was of course to that emergency that she had sacrificed poor Exhibit A—little guessing his relief at the postponement. But what could have obliged her to see Manford so suddenly, when they were to meet at dinner that evening?

The girl had asked no questions: she knew that Manford, true to his profession, preferred putting them. And her chief object, of course, had been to get him to help her about Arthur Wyant. That, she perceived, at first added to his irritation: was he Wyant's keeper, he wanted to know? But he broke off before the next question: "Why the devil can't his own son look after him?" She had seen that question on his very lips; but they shut down on it, and he rose from his chair with a shrug. "Poor devil—if you think I can be of any use? All right, then—I'll drop in on him tomorrow." He and Wyant, ever since the divorce, had met whenever Jim's fate was to be discussed; Wyant felt a sort of humiliated gratitude for Manford's generosity to his son. "Not the money, you know, Nona—damn the money! But taking such an interest in him; helping him to find himself: appreciating him, hang it! He understands Jim a hundred times better than your mother ever did. . ." On this basis the two men came together now and then in a spirit of tolerant understanding. . .

Nona recalled her father's face as it had been when she left him: worried, fagged, yet with that twinkle of gaiety his eyes always had when he looked at her. Now, smoothed out, smiling, slightly replete, it was hard as stone. "Like his own death-mask," the girl thought; "as if he'd done with everything, once for all.— And the way those two women bore him! Mummy put Gladys Toy next to him as a reward—for what?" She smiled at her mother's simplicity in imagining that he was having what Pauline called a "harmless flirtation" with Mrs. Herman Toy. That lady's obvious charms were no more to him, Nona suspected, than those of the florid Bathsheba in the tapestry behind his chair. But Pauline had evidently had some special reason—over and above her usual diffused benevolence— for wanting to put Manford in a good humour. "The Mahatma, probably." Nona knew how her mother hated a fuss: how vulgar and unchristian she always thought it. And it would certainly be inconvenient to give up the rest-cure at Dawnside she had planned for March, when Manford was to go off tarpon-fishing.

Nona's glance, in the intervals of talk with her neighbours, travelled farther, lit on Jim's good-humoured wistful face—Jim was always wistful at his mother's banquets—and flitted on to Aggie Heuston's precise little mask, where everything was narrow and perpendicular, like the head of a saint squeezed into a cathedral niche. But the girl's eyes did not linger, for as they rested on Aggie they abruptly met the latter's gaze. Aggie had been furtively scrutinizing her, and the discovery gave Nona a faint shock. In another instant Mrs. Heuston turned to Parker Greg, the interesting young social reformer whom Pauline had thoughtfully placed next to her, with the optimistic idea that all persons interested in improving the world must therefore be in the fullest sympathy. Nona, knowing Parker Greg's views, smiled at that too. Aggie, she was sure, would feel much safer with her other neighbour, Mr. Herman Toy, who thought, on all subjects, just what all his fellow capitalists did.

Nona caught Stan Heuston's smile, and knew he had read her thought; but from him too she turned. The last thing she wanted was that he should guess her real opinion of his wife. Something deep down and dogged in Nona always, when it came to the touch, made her avert her feet from the line of least resistance.

Manford lent an absent ear first to one neighbour, then the other. Mrs. Toy was saying, in her flat uncadenced voice, like tepid water running into a bath: "I don't see how people can LIVE without lifts in their houses, do you? But perhaps it's because I've never had to. Father's house had the first electric lift at Climax. Once, in England, we went to stay with the Duke of Humber, at Humber Castle—one of those huge parties, royalties and everything— golf and polo all day, and a ball every night; and, will you believe it, WE HAD TO WALK UP AND DOWN STAIRS! I don't know what English people are made of. I suppose they've never been used to what we call comfort. The second day I told Herman I couldn't stand those awful slippery stairs after two rounds of golf, and dancing till four in the morning. It was simply destroying my heart—the doctor has warned me so often! I wanted to leave right away—but Herman said it would offend the Duke. The Duke's such a sweet old man. But, any way, I made Herman promise me a sapphire and emerald plaque from Carrier's before I'd agree to stick it out. . ."

The Marchesa's little ferret face with sharp impassioned eyes darted conversationally forward. "The Duke of Humber? I know him so WELL. Dear old man! Ah, you also stayed at Humber? So often he invites me. We are related . . . yes, through his first wife, whose mother was a Venturini of the Calabrian branch: Donna Ottaviana. Yes. Another sister, Donna Rosmunda, the beauty of the family, married the Duke of Lepanto . . . a mediatized prince. . ."

She stopped, and Manford read in her eyes the hasty inward interrogation: "Will they think that expression queer? I'm not sure myself just what 'mediatized' means. And these Americans! They stick at nothing, but they're shocked at everything." Aloud she continued: "A mediatized prince—but a man of the VERY HIGHEST character."

"Oh—" murmured Mrs. Toy, puzzled but obviously relieved.

Manford's attention, tugging at its moorings, had broken loose again and was off and away.

The how-many-eth dinner did that make this winter? And no end in sight! How could Pauline stand it? Why did she want to stand it? All those rest-cures, massages, rhythmic exercises, devised to restore the health of people who would have been as sound as bells if only they had led normal lives! Like that fool of a woman spreading her blond splendours so uselessly at his side, who couldn't walk upstairs because she had danced all night! Pauline was just like that—never walked upstairs, and then had to do gymnastics, and have osteopathy, and call in Hindu sages, to prevent her muscles from getting atrophied. . . He had a vision of his mother, out on the Minnesota farm, before they moved into Delos— saw her sowing, digging potatoes, feeding chickens; saw her kneading, baking, cooking, washing, mending, catching and harnessing the half-broken colt to drive twelve miles in the snow for the doctor, one day when all the men were away, and his little sister had been so badly scalded. . . And there the old lady sat at Delos, in her nice little brick house, in her hale and hearty old age, built to outlive them all.—Wasn't that perhaps the kind of life Manford himself had been meant for? Farming on a big scale, with all the modern appliances his forbears had lacked, outdoing everybody in the county, marketing his goods at the big centres, and cutting a swathe in state politics like his elder brother? Using his brains, muscles, the whole of him, body and soul, to do real things, bring about real results in the world, instead of all this artificial activity, this spinning around faster and faster in the void, and having to be continually rested and doctored to make up for exertions that led to nothing, nothing, nothing. . .

"Of course we all know YOU could tell us if you would. Everybody knows the Lindons have gone to you for advice." Mrs. Toy's large shallow eyes floated the question toward him on a sea-blue wave of curiosity. "Not a word of truth? Oh, of course you have to say that! But everybody has been expecting there'd be trouble soon. . ."

And, in a whisper, from the Marchesa's side: "Teasing you about that mysterious Mahatma? Foolish woman! As long as dear Pauline believes in him, I'm satisfied. That was what I was saying to Pauline before dinner: 'Whatever you and Dexter approve of, I approve of.' That's the reason why I'm so anxious to have my poor boy come to New York . . . my Michelangelo! If only you could see him I know you'd grow as fond of him as you are of our dear Jim: perhaps even take him into your office. . . Ah, that, dear Dexter, has always been my dream!"

. . . What sort of a life, after all, if not this one? For of course that dream of a Western farm was all rubbish. What he really wanted was a life in which professional interests as far- reaching and absorbing as his own were somehow impossibly combined with great stretches of country quiet, books, horses and children— ah, children! Boys of his own—teaching them all sorts of country things; taking them for long trudges, telling them about trees and plants and birds—watching the squirrels, feeding the robins and thrushes in winter; and coming home in the dusk to firelight, lamplight, a tea-table groaning with jolly things, all the boys and girls (girls too, more little Nonas) grouped around, hungry and tingling from their long tramp—and a woman lifting a calm face from her book: a woman who looked so absurdly young to be their mother; so—

"You're looking at Jim's wife?" The Marchesa broke in. "No wonder! Très en beauté, our Lita!—that dress, the very same colour as her hair, and those Indian emeralds . . . how clever of her! But a little difficult to talk to? Little too silent? No? Ah, not to YOU, perhaps—her dear father! Father-in-law, I mean—"

Silent! The word sent him off again. For in that other world, so ringing with children's laughter, children's wrangles, and all the healthy blustering noises of country life in a big family, there would somehow, underneath it all, be a great pool of silence, a reservoir on which one could always draw and flood one's soul with peace. The vision was vague and contradictory, but it all seemed to meet and mingle in the woman's eyes. . .

Pauline was signalling from her table-end. He rose and offered his arm to the Marchesa.

In the hall the strains of the famous Somaliland orchestra bumped and tossed downstairs from the ball-room to meet them. The ladies, headed by Mrs. Toy, flocked to the mirror-lined lift dissembled behind forced lilacs and Japanese plums; but Amalasuntha, on Manford's arm, set her blunt black slipper on the marble tread.

"I'm used to Roman palaces!"

VII

"At least you'll take a turn?" Heuston said; and Nona, yielding, joined the dancers balancing with slow steps about the shining floor.

Dancing meant nothing; it was like breathing; what would one be doing if one weren't dancing? She could not refuse without seeming singular; it was simpler to acquiesce, and lose one's self among the couples absorbed in the same complicated ritual.

The floor was full, but not crowded: Pauline always saw to that. It was easy to calculate in advance, for every one she asked always accepted, and she and Maisie Bruss, in making out the list, allotted the requisite space per couple as carefully as if they had been counting cubic feet in a hospital. The ventilation was perfect too; neither draughts nor stuffiness. One had almost the sense of dancing out of doors, under some equable southern sky. Nona, aware of what it cost to produce this illusion, marvelled once more at her tireless mother.

"Isn't she wonderful?"

Mrs. Manford, fresh, erect, a faint line of diamonds in her hair, stood in the doorway, her slim foot advanced toward the dancers.

"Perennially! Ah—she's going to dance. With Cosby."

"Yes. I wish she wouldn't."

"Wouldn't with Cosby?"

"Dear, no. In general."

Nona and Heuston had seated themselves, and were watching from their corner the weaving of hallucinatory patterns by interjoined revolving feet.

"I see. You think she dances with a Purpose?"

The girl smiled. "Awfully well—like everything else she does. But as if it were something between going to church and drilling a scout brigade. Mother's too—too tidy to dance."

"Well—this is different," murmured Heuston.

The floor had cleared as if by magic before the advance of a long slim pair: Lita Wyant and Tommy Ardwin. The decorator, tall and supple, had the conventional dancer's silhouette; but he was no more than a silhouette, a shadow on the wall. All the light and music in the room had passed into the translucent creature in his arms. He seemed to Nona like some one who has gone into a spring wood and come back carrying a long branch of silver blossom.

"Good heavens! Quelle plastique!" piped the Marchesa over Nona's shoulder.

The two had the floor to themselves: every one else had stopped dancing. But Lita and her partner seemed unaware of it. Her sole affair was to shower radiance, his to attune his lines to hers. Her face was a small still flower on a swaying stalk; all her expression was in her body, in that long legato movement like a weaving of grasses under a breeze, a looping of little waves on the shore.

"Look at Jim!" Heuston laughed. Jim Wyant, from a doorway, drank the vision thirstily. "Surely," his eyes seemed to triumph, "this justifies the Cubist Cabaret, and all the rest of her crazes."

Lita, swaying near him, dropped a smile, and floated off on the bright ripples of her beauty.

Abruptly the music stopped. Nona glanced across the room and saw Mrs. Manford move away from the musicians' balcony, over which the conductor had just leaned down to speak to her.

There was a short interval; then the orchestra broke into a fox- trot and the floor filled again. Mrs. Manford swept by with a set smile—"the kind she snaps on with her tiara," Nona thought. Well, perhaps it WAS rather bad form of Lita to monopolize the floor at her mother-in-law's ball; but was it the poor girl's fault if she danced so well that all the others stopped to gaze?

Ardwin came up to Nona. "Oh, no," Heuston protested under his breath. "I wanted—"

"There's Aggie signalling."

The girl's arm was already on Ardwin's shoulder. As they circled toward the middle of the room, Nona said: "You show off Lita's dancing marvellously."

He replied, in his high-pitched confident voice: "Oh, it's only a question of giving her her head and not butting in. She and I each have our own line of self-expression: it would be stupid to mix them. If only I could get her to dance just once for Serge Klawhammer; he's scouring the globe to find somebody to do the new 'Herodias' they're going to turn at Hollywood. People are fed up with the odalisque style, and with my help Lita could evolve something different. She's half promised to come round to my place tonight after supper and see Klawhammer. Just six or seven of the enlightened—wonder if you'd join us? He's tearing back to Hollywood tomorrow."

"Is Lita really coming?"

"Well, she said yes and no, and ended on yes."

"All right—I will." Nona hated Ardwin, his sleekness, suppleness, assurance, the group he ruled, the fashions he set, the doctrines he professed—hated them so passionately and undiscerningly that it seemed to her that at last she had her hand on her clue. That was it, of course! Ardwin and his crew were trying to persuade Lita to go into the movies; that accounted for her restlessness and irritability, her growing distaste for her humdrum life. Nona drew a breath of relief. After all, if it were only that—!

The dance over, she freed herself and slipped through the throng in quest of Jim. Should she ask him to take her to Ardwin's? No: simply tell him that she and Lita were off for a final spin at the decorator's studio, where there would be more room and less fuss than at Pauline's. Jim would laugh and approve, provided she and Lita went together; no use saying anything about Klawhammer and his absurd "Herodias."

"Jim? But, my dear, Jim went home long ago. I don't blame the poor boy," Mrs. Manford sighed, waylaid by her daughter, "because I know he has to be at the office so early; and it must be awfully boring, standing about all night and not dancing. But, darling, you must really help me to find your father. Supper's ready, and I can't imagine. . ."

The Marchesa's ferret face slipped between them as she trotted by on Mr. Toy's commodious arm.

"Dear Dexter? I saw him not five minutes ago, seeing off that wonderful Lita—"

"Lita? Lita gone too?" Nona watched the struggle between her mother's disciplined features and twitching nerves. "What impossible children I have!" A smile triumphed over her discomfiture. "I do hope there's nothing wrong with the baby? Nona, slip down and tell your father he must come up. Oh, Stanley, dear, all my men seem to have deserted me. Do find Mrs. Toy and take her in to supper. . ."

In the hall below there was no Dexter. Nona cast about a glance for Powder, the pale resigned butler, who had followed Mrs. Manford through all her vicissitudes and triumphs, seemingly concerned about nothing but the condition of his plate and the discipline of his footmen. Powder knew everything, and had an answer to everything; but he was engaged at the moment in the vast operation of making terrapin and champagne appear simultaneously on eighty-five small tables, and was not to be found in the hall. Nona ran her eye along the line of footmen behind the piled-up furs, found one who belonged to the house, and heard that Mr. Manford had left a few minutes earlier. His motor had been waiting for him, and was now gone. Mrs. James Wyant was with him, the man thought. "He's taken her to Ardwin's, of course. Poor father! After an evening of

Mrs. Toy and Amalasuntha—who can wonder? If only mother would see how her big parties bore him!" But Nona's mother would never see that.

"It's just my indestructible faith in my own genius—nothing else," Ardwin was proclaiming in his jumpy falsetto as Nona entered the high-perched studio where he gathered his group of the enlightened. These privileged persons, in the absence of chairs, had disposed themselves on the cushions and mattresses scattered about a floor painted to imitate a cunning perspective of black and white marble. Tall lamps under black domes shed their light on bare shoulders, heads sleek or tousled, and a lavish show of flesh-coloured legs and sandalled feet. Ardwin, unbosoming himself to a devotee, held up a guttering church-candle to a canvas which simulated a window open on a geometrical representation of brick walls, fire escapes and back-yards. "Sham? Oh, of course. I had the real window blocked up. It looked out on that stupid old 'night-piece' of Brooklyn Bridge and the East River. Everybody who came here said: 'A Whistler nocturne!' and I got so bored. Besides, it was REALLY THERE: and I hate things that are really where you think they are. They're as tiresome as truthful people. Everything in art should be false. Everything in life should be art. Ergo, everything in life should be false: complexions, teeth, hair, wives . . . specially wives. Oh, Miss Manford, that you? Do come in. Mislaid Lita?"

"Isn't she here?"

"IS she?" He pivoted about on the company. When he was not dancing he looked, with his small snaky head and too square shoulders, like a cross between a Japanese waiter and a full-page advertisement for silk underwear. "IS Lita here? Any of you fellows got her dissembled about your persons? Now, then, out with her! Jossie Keiler, YOU'RE not Mrs. James Wyant disguised as a dryad, are you?" There was a general guffaw as Miss Jossie Keiler, the octoroon pianist, scrambled to her pudgy feet and assembled a series of sausage arms and bolster legs in a provocative pose. "Knew I'd get found out," she lisped.

A short man with a deceptively blond head, thick lips under a stubby blond moustache, and eyes like needles behind tortoiseshell- rimmed glasses, stood before the fire, bulging a glossy shirtfront and solitaire pearl toward the company. "Don't this lady dance?" he enquired, in a voice like melted butter, a few drops of which seemed to trickle down his lips and be licked back at intervals behind a thickly ringed hand.

"Miss Manford? Bet she does! Come along, Nona; shed your togs and let's show Mr. Klawhammer here present that Lita's not the only peb—"

"Gracious! Wait till I get into the saddle!" screamed Miss Keiler, tiny hands like blueish mice darting out at the keyboard from the end of her bludgeon arms.

Nona perched herself on the edge of a refectory table. "Thanks. I'm not a candidate for 'Herodias.' My sister-in-law is sure to turn up in a minute."

Even Mrs. Dexter Manford's perfectly run house was not a particularly appetizing place to return to at four o'clock on the morning after a dance. The last motor was gone, the last overcoat and opera cloak had vanished from hall and dressing-rooms, and only one hanging lamp lit the dusky tapestries and the monumental balustrade of the staircase. But empty cocktail glasses and ravaged cigar-boxes littered the hall tables, wisps of torn tulle and trampled orchids strewed the stair-carpet, and the thicket of forced lilacs and Japanese plums in front of the lift drooped mournfully in the hot air. Nona, letting herself in with her latch- key, scanned the scene with a feeling of disgust. What was it all for, and what was left when it was over? Only a huge clearing-up for Maisie and the servants, and a new list to make out for the next time. . . She remembered mild spring nights at Cedarledge, when she was a little girl, and she and Jim used to slip downstairs in stocking feet, go to the lake, loose the canoe, and drift on a silver path among islets fringed with budding dogwood. She hurried on past the desecrated shrubs.

Above, the house was dark but for a line of light under the library door. Funny—at that hour; her father must still be up. Very likely he too had just come in. She was passing on when the door opened and Manford called her.

"'Pon my soul, Nona! That you? I supposed you were in bed long ago."

One of the green-shaded lamps lit the big writing-table. Manford's armchair was drawn up to it, an empty glass and half-consumed cigarette near by, the evening paper sprawled on the floor.

"Was that you I heard coming in? Do you know what time it is?"

"Yes; worse luck! I've been scouring the town after Lita."

"LITA?"

"Waiting for her for hours at Tommy Ardwin's. Such a crew! He told me she was going there to dance for Klawhammer, the Hollywood man, and I didn't want her to go alone—"

Manford's face darkened. He lit another cigarette and turned to his daughter impatiently.

"What the devil made you believe such a yarn? Klawhammer—!"

Nona stood facing him; their eyes met, and he turned away with a shrug to reach for a match.

"I believed it because, just afterward, the servants told me that Lita had left, and as they said you'd gone with her I supposed you'd taken her to Ardwin's, not knowing that I meant to join her there."

"Ah; I see." He lit the cigarette and puffed at it for a moment or two, deliberately. "You're quite right to think she needs looking after," he began again, in a changed tone. "Somebody's got to take on the job, since her husband seems to have washed his hands of it."

"Father! You know perfectly well that if Jim took on that job— running after Lita all night from one cabaret to another—he'd lose the other, the one that keeps them going. Nobody could carry on both."

"Hullo, spitfire! Hands off our brother!"

"Rather." She leaned against the table, her eyes still on him. "And when Ardwin told me about this Klawhammer film—didn't Lita mention it to you?"

He appeared to consider. "She did say Ardwin was bothering her about something of the kind; so when I found Jim had gone I took her home myself."

"Ah—you took her home?"

Manford, settling himself back in his armchair, met the surprise in her voice unconcernedly. "Why, of course. Did you really see me letting her make a show of herself? Sorry you think that's my way of looking after her."

Nona, perched on the arm of his chair, enclosed him in a happy hug. "You goose, you!" she sighed; but the epithet was not for her father.

She poured herself a glass of cherry brandy, dropped a kiss on his thinning hair, and ran up to her room humming Miss Jossie Keiler's jazz-tune. Perhaps after all it wasn't such a rotten world.

VIII

The morning after a party in her own house Pauline Manford always accorded herself an extra half-hour's rest; but on this occasion she employed it in lying awake and wearily reckoning up the next day's tasks. Disenchantment had succeeded to the night's glamour. The glamour of balls never did last: they so quickly became a matter for those domestic undertakers, the charwomen, housemaids and electricians. And in this case the taste of pleasure had soured early. When the doors were thrown open on the beflowered supper tables not one of the hostess's family was left to marshal the guests to their places! Her husband, her daughter and son, her son's wife—all had deserted her. It needed, in that chill morning vigil, all Pauline's self-control to banish the memory. Not that she wanted any of them to feel under any obligation—she was all for personal freedom, self-expression, or whatever they called it nowadays—but still, a ball was a ball, a host was a host. It was too bad of Dexter, really; and of Jim too. On Lita of course no one could count: that was part of the pose people found so fascinating. But Jim—Jim and Nona to forsake her! What a ridiculous position it had put her in—but no, she mustn't think of that now, or those nasty little wrinkles would creep back about her eyes. The masseuse had warned her. . . Gracious! At what time was the masseuse due? She stretched out her hand, turned on the light by the bed (for the windows were still closely darkened), and reached for what Maisie Bruss called the night-list: an upright porcelain tablet on which the secretary recorded, for nocturnal study, the principal "fixtures" of the coming day.

Today they were so numerous that Miss Bruss's tight script had hardly contrived to squeeze them in. Foremost, of course, poor Exhibit A, moved on from yesterday; then a mysterious appointment with Amalasuntha, just before lunch: something urgent, she had hinted. Today of all days! Amalasuntha was so tactless at times. And then that Mahatma business: since Dexter was inflexible, his wife had made up her mind to appeal to the Lindons. It would be awkward, undoubtedly—and she did so hate things that were awkward. Any form of untidiness, moral or material, was unpleasant to her; but something must be done, and at once. She herself hardly knew why she felt so apprehensive, so determined that the matter should have no sequel; except that, if anything DID go wrong, it would upset all her plans for a rest-cure, for new exercises, for all sorts of promised ways of prolonging youth, activity and slenderness, and would oblige her to find a new Messiah who would tell her she was psychic.

But the most pressing item on her list was her address that very afternoon to the National Mothers' Day Association—or, no; wasn't it the Birth Control League? Nonsense! That was her speech at the banquet next week: a big affair at the St. Regis for a group of International Birth-controllers. Wakeful as she felt, she must be half asleep to have muddled up her engagements like that! She extinguished the lamp and sank hopefully to her pillow—perhaps now sleep would really come. But her bed-lamp seemed to have a double switch, and putting it out in the room only turned it on in her head.

Well, she would try reciting scraps of her Mothers' Day address: she seldom spoke in public, but when she did she took the affair seriously, and tried to be at once winning and impressive. She and Maisie had gone carefully over the typed copy; and she was sure it was all right; but she liked getting the more effective passages by heart—it brought her nearer to her audience to lean forward and speak intimately, without having to revert every few minutes to the text.

"Was there ever a hearth or a heart—a mother's heart—that wasn't big enough for all the babies God wants it to hold? Of course there are days when the mother is so fagged out that she thinks she'd give the world if there were nothing at all to do in the nursery, and she could just sit still with folded hands. But the only time when there's nothing at all for a mother to do in the nursery is when there's a little coffin there. It's all quiet enough THEN . . . as some of us here know. . ." (Pause, and a few tears in the audience.) "Not that we want the modern mother to wear herself out: no indeed! The babies themselves haven't any use for worn-out mothers! And the first thing to be considered is what the babies want, isn't it?" (Pause—smiles in the audience). . .

What on earth was Amalasuntha coming to bother her about? More money, of course—but she really couldn't pay all that wretched Michelangelo's debts. There would soon be debts nearer home if Lita went on dressing so extravagantly, and perpetually having her jewellery reset. It cost almost as much nowadays to reset jewels as to buy new ones, and those emeralds. . .

At that hour of the morning things did tend to look ash-coloured; and she felt that her optimism had never been so sorely strained since the year when she had had to read Proust, learn a new dance- step, master Oriental philosophy, and decide whether she should really bob her hair, or only do it to look so. She had come victoriously through those ordeals; but what if worse lay ahead?

Amalasuntha, in one of Mrs. Manford's least successfully made-over dresses, came in looking shabby and humble—always a bad sign. And of course it was Michelangelo's debts. Racing, baccara, and a woman . . . a Russian princess; oh, my dear, AUTHENTIC, quite! Wouldn't Pauline like to see her picture from the "Prattler"? She and Michelangelo had been snapped together in bathing tights at the Lido.

No—Pauline wouldn't. She turned from the proffered effigy with a disgust evidently surprising to the Marchesa, whose own prejudices were different, and who could grasp other people's only piece-meal, one at a time, like a lesson in mnemonics.

"Oh, my boy doesn't do things by halves," the Marchesa averred, still feeling that the occasion was one for boasting.

Pauline leaned back wearily. "I'm as sorry for you as I can be, Amalasuntha; but Michelangelo is not a baby, and if he can't be made to understand that a poor man who wants to spend money must first earn it—"

"Oh, but he does, darling! Venturino and I have always dinned it into him. And last year he tried his best to marry that one-eyed Miss Oxbaum from Oregon, he really did."

"I said EARN," Pauline interposed. "We don't consider that marrying for money is earning it—"

"Oh, mercy—don't you? Not sometimes?" breathed the Marchesa.

"What I mean by earning is going into an office—is—"

"Ah, just so! It was what I said to Dexter last night. It is what Venturino and I most long for: that Dexter should take Michelangelo into his office. That would solve every difficulty. And once Michelangelo is here I'm sure he will succeed. No one is more clever, you know: only, in Rome, young men are in greater danger— there are more temptations—"

Pauline pursed her lips. "I suppose there are." But, since temptations are the privilege of metropolises, she thought it rather impertinent of Amalasuntha to suggest that there were more in a one-horse little place like Rome than in New York; though in a different mood she would have been the first to pronounce the Italian capital a sink of iniquity, and New York the model and prototype of the pure American city. All these contradictions, which usually sat lightly on her, made her head ache today, and she continued, nervously: "Take Michelangelo into his office! But what preparations has he had, what training? Has he ever studied for the law?"

"No; I don't think he has, darling; but he WOULD; I can promise you he would," the Marchesa declared, in the tone of one saying: "In such straits, he would become a street-cleaner."

Pauline smiled faintly. "I don't think you understand. The law is a profession." (Dexter had told her that.) "It requires years of training, of preparation. Michelangelo would have to take a degree at Harvard or Columbia first. But perhaps"—a glance at her wrist- watch told her that her next engagement impended—"perhaps Dexter could suggest some other kind of employment. I don't know, of course. . . I can't promise. . . But meanwhile . . ." She turned to her writing-table, and a cheque passed between them, too small to make a perceptible impression on Michelangelo's deficit, but large enough for Amalasuntha to murmur: "How you do spoil me, darling! Well—for the boy's sake I accept in all simplicity. And about the reception for the Cardinal—I'm sure a cable to Venturino will arrange it. Would that kind Maisie send it off, and sign my name?"

It was well after three o'clock when Pauline came down the Lindons' door-step and said to her chauffeur: "To Mr. Wyant's." And she had still to crowd in her eurythmic exercises (put off from the morning), and be ready at half-past four, bathed, waved and apparelled, for the Mothers' Day Meeting, which was to take place in her own ball-room, with a giant tea to follow.

Certainly, no amount of "mental deep-breathing," and all the other exercises in serenity, could combat the nervous apprehension produced by this breathless New York life. Today she really felt it to be too much for her: she leaned back and closed her lids with a sigh. But she was jerked back to consciousness by the traffic- control signal, which had immobilized the motor just when every moment was so precious. The result of every one's being in such a hurry to get everywhere was that nobody could get anywhere. She looked across the triple row of motors in line with hers, and saw in each (as if in a vista of mirrors) an expensively dressed woman like herself, leaning forward in the same attitude of repressed impatience, the same nervous frown of hurry on her brow.

Oh, if only she could remember to relax!

But how could one, with everything going wrong as it was today? The visit to Fanny Lindon had been an utter failure. Pauline had apparently overestimated her influence on the Lindons, and that discovery in itself was rather mortifying. To be told that the Mahatma business was "a family affair"—and thus be given to understand that she was no longer of the family! Pauline, in her own mind, had never completely ceased to be a Wyant. She thought herself still entitled to such shadowy prerogatives as the name afforded, and was surprised that the Wyants should not think so too. After all, she kept Amalasuntha for them—no slight charge!

But Mrs. Lindon had merely said it was "all too painful"—and had ended, surprisingly: "Dexter himself has specially asked us not to say anything."

The implication was: "If you want to find out, go to him!"—when of course Fanny knew well enough that lawyers' and doctors' wives are the last people to get at their clients' secrets.

Pauline rose to her feet, offended, and not averse from showing it. "Well, my dear, I can only say that if it's so awful that you can't tell ME, I rather wonder at your wanting to tell Tom, Dick and Harry. Have you thought of that?"

Oh, yes, she had, Mrs. Lindon wailed. "But Grant says it's a duty . . . and so does Dexter. . ."

Pauline permitted herself a faint smile. "Dexter naturally takes the lawyer's view: that's HIS duty."

Mrs. Lindon's mind was not alert for innuendos. "Yes; he says we OUGHT to," she merely repeated.

A sudden lassitude overcame Pauline. "At least send Grant to me first—let me talk to him."

But to herself she said: "My only hope now is to get at them through Arthur." And she looked anxiously out of the motor, watching for the signal to shift.

Everything at Arthur Wyant's was swept and garnished for her approach. One felt that cousin Eleanor, whisking the stray cigarette-ends into the fire, and giving the sofa cushions a last shake, had slipped out of the back door as Mrs. Manford entered by the front.

Wyant greeted her with his usual rather overdone cordiality. He had never quite acquired the note on which discarded husbands should welcome condescending wives. In this respect Pauline was his superior. She had found the exact blend of gravity with sisterly friendliness; and the need of having to ask about his health always helped her over the first moments.

"Oh, you see—still mummified." He pointed to the leg stretched out in front of him. "Couldn't even see Amalasuntha to the door—"

"Amalasuntha? Has she been here?"

"Yes. Asked herself to lunch. Rather a to-do for me; I'm not used to entertaining distinguished foreigners, especially when they have to picnic on a tray at my elbow. But she took it all very good- naturedly."

"I should think so," Pauline murmured; adding inwardly: "Trust Amalasuntha not to pay for her own lunch."

"Yes; she's in great feather. Said you'd been so kind to her—as usual."

Pauline sounded the proper deprecation.

"She's awfully pleased at your having promised that Manford would give Michelangelo a leg up if he comes out to try his luck in New York."

"Promised? Well—not quite. But I did say Dexter would do what he could. It seems the only way left of disposing of Michelangelo."

Wyant leaned back, a smile twitching under his moustache. "Yes— that young man's a scourge. And I begin to see why. Did you see his picture in bathing tights with the latest lady?"

Pauline waved away the suggestion. How like Arthur not to realize, even yet, that such things disgusted her!

"Well, he's the best looking piece of human sculpture I've seen since I last went through the Vatican galleries. Regular Apollo. Funny, the Albany Wyants having a hand in turning out a heathen divinity. I was showing the picture to Manford just now, and telling him the fond mother's comment."

Pauline looked up quickly. "Has Dexter been here too?"

"Yes; trying to give ME a leg up." He glanced at his bandages. "Rather more difficult, that. I must get it down first—to the floor. But Manford's awfully kind too—it's catching. He wants me to go off with Jim, down to that island of his, and get a fortnight's real sunshine. Says he can get Jim off by a little wirepulling, some time just before Easter, he thinks. It's tempting—"

Pauline smiled: she was always pleased when the two men spoke of each other in that tone; and certainly it WAS kind of Dexter to offer the hospitality of his southern island to poor Arthur. . . She thought how easy life would be if only every one were kind and simple.

"But about Michelangelo: I was going to tell you what is worrying Amalasuntha. Of course what she means by Michelangelo's going into business in America is marrying an heiress—"

"Oh, of course. And I daresay he will."

"Exactly. She's got her eye on one already. You haven't guessed? Nona!"

Pauline's sense of humour was not unfailing, but this relaxed her taut nerves, and she laughed. "Poor Michelangelo!"

"I thought it wouldn't worry you. But what is worrying Amalasuntha is that he won't be LET—"

"Be let?"

"By Lita. Her theory is that Lita will fall madly in love with Michelangelo as soon as she lays eyes on him—and that when they've had one dance together she'll be lost. And Amalasuntha, for that reason—though she daren't tell you so—thinks it might really be cheaper in the end to pay Michelangelo's debts than to import him. As she says, it's for the family to decide, now she's warned them."

Their laughter mingled. It was the first time, perhaps, since they had been young together; as a rule, their encounters were untinged with levity.

But Pauline dismissed the laugh hurriedly for the Grant Lindons. At the name Wyant's eyes lit up: it was as if she had placed an appetizing morsel before a listless convalescent.

"But you're the very person to tell me all about it—or, no, you can't, of course, if Manford's going to take it up. But no matter— after all, it's public property by this time. Seen this morning's 'Looker-on'—with pictures? Here, where—" In the stack of illustrated papers always at his elbow he could never find the one he wanted, and now began to toss over "Prattlers," "Listeners" and others with helpless hand. How that little symptom of inefficiency took her back to the old days, when his perpetual disorder, and his persistent belief that he could always put his hand on everything, used to be such a strain on her nerves!

"Pictures?" she gasped.

"Rather. The nigger himself, in turban and ritual togs; and a lot of mixed nudes doing leg-work round a patio. The place looks like a Palm Beach Hotel. Fanny Lindon's in a stew because she's recognized Bee in the picture. She says she's going to have the man in jail if they spend their last penny on it. Hullo— here it is, after all."

Pauline shrank back. Would people never stop trying to show her disgusting photographs? She articulated: "You haven't seen Fanny Lindon too?"

"Haven't I? She spent the morning here. She told Amalasuntha everything."

Pauline, with a great effort, controlled her rising anger. "How idiotic! Now it WILL be spread to all the winds!" She saw Fanny and Amalasuntha gloatingly exchanging the images of their progenies' dishonour. It was too indecent . . . and the old New Yorker was as shameless as the demoralized foreigner.

"I didn't know Fanny had been here before me. I've just left her. I've been trying to persuade her to stop; to hush up the whole business before it's too late. I suppose you gave her the same advice?"

Wyant's face clouded: he looked perplexedly at his former wife, and she saw he had lost all sense of the impropriety and folly of the affair in his famished enjoyment of its spicy details.

"I don't know—I understood it WAS too late; and that Manford was urging them to do it."

Pauline made a slight movement of impatience. "Dexter—of course! When he sees a 'case'! I suppose lawyers are all alike. At any rate, I can't make him understand. . ." She broke off, suddenly aware that the rôles were reversed, and that for the first time she was disparaging her second husband to her first. "Besides," she hurried on, "it's no affair of Dexter's if the Lindons choose to dishonour their child publicly. They're not HIS relations; Bee is not HIS cousin's daughter. But you and I—how can we help feeling differently? Bee and Nona and Jim were all brought up together. You must help me to stop this scandal! You must send for Grant Lindon at once. He's sure to listen to you . . . you've always had a great influence on Grant. . ."

She found herself, in her extremity, using the very arguments she had addressed to Manford, and she saw at once that in this case they were more effective. Wyant drew himself up stiffly with a faint smile of satisfaction. Involuntarily he ran a thin gouty hand through his hair, and tried for a glimpse of himself in the mirror.

"Think so—really? Of course when Grant was a boy he used to consider me a great fellow. But now . . . who remembers me in my dingy corner?"

Pauline rose with her clear wintry smile. "A good many of us, it seems. You tell me I'm the third lady to call on you today! You know well enough, Arthur—" she brushed the name in lightly, on the extreme tip of her smile—"that the opinion of people like you still counts in New York, even in these times. Imagine what your mother would have felt at the idea of Fanny and Bee figuring in all the daily headlines, with reporters and photographers in a queue on the doorstep! I'm glad she hasn't lived to see it."

She knew that Wyant's facile irony always melted before an emotional appeal, especially if made in his mother's name. He blinked unsteadily, and flung away the "Looker-on."

"You're dead right: they're a pack of fools. There are no standards left. I'll do what I can; I'll telephone to Grant to look in on his way home this evening. . . I say, Pauline: what's the truth of it all, anyhow? If I'm to give him a talking to I ought to know." His eyes again lit up with curiosity.

"Truth of it? There isn't any—it's the silliest mare's-nest! Why, I'm going to Dawnside for a rest-cure next month, while Dexter's tarpon-fishing. The Mahatma is worlds above all this tattle—it's for the Lindons I'm anxious, not him."

The paper thrown aside by Wyant had dropped to the floor, face upward at a full-page picture—THE picture. Pauline, on her way out, mechanically yielded to her instinct for universal tidying, and bent to pick it up; bent and looked. Her eyes were still keen; passing over the noxious caption "Dawnside Co-Eds," they immediately singled out Bee Lindon from the capering round; then travelled on, amazed, to another denuded nymph . . . whose face, whose movements. . . Incredible! . . . For a second Pauline refused to accept what her eyes reported. Sick and unnerved, she folded the picture away and laid the magazine on a table.

"Oh, don't bother about picking up that paper. Sorry there's no one to show you out!" she heard Wyant calling. She went downstairs, blind, unbelieving, hardly knowing how she got into her motor.

Barely time to get home, change, and be in the Chair, her address before her, when the Mothers arrived in their multitude. . .

IX

Well, perhaps Dexter would understand NOW the need of hushing up the Grant Lindons. . . The picture might be a libel, of course— such things, Pauline knew, could be patched up out of quite unrelated photographs. The dancing circle might have been skilfully fitted into the Dawnside patio, and goodness knew what shameless creatures have supplied the bodies of the dancers. Dexter had often told her that it was a common blackmailing trick.

Even if the photograph were genuine, Pauline could understand and make allowances. She had never seen anything of the kind herself at Dawnside— heaven forbid!—but whenever she had gone there for a lecture, or a new course of exercises, she had suspected that the bare whitewashed room, with its throned Buddha, which received her and other like-minded ladies of her age, all active, earnest and eager for self-improvement, had not let them very far into the mystery. Beyond, perhaps, were other rites, other settings: why not? Wasn't everybody talking about "the return to Nature," and ridiculing the American prudery in which the minds and bodies of her generation had been swaddled? The Mahatma was one of the leaders of the new movement: the Return to Purity, he called it. He was always celebrating the nobility of the human body, and praising the ease of the loose Oriental dress compared with the constricting western garb: but Pauline had supposed the draperies he advocated to be longer and less transparent; above all, she had not expected familiar faces above those insufficient scarves. . .

But here she was at her own door. There was just time to be ready for the Mothers; none in which to telephone to Dexter, or buy up the whole edition of the "Looker-on" (fantastic vision!), or try and get hold of its editor, who had once dined with her, and was rather a friend of Lita's. All these possibilities and impossibilities raced through her brain to the maddening tune of "too late" while she slipped off her street-dress and sat twitching with impatience under the maid's readjustment of her ruffled head. The gown prepared for the meeting, rich, matronly and just the least bit old-fashioned—very different from the one designed for the Birth Control committee—lay spread out beside the copy of her speech, and Maisie Bruss, who had been hovering within call, dashed back breathless from a peep over the stairs.

"They're arriving—"

"Oh, Maisie, rush down! Say I'm telephoning—"

Her incurable sincerity made her unhook the receiver and call out Manford's office number. Almost instantly she heard him. "Dexter, this Mahatma investigation must be stopped! Don't ask me why— there isn't time. Only promise—"

She heard his impatient laugh.

"No?"

"Impossible," came back.

She supposed she had hung up the receiver, fastened on her jewelled "Motherhood" badge, slipped on rings and bracelets as usual. But she remembered nothing clearly until she found herself on the platform at the end of the packed ball-room, looking across rows and rows of earnest confiding faces, with lips and eyes prepared for the admiring reception of her "message." She was considered a very good speaker: she knew how to reach the type of woman represented by this imposing assemblage—delegates from small towns all over the country, united by a common faith in the infinite extent of human benevolence and the incalculable resources of American hygiene. Something of the moral simplicity of her own bringing-up brought her close to these women, who had flocked to the great perfidious city serenely unaware of its being anything more, or other, than the gigantic setting of a Mothers' Meeting. Pauline, at such times, saw the world through their eyes, and was animated by a genuine ardour for the cause of motherhood and domesticity.

As she turned toward her audience a factitious serenity descended on her. She felt in control of herself and of the situation. She spoke.

"Personality—first and last, and at all costs. I've begun my talk to you with that one word because it seems to me to sum up our whole case. Personality— room to develop in: not only elbow-room but body-room and soul-room, and plenty of both. That's what every human being has a right to. No more effaced wives, no more drudging mothers, no more human slaves crushed by the eternal round of housekeeping and child-bearing—"

She stopped, drew a quick breath, met Nona's astonished gaze over rows of bewildered eye-glasses, and felt herself plunging into an abyss. But she caught at the edge, and saved herself from the plunge—

"That's what our antagonists say—the women who are afraid to be mothers, ashamed to be mothers, the women who put their enjoyment and their convenience and what they call their happiness before the mysterious heaven-sent joy, the glorious privilege, of bringing children into the world—"

A round of applause from the reassured mothers. She had done it! She had pulled off her effect from the very jaws of disaster. Only the swift instinct of recovery had enabled her, before it was too late, to pass off the first sentences of her other address, her Birth Control speech, as the bold exordium of her hymn to motherhood! She paused a moment, still inwardly breathless, yet already sure enough of herself to smile back at Nona across her unsuspecting audience—sure enough to note that her paradoxical opening had had a much greater effect than she could have hoped to produce by the phrases with which she had meant to begin.

A hint for future oratory—

Only—the inward nervousness subsisted. The discovery that she could lose not only her self-control but her memory, the very sense of what she was saying, was like a hand of ice pointing to an undecipherable warning.

Nervousness, fatigue, brain-exhaustion . . . had her fight against them been vain? What was the use of all the months and years of patient Taylorized effort against the natural human fate: against anxiety, sorrow, old age—if their menace was to reappear whenever events slipped from her control?

The address ended in applause and admiring exclamations. She had won her way straight to those trustful hearts, still full of personal memories of a rude laborious life, or in which its stout tradition lingered on in spite of motors, money and the final word in plumbing.

Pauline, after the dispersal of the Mothers, had gone up to her room still dazed by the narrowness of her escape. Thank heaven she had a free hour! She threw herself on her lounge and turned her gaze inward upon herself: an exercise for which she seldom had the leisure.

Now that she knew she was safe, and had done nothing to discredit herself or the cause, she could penetrate an inch or two farther into the motive power of her activities; and what she saw there frightened her. To be Chairman of the Mothers' Day Association, and a speaker at the Birth Control banquet! It did not need her daughter's derisive chuckle to give her the measure of her inconsequence. Yet to reconcile these contradictions had seemed as simple as to invite the Chief Rabbi and the Bishop of New York to meet Amalasuntha's Cardinal. Did not the Mahatma teach that, to the initiated, all discords were resolved into a higher harmony? When her hurried attention had been turned for a moment on the seeming inconsistency of encouraging natality and teaching how to restrict it, she had felt it was sufficient answer to say that the two categories of people appealed to were entirely different, and could not be "reached" in the same way. In ethics, as in advertising, the main thing was to get at your public. Hitherto this argument had satisfied her. Feeling there was much to be said on both sides, she had thrown herself with equal zeal into the propagation of both doctrines; but now, surveying her attempt with a chastened eye, she doubted its expediency.

Maisie Bruss, appearing with notes and telephone messages, seemed to reflect this doubt in her small buttoned-up face.

"Oh, Maisie! Is there anything important? I'm dead tired." It was an admission she did not often make.

"Nothing much. Three or four papers have 'phoned for copies of your address. It was a great success."

A faint glow of satisfaction wavered through Pauline's perplexities. She did not pretend to eloquence; she knew her children smiled at her syntax. Yet she had reached the hearts of her audience, and who could deny that that was success?

"Oh, Maisie—I don't think it's good enough to appear in print . . ."

The secretary smiled, made a short-hand memorandum, and went on: "The Marchesa telephoned that her son is sailing on Wednesday—and I've sent off her cable about the Cardinal, answer paid."

"Sailing on Wednesday? But it can't be—the day after tomorrow!" Pauline raised herself on an anxious elbow. She had warned her husband, and he wouldn't listen. "Telephone downstairs, please, Maisie—find out if Mr. Manford has come in." But she knew well enough what the answer would be. Nowadays, whenever there was anything serious to be talked over, Dexter found some excuse for avoiding her. She lay back, her lids dropped over her tired eyes, and waited for the answer: "Mr. Manford isn't in yet."

Something had come over Dexter lately: no closing of her eyes would shut that out! She supposed it was over-work—the usual reason. Rich men's doctors always said they were over-worked when they became cross and trying at home.

"Dinner at the Toys' at 8.30." Miss Bruss continued her recital; and Pauline drew in her lips on a faintly bitter smile. At the Toys'—he wouldn't forget that! Whenever there was a woman who attracted him . . . why, Lita even . . . she'd seen him in a flutter once when he was going to the cinema with Lita, and thought she had forgotten to call for him! He had stamped up and down, watch in hand. . . Well, she supposed it was one of the symptoms of middle age: a passing phase. She could afford to be generous, after twenty years of his devotion; and she meant to be. Men didn't grow old as gracefully as women— she knew enough not to nag him about his little flirtations, and was really rather grateful to that silly Gladys Toy for making a fuss over him.

But when it came to serious matters, like this of the Mahatma, it was different, Dexter owed it to her to treat her opinions with more consideration— a woman whose oratory was sought for by a dozen newspapers! And that tiresome business of Michelangelo; another problem he had obstinately shirked. Discouragement closed in on Pauline. Of what use were eurythmics, cold douches, mental deep- breathings and all the other panaceas?

If things went on like this she would have to have her face lifted.

X

It was exasperating, the way the Vollard girl lurked and ogled. . . Undoubtedly she was their best typist: mechanically perfect, with a smattering of French and Italian useful in linguistic emergencies. There could be no question of replacing her. But, apart from her job, what a poor Poll! And always—there was no denying it, the office smiled over it—always finding excuses to intrude on Manford's privacy: a hurry trunk-call, a signature forgotten, a final question to ask, a message from one of the other members of the firm . . . she seized her pretexts cleverly. . . And when she left him nowadays, he always got up, squared his shoulders, studied himself critically in the mirror over the mantelpiece, and hated her the more for having caused him to do anything so silly.

This afternoon her excuse had been flimsier than usual: a new point to be noted against her. "One of the gentlemen left it on his desk. There's a picture in it that'll amuse you. Oh, you don't mind my bringing it in?" she gasped.

Manford was just leaving; overcoat on, hat and stick in hand. He muttered: "Oh, thanks," and took the "Looker-on" in order to cut short her effusions. A picture that might amuse him! The simpleton. . . Probably some of those elaborate "artistic" studies of the Cedarledge gardens. He remembered that his wife had allowed the "Looker-on" photographers to take them last summer. She thought it a duty: it might help to spread the love of gardening (another of her hobbies); and besides it was undemocratic to refuse to share one's private privileges with the multitude. He knew all her catch-words and had reached the point of wondering how much she would have valued her privileges had the multitude not been there to share them.

He thrust the magazine under his arm, and threw it down, half an hour later, in Lita Wyant's boudoir. It was so quiet and shadowy there that he was almost glad Lita was not in, though sometimes her unpunctuality annoyed him. This evening, after the rush and confusion of the day, he found it soothing to await her in this half-lit room, with its heaped-up cushions still showing where she had leaned, and the veiled light on two arums in a dark bowl. Wherever Lita was, there were some of those smooth sculptural arums.

When she came, the stillness would hardly be disturbed. She had a way of deepening it by her presence: noise and hurry died on her threshold. And this evening all the house was quiet. Manford, as usual, had tiptoed up to take a look at the baby, in the night nursery where there were such cool silver-coloured walls, and white hyacinths in pots of silvery lustre. The baby slept, a round pink Hercules with defiant rosy curls, his pink hands clenched on the coverlet. Even the nurse by the lamp sat quiet and silver-coloured as a brooding pigeon.

A house without fixed hours, engagements, obligations . . . where none of the clocks went, and nobody was late, because there was no particular time for anything to happen. Absurd, of course, maddeningly unpractical—but how restful after a crowded day! And what a miracle to have achieved, in the tight pattern of New York's tasks and pleasures—in the very place which seemed doomed to collapse and vanish if ever its clocks should stop!

These late visits had begun by Manford's dropping in on the way home for a look at the baby. He liked babies in their cribs, and especially this fat rascal of Jim's. Next to Nona, there was no one he cared for as much as Jim; and seeing Jim happily married, doing well at his bank, and with that funny little chap upstairs, stirred in the older man all his old regrets that he had no son.

Jim seldom got back early enough to assist at these visits; and Lita too, at first, was generally out. But in the last few months Manford had more often found her—or at least, having fallen into the habit of lingering over a cigarette in her boudoir, had managed to get a glimpse of her before going on to that other house where all the clocks struck simultaneously, and the week's engagements, in Maisie Bruss's hand, jumped out at him as he entered his study.

This evening he felt more than usually tired—of his day, his work, his life, himself—oh, especially himself; so tired that, the deep armchair aiding, he slipped into a half-doze in which the quietness crept up round him like a tide.

He woke with a start, imagining that Lita had entered, and feeling the elderly man's discomfiture when beauty finds him napping. . . But the room was empty: a movement of his own had merely knocked Miss Vollard's magazine to the floor. He remembered having brought it in to show Lita the photographs of Cedarledge which he supposed it to contain. Would there be time? He consulted his watch—an anachronism in that house—lit another cigarette, and leaned back contentedly. He knew that as soon as he got home Pauline, who had telephoned again that afternoon about the Mahatma, would contrive to corner him and reopen the tiresome question, together with another, which threatened to be almost equally tiresome, about paying that rotten Michelangelo's debts. "If we don't, we shall have him here on our hands: Amalasuntha is convinced you'll take him into the firm. You'd better come home in time to talk things over—." Always talking over, interfering, adjusting! He had enough of that in his profession. Pity Pauline wasn't a lawyer: she might have worked off her steam in office hours. He would sit quietly where he was, taking care to reach his house only just in time to dress and join her in the motor. They were dining out, he couldn't remember where.

For a moment his wife's figure stood out before him in brilliant stony relief, like a photograph seen through a stereopticon; then it vanished in the mist of his well-being, the indolence engendered by waiting there alone and undisturbed for Lita. Queer creature, Lita! His lips twitched into a reminiscent smile. One day she had come up noiselessly behind him and surprised him by a light kiss on his hair. He had thought it was Nona. . . Since then he had sometimes feigned to doze while he waited; but she had never kissed him again. . .

What sort of a life did she really lead, he wondered? And what did she make of Jim, now the novelty was over? He could think of no two people who seemed less made for each other. But you never could tell with a woman. Jim was young and adoring; and there was that red-headed boy. . .

Luckily Lita liked Nona, and the two were a good deal together. Nona was as safe as a bank—and as jolly as a cricket. Everything was sure to be right when she was there. But there were all the other hours, intervals that Manford had no way of accounting for; and Pauline always said the girl had had a queer bringing-up, as indeed any girl must have had at the hands of Mrs. Percy Landish. Pauline had objected to the marriage on that ground, though the modern mother's respect for the independence of her children had reduced her objection to mere shadowy hints of which Jim, in his transports, took no heed.

Manford also disliked the girl at first, and deplored Jim's choice. He thought Lita positively ugly, with her high cheekbones, her too small head, her glaring clothes and conceited lackadaisical airs. Then, as time passed, and the marriage appeared after all to be turning out well, he tried to interest himself in her for Jim's sake, to see in her what Jim apparently did. But the change had not come till the boy's birth. Then, as she lay in her pillows, a new shadowiness under her golden lashes, one petal of a hand hollowed under the little red head at her side, the vision struck to his heart. The enchantment did not last; he never recaptured it; there were days when what he called her "beauty airs" exasperated him, others when he was chilled by her triviality. But she never bored him, never ceased to excite in him a sort of irritated interest. He told himself that it was because one could never be sure what she was up to; speculating on what went on behind that smooth round forehead and those elusive eyes became his most absorbing occupation.

At first he used to be glad when Nona turned up, and when Jim came in from his bank, fagged but happy, and the three young people sat talking nonsense, and letting Manford smoke and listen. But gradually he had fallen into the way of avoiding Nona's days, and of coming earlier (extricating himself with difficulty from his professional engagements), so that he might find Lita alone before Jim arrived.

Lately she had seemed restless, vaguely impatient with things; and Manford was determined to win her confidence and get at the riddle behind that smooth round brow. He could not bear the idea that Jim's marriage might turn out to be a mere unsuccessful adventure, like so many others. Lita must be made to understand what a treasure she possessed, and how easily she might lose it. Lita Cliffe—Mrs. Percy Landish's niece—to have had the luck to marry Jim Wyant, and to risk estranging him! What fools women were! If she could be got away from the pack of frauds and flatterers who surrounded her, Manford felt sure he could bring her to her senses. Sometimes, in her quiet moods, she seemed to depend on his judgment, to defer rather touchingly to what he said. . .

The thing would be to coax her from jazz and night-clubs, and the pseudo-artistic rabble of house-decorators, cinema stars and theatrical riff-raff who had invaded her life, to get her back to country joys, golf and tennis and boating, all the healthy outdoor activities. She liked them well enough when there were no others available. She had owned to Manford that she was sick of the rush and needed a rest; had half promised to come to Cedarledge with the boy for Easter. Jim would be taking his father down to the island off the Georgia coast; and Jim's being away might be a good thing. These modern young women soon tired of what they were used to; Lita would appreciate her husband all the more after a separation.

Well, only a few weeks more, and perhaps it would come true. She had never seen the Cedarledge dogwood in bud, the woods trembling into green. Manford, smiling at the vision, stooped to pick up the "Looker-on" and refresh his memory.

But it wasn't the right number: there were no gardens in it. Why had Miss Vollard given it to him? As he fluttered the pages they dropped open at: "Oriental Sage in Native Garb"—. Oh, damn the Mahatma! "Dawnside Co-Eds"—oh, damn. . .

He stood up to thrust the paper under one of the heavily-shaded lamps. At home, where Pauline and reason ruled, the lighting was disposed in such a way that one could always read without moving from one's chair; but in this ridiculous house, where no one ever opened a book, the lamps were so perversely placed, and so deeply shrouded, that one had to hold one's paper under the shade to make out anything.

He scrutinized the picture, shrugged away his disgusted recognition of Bee Lindon, looked again and straightened his eye-glasses on his nose to be doubly sure—the lawyer's instinct of accuracy prevailing over a furious inward tremor.

He walked to the door, and then turned back and stood irresolute. To study the picture he had lifted the border of the lampshade, and the light struck crudely on the statue above Lita's divan; the statue of which Pauline (to her children's amusement) always said a little apprehensively that she supposed it must be Cubist. Manford had hardly noticed the figure before, except to wonder why the young people admired ugliness: half lost in the shadows of the niche, it seemed a mere bundle of lumpy limbs. Now, in the glare— "Ah, you carrion, you!" He clenched his fist at it. "THAT'S what they want—that's their brutish idol!" The words came stammering from him in a blur of rage. It was on Jim's account . . . the shock, the degradation. . . The paper slipped to the floor, and he dropped into his seat again.

Slowly his mind worked its way back through the disgust and confusion. Pauline had been right: what could one expect from a girl brought up in that Landish house? Very likely no one had ever thought of asking where she was, where she had been—Mrs. Landish, absorbed in her own silly affairs, would be the last person to know.

Well, what of that? The modern girl was always free, was expected to know how to use her freedom. Nona's independence had been as scrupulously respected as Jim's; she had had her full share of the perpetual modern agitations. Yet Nona was firm as a rock: a man's heart could build on her. If a woman was naturally straight, jazz and night-clubs couldn't make her crooked. . .

True, in Nona's case there had been Pauline's influence: Pauline who, whatever her faults, was always good-humoured and usually wise with her children. The proof was that, while they laughed at her, they adored her: he had to do her that justice. At the thought of Pauline a breath of freshness and honesty swept through him. He had been unfair to her lately, critical, irritable. He had been absorbing a slow poison, the poison emanating from this dusky self- conscious room, with all its pernicious implications. His first impression of Lita, when he had thought her ugly and pretentious, rushed back on him, dissipating the enchantment.

"Oh, I'm glad you waited—" She was there before him, her little heart-shaped face deep in its furs, like a bird on the nest. "I wanted to see you today; I WILLED you to wait." She stood there, her head slightly on one side, distilling her gaze through half- parted lids like some rare golden liquid.

Manford stared back. Her entrance had tangled up the words in his throat: he stood before her choked with denunciation and invective. And then it occurred to him how much easier it was just to say nothing—and to go. Of course he meant to go. It was no business of his: Jim Wyant was not his son. Thank God he could wash his hands of the whole affair.

He mumbled: "Dining out. Can't wait."

"Oh, but you must!" Her hand was on his arm, as light as a petal. "I want you." He could just see the twinkle of small round teeth as her upper lip lifted. . . "Can't . . . can't." He tried to disengage his voice, as if that too were tangled up in her.

He moved away toward the door. The "Looker-on" lay on the floor between them. So much the better; she would find it when he was gone! She would understand then why he hadn't waited. And no fear of Jim's getting hold of the paper; trust her to make it disappear!

"Why, what's that?" She bent her supple height to pick it up and moved to the lamp, her face alight.

"You darling, you—did you bring me this? What luck! I've been all over the place hunting for a copy—the whole edition's sold out. I had the original photograph somewhere, but couldn't put my hand on it."

She had reached the fatal page; she was spreading it open. Her smile caressed it; her mouth looked like a pink pod bursting on a row of pearly seeds. She turned to Manford almost tenderly. "After you prevented my going to Ardwin's I had to swear to send this to Klawhammer, to show that I really CAN dance. Tommy telephoned at daylight that Klawhammer was off to Hollywood, and that when I chucked last night they all said it was because I knew I couldn't come up to the scratch." She held out the picture with an air of pride. "Doesn't look much like it, does it? . . . Why, what are you staring at? Didn't you know I was going in for the movies? Immobility was never my strong point. . ." She threw the paper down, and began to undo her furs with a lazy smile, sketching a dance step as she did so. "Why do you look so shocked? If I don't do that I shall run away with Michelangelo. I suppose you know that Amalasuntha's importing him? I can't stick this sort of thing much longer. . . Besides, we've all got a right to self- expression, haven't we?"

Manford continued to look at her. He hardly heard what she was saying, in the sickness of realizing what she was. Those were the thoughts, the dreams, behind those temples on which the light laid such pearly circles!

He said slowly: "This picture—it's true, then? You've been there?"

"Dawnside? Bless you—where'd you suppose I learnt to dance? Aunt Kitty used to plant me out there whenever she wanted to go off on her own—which was pretty frequently." She had tossed of her hat, slipped out of her furs, and lowered the flounce of the lamp-shade; and there she stood before him in her scant slim dress, her arms, bare to the shoulder, lifted in an amphora-gesture to her little head.

"Oh, children—but I'm bored!" she yawned.

BOOK II

XI

Pauline Manford was losing faith in herself; she felt the need of a new moral tonic. Could she still obtain it from the old sources? The morning after the Toys' dinner, considering the advisability of repairing to that small bare room at Dawnside where the Mahatma gave his private audiences, she felt a chill of doubt. She would have preferred, just then, not to be confronted with the sage; in going to him she risked her husband's anger, and prudence warned her to keep out of the coming struggle. If the Mahatma should ask her to intervene she could only answer that she had already done so unsuccessfully; and such admissions, while generally useless, are always painful. Yet guidance she must have: no Papist in quest of "direction" (wasn't that what Amalasuntha called it?) could have felt the need more acutely. Certainly the sacrament of confession, from which Pauline's ingrained Protestantism recoiled in horror, must have its uses at such moments. But to whom, if not to the Mahatma, could she confess?

Dexter had gone down town without asking to see her; she had been sure he would, after their drive to and from the Toys' the evening before. When he was in one of his moods of clenched silence—they were becoming more frequent, she had remarked—she knew the uselessness of interfering. Echoes of the Freudian doctrine, perhaps rather confusedly apprehended, had strengthened her faith in the salutariness of "talking things over," and she longed to urge this remedy again on Dexter; but the last time she had done so he had wounded her by replying that he preferred an aperient. And in his present mood of stony inaccessibility he might say something even coarser.

She sat in her boudoir, painfully oppressed by an hour of unexpected leisure. The facial-massage artist had the grippe, and had notified her only at the last moment. To be sure, she had skipped her "Silent Meditation" that morning; but she did not feel in the mood for it now. And besides, an hour is too long for meditation—an hour is too long for anything. Now that she had one to herself, for the first time in years, she didn't in the least know what to do with it. That was something which no one had ever thought of teaching her; and the sense of being surrounded by a sudden void, into which she could reach out on all sides without touching an engagement or an obligation, produced in her a sort of mental dizziness. She had taken plenty of rest-cures, of course; all one's friends did. But during a rest-cure one was always busy resting; every minute was crammed with passive activities; one never had this queer sense of inoccupation, never had to face an absolutely featureless expanse of time. It made her feel as if the world had rushed by and forgotten her. An hour—why, there was no way of measuring the length of an empty hour! It stretched away into infinity like the endless road in a nightmare; it gaped before her like the slippery sides of an abyss. Nervously she began to wonder what she could do to fill it—if there were not some new picture show or dressmakers' opening or hygienic exhibition that she might cram into it before the minute hand switched round to her next engagement. She took up her list to see what that engagement was.

"11.45. Mrs. Swoffer."

Oh, to be sure . . . Mrs. Swoffer. Maisie had reminded her that morning. The relief was instantaneous. Only, who WAS Mrs. Swoffer? Was she the President of the Militant Pacifists' League, or the Heroes' Day delegate, or the exponent of the New Religion of Hope, or the woman who had discovered a wonderful trick for taking the wrinkles out of the corners of your eyes? Maisie was out on an urgent commission, and could not be consulted; but whatever Mrs. Swoffer's errand was, her arrival would be welcome—especially if she came before her hour. And she did.

She was a small plump woman of indefinite age, with faded blond hair and rambling features held together by a pair of urgent eye- glasses. She asked if she might hold Pauline's hand just a moment while she looked at her and reverenced her—and Pauline, on learning that this was the result of reading her Mothers' Day speech in the morning papers, acceded not unwillingly.

Not that that was what Mrs. Swoffer had come for; she said it was just a flower she wanted to gather on the way. A rose with the dew on it—she took off her glasses and wiped them, as if to show where the dew had come from. "You speak for so MANY of us," she breathed, and recovered Pauline's hand for another pressure.

But she HAD come for the children, all the same; and that was really coming for the mothers, wasn't it? Only she wanted to reach the mothers through the children—reversing the usual process. Mrs. Swoffer said she believed in reversing almost everything. Standing on your head was one of the most restorative physical exercises, and she believed it was the same mentally and morally. It was a good thing to stand one's SOUL upside down. And so she'd come about the children. . .

The point was to form a League—a huge International League of Mothers—against the dreadful old practice of telling children they were naughty. Had Mrs. Manford ever stopped to think what an abominable thing it was to suggest to a pure innocent child that there was such a thing in the world as Being Naughty? What did it open the door to? Why, to the idea of Wickedness, the most awful idea in the whole world.

Of course Mrs. Manford would see at once what getting rid of the idea of Wickedness would lead to. How could there be bad men if there were no bad children? And how could there be bad children if children were never allowed to know that such a thing as badness existed? There was a splendid woman—Orba Clapp; no doubt Mrs. Manford had heard of her?—who was getting up a gigantic world-wide movement to boycott the manufacturers and sellers of all military toys, tin soldiers, cannon, toy rifles, water-pistols and so on. It was a grand beginning, and several governments had joined the movement already: the Philippines, Mrs. Swoffer thought, and possibly Montenegro. But that seemed to her only a beginning: much as she loved and revered Orba Clapp, she couldn't honestly say that she thought the scheme went deep enough. She, Mrs. Swoffer, wanted to go right down to the soul: the collective soul of all the little children. The great Teacher, Alvah Loft—she supposed Mrs. Manford knew about HIM? No? She was surprised that a woman like Mrs. Manford—"one of our beacon-lights"—hadn't heard of Alvah Loft. She herself owed everything to him. No one had helped her as he had: he had pulled her out of the very depths of scepticism. But didn't Mrs. Manford know his books, even: "Spiritual Vacuum-Cleaning" and "Beyond God"?

Pauline had grown a little listless while the children were to the fore. She would help, of course; lend her name; subscribe. But that string had been so often twanged that it gave out rather a deadened note: whereas the name of a new Messiah immediately roused her. "Beyond God" was a tremendous title; she would get Maisie to telephone for the books at once. But what exactly did Alvah Loft teach?

Mrs. Swoffer's eye-glasses flashed with inspiration. "He doesn't teach: he absolutely refuses to be regarded as a TEACHER. He says there are too many already. He's an Inspirational Healer. What he does is to ACT on you—on your spirit. He simply relieves you of your frustrations."

Frustrations! Pauline was fascinated by the word. Not that it was new to her. Her vocabulary was fairly large, far more so, indeed, than that of her daughter's friends, whose range was strictly limited to sport and dancing; but whenever she heard a familiar word used as if it had some unsuspected and occult significance it fascinated her like a phial containing a new remedy.

Mrs. Swoffer's glasses were following Pauline's thoughts as they formed. "Will you let me speak to you as I would to an old friend? The moment I took your hand I KNEW you were suffering from frustrations. To any disciple of Alvah Loft's the symptoms are unmistakeable. Sometimes I almost wish I didn't see it all so clearly . . . it gives one such a longing to help. . ."

Pauline murmured: "I DO want help."

"Of course you do," Mrs. Swoffer purred, "and you want HIS help. Don't you know those wonderful shoe-shops where they stock every size and shape the human foot can require? I tell Alvah Loft he's like that; he's got a cure for everybody's frustrations. Of course," she added, "there isn't time for everybody; he has to choose. But he would take YOU at once." She drew back, and her glasses seemed to suck Pauline down as if they had been quicksands. "You're psychic," she softly pronounced.

"I believe I am," Pauline acknowledged. "But—"

"Yes; I know; those frustrations! All the things you think you ought to do, AND CAN'T; that's it, isn't it?" Mrs. Swoffer stood up. "Dear friend, come with me. Don't look at your watch. Just come!"

An hour later Pauline, refreshed and invigorated, descended the Inspirational Healer's brown-stone doorstep with a springing step. It had been worth while breaking three or four engagements to regain that feeling of moral freedom. Why had she never heard of Alvah Loft before? His method was so much simpler than the Mahatma's: no eurythmics, gymnastics, community life, no mental deep-breathing, or long words to remember. Alvah Loft simply took out your frustrations as if they'd been adenoids; it didn't last ten minutes, and was perfectly painless. Pauline had always felt that the Messiah who should reduce his message to tabloid form would outdistance all the others; and Alvah Loft had done it. He just received you in a boarding-house back-parlour, with bunches of pampas-grass on the mantelpiece, while rows of patients sat in the front room waiting their turn. You told him what was bothering you, and he said it was just a frustration, and he could relieve you of it, and make it so that it didn't exist, by five minutes of silent communion. And he sat and held you by the wrist, very lightly, as if he were taking your temperature, and told you to keep your eyes on the Ella Wheeler Wilcox line-a-day on the wall over his head. After it was over he said: "You're a good subject. The frustrations are all out. Go home, and you'll hear something good before dinner. Twenty-five dollars." And a pasty-faced young man with pale hair, who was waiting in the passage, added: "Pass on, please," and steered Pauline out by the elbow.

Of course she wasn't naturally credulous; she prided herself on always testing everything by reason. But it WAS marvellous, how light she felt as she went down the steps! The buoyancy persisted all day, perhaps strengthened by an attentive study of the reports of the Mothers' Day Meeting, laid out by the vigilant Maisie for perusal. Alvah Loft had told her that she would hear of something good before dinner, and when, late in the afternoon, she went up to her boudoir, she glanced expectantly at the writing-table, as if revelation might be there. It was, in the shape of a telephone message.

"Mr. Manford will be at home by seven. He would like to see you for a few minutes before dinner."

It was nearly seven, and Pauline settled herself by the fire and unfolded the evening paper. She seldom had time for its perusal, but today there might be some reference to the Mothers' Day Meeting; and her newly-regained serenity made it actually pleasant to be sitting there undisturbed, waiting for her husband.

"Dexter—how tired you look!" she exclaimed when he came in. It occurred to her at once that she might possibly insinuate an allusion to the new healer; but wisdom counselled a waiting policy, and she laid down her paper and smiled expectantly.

Manford gave his shoulders their usual impatient shake. "Everybody looks tired at the end of a New York day; I suppose it's what New York is for." He sat down in the armchair facing hers, and stared at the fire.

"I wanted to see you to talk about plans—a rearrangement," he began. "It's so hard to find a quiet minute."

"Yes; but there's no hurry now. The Delavans don't dine till half- past eight."

"Oh, are we dining there?" He reached for a cigarette.

She couldn't help saying: "I'm sure you smoke too much, Dexter. The irritation produced by the paper—"

"Yes; I know. But what I wanted to say is: I should like you to ask Lita and the boy to Cedarledge while Jim and Wyant are at the island."

This was a surprise; but she met it with unmoved composure. "Of course, if you like. But do you think Lita'll go, all alone? You'll be off tarpon-fishing, Nona

62

is going to Asheville for a fortnight's change, and I had intended—" She pulled up suddenly. She had meant, of course, to take her rest-cure at Dawnside.

Manford sat frowning and studying the fire. "Why shouldn't we all go to Cedarledge instead?" he began. "Somebody ought to look after Lita while Jim's away; in fact, I don't believe he'll go with Wyant if we don't. She's dead-beat, and doesn't know it, and with all the fools she has about her the only way to ensure her getting a real rest is to carry her off to the country with the boy."

Pauline's face lit up with a blissful incredulity. "Oh, Dexter— would you really come to Cedarledge for Easter? How splendid! Of course I'll give up my rest-cure. As you say, there's no place like the country."

She was already raising an inward hymn to Alvah Loft. An Easter holiday in the country, all together—how long it was since that had happened! She had always thought it her duty to urge Dexter to get away from the family when he had the chance; to travel or shoot or fish, and not feel himself chained to her side. And here at last was her reward—of his own accord he was proposing that they should all be together for a quiet fortnight. A softness came about her heart: the stiff armour of her self-constraint seemed loosened, and she saw the fire through a luminous blur. "It will be lovely," she murmured.

Manford lit another cigarette, and sat puffing it in silence. It seemed as though a weight had been lifted from him too; yet his face was still heavy and preoccupied. Perhaps before their talk was over she might be able to say a word about Alvah Loft; she was so sure that Dexter would see everything differently if only he could be relieved of his frustrations.

At length he said: "I don't see why this should interfere with your arrangements, though. Hadn't you meant to go somewhere for a rest-cure?"

He had thought of that too! She felt a fresh tremor of gratitude. How wicked she had been ever to doubt the designs of Providence, and the resolving of all discords in the Higher Harmony!

"Oh, my rest-cure doesn't matter; being with you all at Cedarledge will be the best kind of rest."

His obvious solicitude for her was more soothing than any medicine, more magical even than Alvah Loft's silent communion. Perhaps the one thing she had lacked, in all these years, was to feel that some one was worrying about her as she worried about the universe.

"It's awfully unselfish of you, Pauline. But running a big house is never restful. Nona will give up Asheville and come to Cedarledge to look after us; you mustn't change your plans."

She smiled a little. "But I MUST, dear; because I'd meant to go to Dawnside, and now, of course, in any case—"

Manford stood up and went and leaned against the chimney-piece. "Well, that will be all right," he said.

"All right?"

He was absently turning about in his hand a little bronze statuette. "Yes. If you think the fellow does you good. I've been thinking over what you said the other day; and I've decided to advise the Lindons not to act . . . too precipitately.

. ." He coughed and put the statuette back on the mantelshelf. "They've abandoned the idea. . ."

"Oh, Dexter—" She started to her feet, her eyes brimming. He had actually thought over what she had said to him—when, at the time, he had seemed so obdurate and sneering! Her heart trembled with a happy wonder in which love and satisfied vanity were subtly mingled. Perhaps, after all, what her life had really needed was something much simpler than all the complicated things she had put into it.

"I'm so glad," she murmured, not knowing what else to say. She wanted to hold out her arms, to win from him some answering gesture. But he was already glancing at his watch. "That's all right. Jove, though—we'll be late for dinner. . . Opera afterward, isn't there?"

The door closed on him. For a moment or two she stood still, awed by the sense of some strange presence in the room, something as fresh and strong as a spring gale. It must be happiness, she thought.

XII

"Yes; this morning I think you CAN see her. She seems ever so much better; not in such a fearful hurry, I mean."

Pauline, from her dressing-room, overheard Maisie Bruss. She smiled at the description of herself, sent a thought of gratitude to Alvah Loft, and called out: "Is that Nona? I'll be there in a minute. Just finishing my exercises. . ."

She appeared, fresh and tingling, draped in a restful dove-coloured wrapper, and offered Nona a smooth cheek. Miss Bruss had vanished, and mother and daughter had to themselves the sunny room, full of flowers and the scent of a wood-fire.

"How wonderful you look, mother! All made over. Have you been trying some new exercises?"

Pauline smiled and pulled up the soft eiderdown coverlet at the foot of her lounge. She sank comfortably back among her cushions.

"No, dear: it's just—understanding a little better, I think."

"Understanding?"

"Yes; that things ALWAYS come out right if one just keeps on being brave and trustful."

"Oh—." She fancied she caught a note of disappointment in Nona's voice. Poor Nona—her mother had long been aware that she had no enthusiasm, no transports of faith. She took after her father. How tired and sallow she looked in the morning light, perched on the arm of a chair, her long legs dangling!

"You really ought to try to believe that yourself, darling," said Pauline brightly.

Nona gave one of her father's shrugs. "Perhaps I will when I have more time."

"But one can always MAKE time, dear." ("Just as I do," the smile suggested.) "You look thoroughly fagged out, Nona. I do wish you'd go to the wonderful new man I've just—"

"All right, mother. Only, this morning I haven't come to talk about myself. It's Lita."

"Lita?"

"I've been wanting to speak to you about her for a long time. Haven't you noticed anything?"

Pauline still wore her alert and sympathizing smile. "Tell me what, dear—let's talk it all over."

Nona's brows were drawn in a troubled frown.

"I'm afraid Jim's not happy," she said.

"Jim? But, darling, he's been so dreadfully over-worked—that's the trouble. Your father spoke to me about it the other day. He's sending Jim and Arthur down to the island next month for a good long rest."

"Yes; it's awfully nice of father. But it's not that—it's Lita," Nona doggedly repeated.

A faint shadow brushed Pauline's cloudless horizon; but she resolutely turned her eyes from it. "Tell me what you think is wrong."

"Why, that she's bored stiff—says she's going to chuck the whole thing. She says the life she's leading prevents her expressing her personality."

"Good gracious—she dares?" Pauline sat bolt upright, the torn garment of her serenity fluttering away like a wisp of vapour. Was there never to be any peace for her, she wondered? She had a movement of passionate rebellion—then a terror lest it should imperil Alvah Loft's mental surgery. After a physical operation the patient's repose was always carefully guarded—but no one thought of sparing HER, though she had just been subjected to so radical an extirpation. She looked almost irritably at Nona.

"Don't you think you sometimes imagine things, my pet? Of course, the more we yield to suggestions of pain and distress the more—"

"Yes; I know. But this isn't a suggestion, it's a fact. Lita says she's got to express her personality, or she'll do something dreadful. And if she does it will break Jim's heart."

Pauline leaned back, vaguely fortified by so definite a menace. It was laughable to think of Lita Cliffe's threatening to do something dreadful to a Wyant!

"Don't you think she's just over-excited, perhaps? She leads such a crazy sort of life—all you children do. And she hasn't been very strong since the baby's birth. I believe she needs a good rest as much as Jim does. And you know your father has been so wise about that; he's going to persuade her to go to Cedarledge for two or three weeks while Jim's in Georgia."

Nona remained unimpressed. "Lita won't go to Cedarledge alone—you know she won't."

"She won't have to, dear. Your father has thought of that too; he finds time to think of everything."

"Who's going, then?"

"We ALL are. At least, your father hopes you will; and he's giving up his tarpon-fishing on purpose to join us."

"Father is?" Nona stood up, her gaze suddenly fixed on her mother.

"Your father's wonderful," Pauline triumphed.

"Yes, I know." The girl's voice flagged again. "But all this is weeks away. And meanwhile I'm afraid—I'm afraid."

"Little girls mustn't be afraid. If you are, send Lita to ME. I'm sure it's just a case of frustration—"

"Frustration?"

"Yes; the new psychological thing. I'll take her with me to see Alvah Loft. He's the great Inspirational Healer. I've only had three treatments, and it's miraculous. It doesn't take ten minutes, and all one's burdens are lifted." Pauline threw back her head with a sigh which seemed to luxuriate in the remembrance of her own release. "I wish I could take you ALL to him!" she said.

"Well, perhaps you'd better begin with Lita." Nona was half- smiling too, but it was what her mother secretly called her disintegrating smile. "I wish the poor child were more constructive—but I suppose she's inherited her father's legal mind," Pauline thought.

Nona stood before her irresolutely. "You know, mother, if things do go wrong Jim will never get over it."

"There you are again—jumping at the conclusion that things will go wrong! As for Lita, to me it's a clear case of frustration. She says she wants to express her personality? Well, every one has the right to do that—I should think it wrong of me to interfere. That wouldn't be the way to make Jim happy. What Lita needs is to have her frustrations removed. That will open her eyes to her happiness, and make her see what a perfect home she has. I wonder where my engagement-list is? Maisie! . . . Oh, here. . ." She ran her eyes rapidly over the tablet. "I'll see Lita tomorrow— I'll make a point of it. We'll have a friendly simple talk— perfectly frank and affectionate. Let me see: at what time should I be likely to find her? . . . And, no, of course not, darling; I wouldn't think of saying a word to Jim. But your father—surely I may speak to your father?"

Nona hesitated. "I think father knows about it—as much as he need," she answered, her hand on the door.

"Ah, your father always knows everything," Pauline placidly acquiesced.

The prospect of the talk with her daughter-in-law barely ruffled her new-found peace. It was a pity Lita was restless; but nowadays all the young people were restless. Perhaps it would be as well to say a word to Kitty Landish; flighty and inconsequent as she was, it might open her eyes to find that she was likely to have her niece back on her hands. Mrs. Percy Landish's hands were always full to overflowing with her own difficulties. A succession of ingenious theories of life, and the relentless pursuit of originality, had landed her in a state of chronic embarrassment, pecuniary, social and sentimental. The announcement that Lita was tired of Jim, and threatened to leave him, would fall like a bombshell on that precarious roof which figured in the New York Directory as somewhere in the

East Hundreds, but was recorded in the "Social Register" as No. 1 Viking Court. Mrs. Landish's last fad had been to establish herself on the banks of the East River, which she and a group of friends had adorned with a cluster of reinforced-cement bungalows, first christened El Patio, but altered to Viking Court after Mrs. Landish had read in an illustrated weekly that the Vikings, who had discovered America ages before Columbus, had not, as previously supposed, effected their first landing at Vineyard Haven, but at a spot not far from the site of her dwelling. Cement, at an early stage, is malleable, and the Alhambra motifs had hastily given way to others from the prows of Nordic ships, from silver torques and Runic inscriptions, the latter easily contrived out of Arabic sourats from the Koran. Before these new ornaments were dry, Mrs. Landish and her friends were camping on the historic spot; and after four years of occupancy they were camping still, in Mrs. Manford's sense of the word.

A hurried telephone call had assured Pauline that she could see Mrs. Landish directly after lunch; and at two o'clock her motor drove up to Viking Court, which opened on a dilapidated river-front and was cynically overlooked by tall tenement houses with an underpinning of delicatessen stores.

Mrs. Landish was nowhere to be found. She had had to go out to lunch, a melancholy maid-servant said, because the cook had just given notice; but she would doubtless soon be back. With gingerly steps Pauline entered the "living-room," so called (as visitors were unfailingly reminded) because Mrs. Landish ate, painted, modelled in clay, sculptured in wood, and received her friends there. The Vikings, she added, had lived in that way. But today all traces of these varied activities had disappeared, and the room was austerely empty. Mrs. Landish's last hobby was for what she called "purism," and her chief desire to make everything in her surroundings conform to the habits and industries of a mythical past. Ever since she had created Viking Court she had been trying to obtain rushes for the floor: but as the Eastern States of America did not produce the particular variety of rush which the Vikings were said to have used she had at last decided to have rugs woven on handlooms in Abyssinia, some one having assured her that an inscription referring to trade-relations between the Vikings and the kingdom of Prester John had been discovered in the ruins of Petra.

The difficulty of having these rugs made according to designs of the period caused the cement floor of Mrs. Landish's living-room to remain permanently bare, and most of the furniture having now been removed, the room had all the appearance of a garage, the more so as Mrs. Landish's latest protégé, a young cabaret-artist who performed on a motor-siren, had been suffered to stable his cycle in one corner.

In addition to this vehicle, the room contained only a few relentless-looking oak chairs, a long table bearing an hour-glass (for clocks would have been an anachronism), and a scrap of dusty velvet nailed on the cement wall, as to which Mrs. Landish explained that it was a bit of a sixth century Coptic vestment, and that the nuns of a Basilian convent in Thessaly were reproducing it for eventual curtains and chair-cushions. "It may take fifty years."

Mrs. Landish always added, "but I would rather go without it than live with anything less perfect."

The void into which Pauline advanced gave prominence to the figure of a man who stood with his back to her, looking through the window at what was to be a garden when Viking horticulture was revived. Meanwhile it was fully occupied by neighbouring cats and by swirls of wind-borne rubbish.

The visitor, duskily blocked against a sullen March sky, was at first not recognizable; but half way toward him Pauline exclaimed: "Dexter!" He turned, and his surprise met hers.

"I never dreamed of its being you!" she said.

He faced her with a certain defiant jauntiness. "Why not?"

"Because I never saw you here before. I've tried often enough to get you to come—"

"Oh, to lunch or dine!" He sent a grimace about the room. "I never thought that was among my duties."

She did not take this up, and a moment's silence hung between them. Finally Manford said: "I came about Lita."

Pauline felt a rush of relief. Her husband's voice had been harsh and impatient: she saw that her arrival had mysteriously put him out. But if anxiety about Lita were the cause of his visit it not only explained his perturbation but showed his revived solicitude for herself. She sent back another benediction to the Inspirational Healer, so sweet it was to find that she and Dexter were once more moved by the same impulses.

"It's awfully kind of you, dear. How funny that we should meet on the same errand!"

He stared: "Why, have you—?"

"Come about Lita? Well, yes. She's been getting rather out of hand, hasn't she? Of course a divorce would kill poor Jim— otherwise I shouldn't so much mind—"

"A divorce?"

"Nona tells me it's Lita's idea. Foolish child! I'm to have a talk with her this afternoon. I came here first to see if Kitty's influence—"

"Oh: Kitty's influence!"

"Yes; I know." She broke off, and glanced quickly at Manford. "But if you don't believe in her influence, why did you come here yourself?"

The question seemed to take her husband by surprise, and he met it by a somewhat rigid smile. How old he looked in the hard slaty light! The crisp hair was almost as thin on his temples as higher up. If only he would try that wonderful new "Radio-scalp"! "And he used to be so handsome!" his wife said to herself, with the rush of vitality she always felt when she noted the marks of fatigue or age in her contemporaries. Manford and Nona, she reflected, had the same way of turning sallow and heavy-cheeked when they were under any physical or moral strain.

Manford said: "I came to ask Mrs. Landish to help us get Lita away for Easter. I thought she might put in a word—"

It was Pauline's turn to smile. "Perhaps she might. What I came for was to say that if Lita doesn't quiet down and behave reasonably she may find herself thrown on her aunt's hands again. I think that will produce an effect on Kitty. I shall make it perfectly clear that they are not to count on me financially if Lita leaves Jim." She glanced brightly at Manford, instinctively awaiting his approval.

But the expected response did not come. His face grew blurred and uncertain, and for a moment he said nothing. Then he muttered: "It's all very unfortunate . . . a stupid muddle. . ."

Pauline caught the change in his tone. It suggested that her last remark, instead of pleasing him, had raised between them one of those invisible barriers against which she had so often bruised her perceptions. And just as she had thought that he and she were really in touch again!

"We mustn't be hard on her . . . we mustn't judge her without hearing both sides . . ." he went on.

"But of course not." It was just the sort of thing she wanted him to say, but not in the voice in which he said it. The voice was full of hesitation and embarrassment. Could it be her presence which embarrassed him? With Manford one could never tell. She suggested, almost timidly: "But why shouldn't I leave you to see Kitty alone? Perhaps we needn't both. . ."

His look of relief was unconcealable; but her bright resolution rose above the shock. "You'll do it so much better," she encouraged him.

"Oh, I don't know. But perhaps two of us . . . looks rather like the Third Degree, doesn't it?"

She assented nervously: "All I want is to smooth things over. . ."

He gave an acquiescent nod, and followed her as she moved toward the door. "Perhaps, though—look here, Pauline—"

She sparkled with responsiveness.

"Hadn't you better wait before sending for Lita? It may not be necessary, if—"

Her first impulse was to agree; but she thought of the Inspirational Healer. "You can trust me to behave with tact, dear; but I'm sure it will help Lita to talk things out, and perhaps I shall know better than Kitty how to get at her. . . Lita and I have always been good friends, and there's a wonderful new man I want to persuade her to see . . . some one really psychic. . ."

Manford's lips narrowed in a smile; again she had a confused sense of new deserts widening between them. Why had he again become suddenly sardonic and remote? She had no time to consider, for the new gospel of frustrations was surging to her lips.

"NOT a teacher; he repudiates all doctrines, and simply ACTS on you. He—"

"Pauline darling! Dexter! Have you been waiting long? Oh, dear— my hourglass seems to be quite empty!"

Mrs. Percy Landish was there, slipping toward them with a sort of aerial shuffle, as if she had blown in on a March gust. Her tall swaying figure produced, at a distance, an effect of stateliness which vanished as she approached, as if she had suddenly got out of focus. Her face was like an unfinished sketch, to which the artist had given heaps of fair hair, a lovely nose, expressive eyes, and no mouth. She laid down some vague parcels and shook the hour- glass irritably, as if it had been at fault.

"How dear of you!" she said to her visitors. "I don't often get you together in my eyrie."

The expression puzzled Pauline, who knew that in poetry an eyrie was an eagle's nest, and wondered how this term could be applied to a cement bungalow in the East Hundreds. . . But there was no time to pursue such speculations.

Mrs. Landish was looking helplessly about her. "It's cold—you're both freezing, I'm afraid?" Her eyes rested tragically on the empty hearth. "The fact is, I can't have a fire because my andirons are WRONG."

"Not high enough? The chimney doesn't draw, you mean?" Pauline in such emergencies was in her element; she would have risen from her deathbed to show a new housemaid how to build a fire. But Mrs. Landish shook her head with the look of a woman who never expects to be understood by other women.

"No, dear; I mean they were not of the period. I always suspected it, and Dr. Ygrid Bjornsted, the great authority on Nordic art, who was here the other day, told me that the only existing pair is in the Museum at Christiania. So I have sent an order to have them copied. But you ARE cold, Pauline! Shall we go and sit in the kitchen? We shall be quite by ourselves, because the cook has just given notice."

Pauline drew her furs around her in silent protest at this new insanity. "We shall be very well here, Kitty. I suppose you know it's about Lita—"

Mrs. Landish seemed to drift back to them from incalculable distances. "Lita? Has Klawhammer really engaged her? It was for his 'Herodias,' wasn't it?" She was all enthusiasm and participation.

Pauline's heart sank. She had caught the irritated jut of Manford's brows. No—it was useless to try to make Kitty understand; and foolish to risk her husband's displeasure by staying in this icy room for such a purpose. She wrapped herself in sweetness as in her sables. "It's something much more serious than that cinema nonsense. But I'm going to leave it to Dexter to explain. He will do it ever so much better than I could. . . Yes, Kitty dear, I remember there's a step missing in the vestibule. Please don't bother to see me out—you know Dexter's minutes are precious." She thrust Mrs. Landish softly back into the room, and made her way unattended across the hall. As she did so, the living- room door, the lock of which had responded reluctantly to her handling, swung open again, and she heard Manford ask, in his dry cross-examining voice: "Will you please tell me exactly when and for how long Lita was at Dawnside, Mrs. Landish?"

XIII

"I believe it's the first time in a month that I've heard Nona laugh," Stanley Heuston said with a touch of irony—or was it simply envy?

Nona was still in the whirlpool of her laugh. She struggled to its edge only to be caught back, with retrospective sobs and gasps, into its central coil. "It was too screamingly funny," she flung at them out of the vortex.

She was perched sideways, as her way was, on the arm of the big chintz sofa in Arthur Wyant's sitting-room. Wyant was stretched out in his usual armchair, behind a crumby messy tea-table, on the other side of which sat his son and Stanley Heuston.

"She didn't hesitate for more than half a second—just long enough to catch my eye—then round she jerked, grabbed hold of her last word and fitted it into a beautiful new appeal to the Mothers. Oh— oh—oh! If you could have seen them!"

"I can." Jim's face suddenly became broad, mild and earnestly peering. He caught up a pair of his father's eye-glasses, adjusted them to his blunt nose, and murmured in a soft feminine drawl: "Mrs. Manford is one of our deepest-souled women. She has a vital message for all Mothers."

Wyant leaned back and laughed. His laugh was a contagious chuckle, easily provoked and spreading in circles like a full spring. Jim gave a large shout at his own mimicry, and Heuston joined the chorus on a dry note that neither spread nor echoed, but seemed suddenly to set bounds to their mirth. Nona felt a momentary resentment of his tone. Was he implying that they were ridiculing their mother? They weren't, they were only admiring her in their own way, which had always been humorous and half-parental. Stan ought to have understood by this time—and have guessed why Nona, at this moment, caught at any pretext to make Jim laugh, to make everything in their joint lives appear to him normal and jolly. But Stanley always seemed to see beyond a joke, even when he was in the very middle of it. He was like that about everything in life; forever walking around things, weighing and measuring them, and making his disenchanted calculations. Poor fellow—well, no wonder!

Jim got up, the glasses still clinging to his blunt nose. He gathered an imaginary cloak about him, picked up inexistent gloves and vanity-bag, and tapped his head as if he were settling a feathered hat. The laughter waxed again, and Wyant chuckled: "I wish you young fools would come oftener. It would cure me a lot quicker than being shipped off to Georgia." He turned half-apologetically to Nona. "Not that I'm not awfully glad of the chance—"

"I know, Exhibit dear. It'll be jolly enough when you get down there, you and Jim."

"Yes; I only wish you were coming too. Why don't you?"

Jim's features returned to their normal cast, and he removed the eye-glasses. "Because mother and Manford have planned to carry off Lita and the kid to Cedarledge at the same time. Good scheme, isn't it? I wish I could be in both places at once. We're all of us fed up with New York."

His father glanced at him. "Look here, my boy, there's no difficulty about your being in the same place as your wife. I can take my old bones down to Georgia without your help, since Manford's kind enough to invite me."

"Thanks a lot, dad; but part of Lita's holiday is getting away from domestic cares, and I'm the principal one. She has to order dinner for me. And I don't say I shan't like my holiday too . . . sand and sun, any amount of 'em. That's my size at present. No more superhuman efforts." He stretched his arms over his head with a yawn.

"But I thought Manford was off to the south too—to his tarpon? Isn't this Cedarledge idea new?"

"It's part of his general kindness. He wanted me to go with an easy mind, so he's chucked his fishing and mobilized the whole group to go and lead the simple life at Cedarledge with Lita."

Wyant's sallow cheek-bones reddened slightly. "It's awfully kind, as you say; but if my going south is to result in upsetting everybody else's arrangements—"

"Oh, rot, father." Jim spoke with sudden irritability. "Manford would hate it if you chucked now; wouldn't he, Nona? And I do want Lita to get away somewhere, and I'd rather it was to Cedarledge than anywhere." The clock struck, and he pulled himself out of his chair. Nona noticed with a pang how slack and half-hearted all his movements were. "Jove—I must jump!" he said. "We're due at some cabaret show that begins early; and I believe we dine at Ardwin's first, with a bunch of freaks. By-bye, Nona. . . Stan. . . Goodbye, father. Only a fortnight now before we cut it all!"

The door shut after him on a silence. Wyant reached for his pipe and filled it. Heuston stared at the tea-table. Suddenly Wyant questioned: "Look here— why is Jim being shipped off to the island with me when his wife's going to Cedarledge?"

Nona dropped from her sofa-arm and settled into an armchair. "Simply for the reasons he told you. They both want a holiday from each other."

"I don't believe Jim really wants one from Lita."

"Well, so much the worse for Jim. Lita's temporarily tired of dancing and domesticity, and the doctor says she ought to go off for a while by herself."

Wyant was slowly drawing at his pipe. At length he said: "Your mother's doctor told her that once; and she never came back."

Nona's colour rose through her pale cheeks to her very forehead. The motions of her blood were not impetuous, and she now felt herself blushing for having blushed. It was unlike Wyant to say that—unlike his tradition of reticence and decency, which had always joined with Pauline's breezy optimism in relegating to silence and non-existence whatever it was painful or even awkward to discuss. For years the dual family had lived on the assumption that they were all the best friends in the world, and the vocabulary of that convention had become their natural idiom.

Stanley Heuston seemed to catch the constraint in the air. He got up as if to go. "I suppose we're dining somewhere too—." He pronounced the "we" without conviction, for every one knew that he and his wife seldom went out together.

Wyant raised a detaining hand. "Don't go, Stan. Nona and I have no secrets—if we had, you should share them. Why do you look so savage, Nona? I suppose I've said something stupid. . . Fact is, I'm old-fashioned; and this idea of people who've chosen to live together having perpetually to get away from each other. . . When I remember my father and mother, for sixty-odd years. . . New York in winter, Hudson in summer. . . Staple topics: snow for six months, mosquitoes the other. I suppose that's the reason your generation have got the fidgets!"

Nona laughed. "It's a good enough reason; and anyhow there's nothing to be done about it."

Wyant frowned. "Nothing to be done about it—in Lita's case? I hope you don't mean that. My son—God, if ever a man has slaved for a woman, made himself a fool for her. . ."

Heuston's dry voice cut the diatribe. "Well, sir, you wouldn't deprive him of man's peculiar privilege: the right to make a fool of himself?"

Wyant sank back grumbling among his cushions. "I don't understand you, any of you," he said, as if secretly relieved by the admission.

"Well, Exhibit dear, strictly speaking you don't have to. We're old enough to run the show for ourselves, and all you've got to do is to look on from the front row and admire us," said Nona, bending to him with a caress.

In the street she found herself walking silently at Heuston's side. These weekly meetings with him at Wyant's were becoming a tacit arrangement: the one thing in her life that gave it meaning. She thought with a smile of her mother's affirmation that everything always came out right if only one kept on being brave and trustful, and wondered where, under that formula, her relation to Stanley Heuston could be fitted in. It was anything but brave—letting herself drift into these continual meetings, and refusing to accept their consequences. Yet every nerve in her told her that these moments were the best thing in life, the one thing she couldn't do without: just to be near him, to hear his cold voice, to say something to provoke his disenchanted laugh; or, better still, to walk by him as now without talking, with a furtive glance now and then at his profile, ironic, dissatisfied, defiant—yes, and so weak under the defiance. . . The fact that she judged and still loved showed that her malady was mortal.

"Oh, well—it won't last; nothing lasts for our lot," she murmured to herself without conviction. "Or at the worst it will only last as long as I do; and that's a date I can fix as I choose."

What nonsense, though, to talk like that, when all those others needed her: Jim and his silly Lita, her father, yes, even her proud self-confident father, and poor old Exhibit A and her mother who was so sure that nothing would ever go wrong again, now she had found a new Healer! Yes; they all needed help, though they didn't know it, and Fate seemed to have put her, Nona, at the very point where all their lives intersected, as a First-Aid station is put at the dangerous turn of a race-course, or a points-man at the shunting point of a big junction.

"Look here, Nona: my dinner-engagement was a fable. Would the heavens fall if you and I went and dined somewhere by ourselves, just as we are?"

"Oh, Stan—" Her heart gave a leap of joy. In these free days, when the young came and went as they chose, who would have believed that these two had never yet given themselves a stolen evening? Perhaps it was just because it was so easy. Only difficult things tempted Nona, and the difficult thing was always to say "No."

Yet was it? She stole a glance at Heuston's profile, as a street- lamp touched it, saw the set lips already preparing a taunt at her refusal, and wondered if saying no to everything required as much courage as she liked to think. What if moral cowardice were the core of her boasted superiority? She didn't want to be "like the others"—but was there anything to be proud of in that? Perhaps her disinterestedness was only a subtler vanity, not unrelated, say, to Lita's refusal to let a friend copy her new dresses, or Bee Lindon's perpetual craving to scandalize a world sated with scandals. Exhibitionists, one and all of them, as the psycho- analysts said—and, in her present mood, moral exhibitionism seemed to her the meanest form of the display.

"How mid-Victorian, Stan!" she laughed. "As if there were any heavens to fall! Where shall we go? It will be the greatest fun. Isn't there rather a good little Italian restaurant somewhere near here? And afterward there's that nigger dancing at the Housetop."

"Come along, then!"

She felt as little and light as a wisp of straw carried out into the rushing darkness of a sea splashed with millions of stars. Just the thought of a friendly evening, an evening of simple comradeship, could do that; could give her back her youth, yes, and the courage to persevere. She put her hand through his arm, and knew by his silence that he was thinking her thoughts. That was the final touch of magic.

"You really want to go to the Housetop?" he questioned, leaning back to light his cigar with a leisurely air, as if there need never again be any hurrying about anything. Their dinner at the little Italian restaurant was nearly over. They had conscientiously explored the paste, the frutte di mare, the fritture and the cheese-and-tomato mixtures, and were ending up with a foaming sabaione. The room was low-ceilinged, hot, and crowded with jolly noisy people, mostly Italians, over whom, at unnoticed intervals, an olive-tinted musician with blue-white eyeballs showered trills and twangings. His music did not interrupt the conversation, but merely obliged the diners to shout a little louder; a pretext of which they joyfully availed themselves. Nona, at first, had found the noise a delicious shelter for her talk with Heuston; but now it was beginning to stifle her. "Let's get some fresh air first," she said.

"All right. We'll walk for a while."

They pushed back their chairs, wormed a way through the packed tables, got into their wraps, and stepped out of the swinging doors into long streamers of watery lamplight. The douche of a cold rain received them.

"Oh, dear—the Housetop, then!" Nona grumbled. How sweet the rain would have been under the budding trees of Cedarledge! But here, in these degraded streets. . .

Heuston caught a passing taxi. "A turn, first—just round the Park?"

"No; the Housetop."

He leaned back and lit a cigarette. "You know I'm going to get myself divorced: it's all settled," he announced.

"Settled—with Aggie?"

"No: not yet. But with the lady I'm going off with. My word of honour. I am; next week."

Nona gave an incredulous laugh. "So this is good-bye?"

"Very nearly."

"Poor Stan!"

"Nona . . . listen . . . look here. . ."

She took his hand. "Stan, hang next week!"

"Nona—?"

She shook her head, but let her hand lie in his.

"No questions—no plans. Just being together," she pleaded.

He held her in silence and their lips met. "Then why not—?"

"No: the Housetop—the Housetop!" she cried, pulling herself out of his arms.

"Why, you're crying!"

"I'm not! It's the rain. It's—"

"Nona!"

"Stan, you know it's no earthly use."

"Life's so rotten—"

"Not like this."

"This? This—what?"

She struggled out of another enfolding, put her head out of the window, and cried: "The Housetop!"

They found a corner at the back of the crowded floor. Nona blinked a little in the dazzle of light-garlands, the fumes of smoke, the clash of noise and colours. But there he and she sat, close together, hidden in their irresistible happiness, and though his lips had their moody twist she knew the same softness was in his veins as in hers, isolating them from the crowd as completely as if they had still been in the darkness of the taxi. That was the way she must take her life, she supposed; piece-meal, a tiny scrap of sweetness at a time, and never more than a scrap—never once! Well— it would be worse still if there were no moments like this, short and cruel as they seemed when they came.

The Housetop was packed. The low balcony crammed with fashionable people overhung them like a wreath of ripe fruits, peachy and white and golden, made of painted faces, bare arms, jewels, brocades and fantastic furs. It was the music-hall of the moment.

The curtain shot up, and the little auditorium was plunged in shadow. Nona could leave her hand in Heuston's. On the stage—a New Orleans cotton-market—black dancers tossed and capered. They were like ripe fruits too, black figs flung about in hot sunshine, falling to earth with crimson bursts of laughter splitting open on white teeth, and bounding up again into golden clouds of cotton- dust. It was all warm and jolly and inconsequent. The audience forgot to smoke and chatter: little murmurs of enjoyment rippled over it.

The curtain descended, the light-garlands blossomed out, and once more floor and balcony were all sound and movement.

"Why, there's Lita up there in the balcony," Nona exclaimed, "just above the stage. Don't you see—with Ardwin, and Jack Staley, and Bee Lindon, and that awful Keiler woman?"

She had drawn her hand away at the sight of the box full. "I don't see Jim with them after all. Oh, how I hate that crowd!" All the ugly and disquieting realities she had put from her swept back with a rush. If only she could have had her one evening away from them! "I didn't think we should find them here—I thought Lita had been last week."

"Well, don't that crowd always keep on going to the same shows over and over again? There's nothing they hate as much as novelty— they're so fed up with it! And besides, what on earth do you care? They won't bother us."

She wavered a moment, and then said: "You see, Lita always bothers me."

"Why? Anything new?"

"She says she's tired of everything, Jim included, and is going to chuck it, and go in for the cinema."

"Oh, that—?" He manifested no surprise. "Well, isn't it where she belongs?"

"Perhaps—but Jim!"

"Poor Jim. We've all got to swallow our dose one day or another."

"Yes; but I can't bear it. Not for Jim. Look here, Stan—I'm going up there to join them," she suddenly declared.

"Oh, nonsense, Nona; they don't want you. And besides I hate that crowd as much as you do. . . I don't want you mixed up with it. That cad Staley, and the Keiler woman. . ."

She gave a dry laugh. "Afraid they'll compromise me?"

"Oh, rot! But what's the use of their even knowing you're here? They'll hate your butting in, Lita worst of all."

"Stan, I'm going up to them."

"Oh, damn it. You always—"

She had got up and was pushing away the little table in front of them. But suddenly she stopped and sat down again. For a moment or two she did not speak, nor look at Heuston. She had seen the massive outline of a familiar figure rising from a seat near the front and planting itself there for a slow gaze about the audience.

"Hallo—your father? I didn't know he patronized this kind of show," Heuston said.

Nona groped for a careless voice, and found it. "Father? So it is! Oh, he's really very frivolous—my influence, I'm afraid." The voice sounded sharp and rattling in her own ears. "How funny, though! You don't happen to see mother and Amalasuntha anywhere? That would make the family party complete."

She could not take her eyes from her father. How queer he looked— how different! Strained and vigilant; she didn't know how else to put it. And yet tired, inexpressibly tired, as if with some profound inner fatigue which made him straighten himself a little too rigidly, and throw back his head with a masterful young-mannish air as he scanned the balcony just above him. He stood there for a few moments, letting the lights and the eyes concentrate on him, as if lending himself to the display with a certain distant tolerance; then he began to move toward one of the exits. But half way he stopped, turned with his dogged jerk of the shoulders, and made for a gangway leading up to the balcony.

"Hullo," Heuston exclaimed. "Is he going up to Lita?"

Nona gave a little laugh. "I might have known it! How like father— when he undertakes anything!"

"Undertakes what?"

"Why, looking after Lita. He probably found out at the last minute that Jim couldn't come, and made up his mind to replace him. Isn't it splendid, how he's helping us? I know he loathes this sort of place—and the people she's with. But he told me we oughtn't to lose our influence on her, we ought to keep tight hold of her—"

"I see."

Nona had risen again and was beginning to move toward the passageway. Heuston followed her, and she smiled back at him over her shoulder. She felt as if she must cram every cranny in their talk with more words. The silence which had enclosed them as in a crystal globe had been splintered to atoms, and had left them stammering and exposed.

"Well, I needn't go up to Lita after all; she really doesn't require two dragons. Thank goodness, father has replaced me, and I don't have to be with that crew . . . just this evening," she whispered, slipping her arm through Heuston's. "I should have hated to have it end in that way." By this time they were out in the street.

On the wet pavement he detained her. "Nona, how IS it going to end?"

"Why, by your driving me home, I hope. It's too wet to walk, worse luck."

He gave a resigned shrug, called a taxi, wavered a moment, and jumped in after her. "I don't know why I come," he grumbled.

She kept a bright hold on herself, lit a cigarette at his lighter, and chattered resolutely of the show till the motor turned the corner of her street.

"Well, my child, it's really good-bye now. I'm off next week with the other lady," Heuston said as they stopped before the Manford door. He paid the taxi and helped her out, and she stood in the rain in front of him. "I don't come back till Aggie divorces me, you understand," he continued.

"She won't!"

"She'll have to."

"It's hideous—doing it in that way."

"Not as hideous as the kind of life I'm leading."

She made no answer, and he followed her silently up the doorstep while she fumbled for her latchkey. She was trembling now with weariness and disappointment, and a feverish thirst for the one more kiss she was resolved he should not take.

"Other people get their freedom. I don't see why I shouldn't have mine," he insisted.

"Not in that way, Stan! You mustn't. It's too horrible."

"That way? You know there's no other."

She turned the latchkey, and the ponderous vestibule door swung inward. "If you do, don't imagine I'll ever marry you!" she cried out as she crossed the threshold; and he flung back furiously: "Wait till I ask you!" and plunged away into the rain.

XIV

Pauline Manford left Mrs. Landish's door with the uncomfortable sense of having swallowed a new frustration. In this crowded life of hers they were as difficult to avoid as germs—and there was not always time to have them extirpated!

Manford had evidently found out about Lita's Dawnside frequentations; found it out, no doubt, as Pauline had, by seeing her photograph in that loathsome dancing group in the "Looker-on." Well, perhaps it was best that he should know; it would certainly confirm his resolve to stop any action against the Mahatma.

Only—if he had induced the Lindons to drop the investigation, why was he still preoccupied by it? Why had he gone to Mrs. Landish to make that particular inquiry about Lita? Pauline would have liked to shake off the memory of his voice, and of the barely disguised impatience with which he had waited for her to go before putting his question. Confronted by this new riddle (when there were already so many others in her path) she felt a reasonless exasperation against the broken doorknob which had let her into the secret. If only Kitty Landish, instead of dreaming about Mesopotamian embroideries, would send for a locksmith and keep her house in repair!

All day Pauline was oppressed by the nervous apprehension that Manford might have changed his mind about dropping the investigation. If there had been time she would have gone to Alvah Loft for relief; she had managed so far to squeeze in a daily séance, and had come to depend on it as "addicts" do on their morphia. The very brevity of the treatment, and the blunt negative face and indifferent monosyllables of the Healer, were subtly stimulating after the verbiage and flummery of his predecessors. Such stern economy of means impressed Pauline in much the same way as a new labour-saving device; she liked everything the better for being a short-cut to something else, and even spiritual communion for resembling an improved form of stenography. As Mrs. Swoffer said, Alvah Loft was really the Busy Man's Christ.

But that afternoon there was literally not time for a treatment. Manford's decision to spend the Easter holidays at Cedarledge necessitated one of those campaigns of intensive preparation in which his wife and Maisie Bruss excelled. Leading the simple life at Cedarledge involved despatching there a part of the New York domestic staff at least ten days in advance, testing and lighting three complicated heating systems, going over all the bells and electric wiring, and making sure that the elaborate sanitary arrangements were in irreproachable order.

Nor was this all. Pauline, who prided herself on the perfect organization of every detail of both her establishments, had lately been studying the estimate for a new and singularly complete system of burglar-alarm at Cedarledge, and also going over the bills for the picturesque engine-house and up-to-date fire-engine with which she had just endowed the village patriarchally clustered below the Cedarledge hill. All these matters called for deep thought and swift decision; and the fact gave her a sudden stimulus. No rest- cure in the world was as refreshing to her as a hurried demand on her practical activity; she thrilled to it like a war-horse to a trumpet, and compelled the fagged Maisie to thrill in unison.

In this case their energy was redoubled by the hope that, if Manford found everything to his liking at Cedarledge, he might take a fancy to spending more time there. Pauline's passionate interest in plumbing and electric wiring was suffused with a romantic glow at the thought that they might lure her husband back to domestic intimacy. "The heating of the new swimming-pool must be finished too, and the workmen all out of the way—you'll have to go there next week, Maisie, and impress on everybody that there must not be a workman visible anywhere when we arrive."

Breathless, exultant, Pauline hurried home for a late cup of tea in her boudoir, and settled down, pencil in hand, with plans and estimates, as eagerly as her husband, in the early days of his legal career, used to study the documents of a new case.

Maisie, responding as she always did to the least touch of the spur, yet lifted a perplexed brow to murmur: "All right. But I don't see how I can very well leave before the Birth Control dinner. You know you haven't yet rewritten the opening passage that you used by mistake at the—"

Pauline's colour rose. Maisie's way of putting it was tactless; but the fact remained that the opening of that unlucky speech had to be rewritten, and that Pauline was never very sure of her syntax unless Maisie's reinforced it. She had always meant to be cultivated—she still thought she was when she looked at her bookshelves. But when she had to compose a speech, though words never failed her, the mysterious relations between them sometimes did. Wealth and extensive social activities were obviously incompatible with a complete mastery of grammar, and secretaries were made for such emergencies. Yes; Maisie, fagged as she looked, could certainly not be spared till the speech was remodelled.

The telephone, ringing from downstairs, announced that the Marchesa was on her way up to the boudoir. Pauline's pencil fell from her hand. On her way

up! It was really too inconsiderate. . . Amalasuntha must be made to understand.
. . But there was the undaunted lady.

"The footman swore you were out, dear; but I knew from his manner that I
should find you. (With Powder, now, I never can tell.) And I simply HAD to
rush in long enough to give you a good hug." The Marchesa glanced at Maisie,
and the secretary effaced herself after another glance, this time from her
employer, which plainly warned her: "Wait in the next room; I won't let her
stay."

To her visitor Pauline murmured somewhat coldly: "I left word that I was
out because I'm desperately busy over the new plumbing and burglar-alarm
systems at Cedarledge. Dexter wants to go there for Easter, and of course
everything must be in order before we arrive. . ."

The Marchesa's eyes widened. "Ah, this marvellous American plumbing! I
believe you all treat yourselves to a new set of bathrooms every year. There's
only one bath at San Fedele, and my dear parents-in-law had it covered with a
wooden lid so that it could be used to do the boots on. It's really rather
convenient— and out of family feeling Venturino has always reserved it for that
purpose. But that's not what I came to talk about. What I want is to find words
for my gratitude. . ."

Pauline leaned back, gazing wearily at Amalasuntha's small sharp face, which
seemed to glitter with a new and mysterious varnish of prosperity. "For what?
You've thanked me already more than my little present deserved."

The Marchesa gave her a look of puzzled retrospection. "Oh—that lovely
cheque the other day? Of course my thanks include that too. But I'm entirely
overwhelmed by your new munificence."

"My new munificence?" Pauline echoed between narrowed lips. Could this
be an adroit way of prefacing a fresh appeal? With the huge Cedarledge
estimates at her elbow she stiffened herself for refusal. Amalasuntha must really
be taught moderation.

"Well, Dexter's munificence, then—his royal promise! I left him only an
hour ago," the Marchesa cried with rising exultation.

"You mean he's found a job for Michelangelo? I'm very glad," said Pauline,
still without enthusiasm.

"No, no; something ever so much better than that. At least," the Marchesa
hastily corrected herself, "something more immediately helpful. His debts, dear,
my silly boy's debts! Dexter has promised . . . has authorized me to cable that he
need not sail, as everything will be paid. It's more, far more, than I could have
hoped!" The happy mother possessed herself of Mrs. Manford's unresponsive
hand.

Pauline freed the hand abruptly. She felt the need of assimilating and
interpreting this news as rapidly as possible, without betraying undue
astonishment and yet without engaging her responsibility; but the effort was
beyond her, and she could only sit and stare. Dexter had promised to pay
Michelangelo's debts— but with whose money? And why?

"I'm sure Dexter wants to do all he can to help you about Michelangelo—
we both do. But—"

Pauline's brain was whirling; she found it impossible to go on. She knew by
heart the extent of Michelangelo's debts. Amalasuntha took care that everyone
did. She seemed to feel a sort of fatuous pride in their enormity, and was always
dinning it into her cousin's ears. Dexter, if he had really made such a promise,
must have made it in his wife's name; and to do so without consulting her was
so unlike him that the idea deepened her bewilderment.

"Are you sure? I'm sorry, Amalasuntha—but this comes as a surprise. . .
Dexter and I were to talk the matter over . . . to see what could be done. . ."

"Darling, it's so like you to belittle your own generosity—you always do!
And so does Dexter. But in this case—well, the cable's gone; so why deny it?"
triumphed the Marchesa.

When Maisie Bruss returned, Pauline was still sitting with an idle pencil
before the pile of bills and estimates. She fixed an unseeing eye on her secretary.
"These things will have to wait. I'm dreadfully tired, I don't know why. But I'll
go over them all early tomorrow, before you come; and—Maisie—I hate to ask
it; but do you think you could get here by eight o'clock instead of nine? There's
so much to be done; and I want to get you off to Cedarledge as soon as
possible."

Maisie, a little paler and more drawn than usual, declared that of course she
would turn up at eight.

Even after she had gone Pauline did not move, or give another glance to the
papers. For the first time in her life she had an obscure sense of moving among
incomprehensible and overpowering forces. She could not, to herself, have put
it even as clearly as that—she just dimly felt that, between her and her usual firm
mastery of facts, something nebulous and impenetrable was closing in. . .
Nona—what if she were to consult Nona? The girl sometimes struck her as
having an uncanny gift of divination, as getting at certain mysteries of mood and
character more quickly and clearly than her mother. . . "Though, when it comes
to practical things, poor child, she's not much more use than Jim. . ."

Jim! His name called up the other associated with it. Lita was now another
source of worry. Whichever way Pauline looked, the same choking obscurity
enveloped her. Even about Jim and Lita it clung in a dense fog, darkening and
distorting what, only a short time ago, had seemed a daylight case of domestic
harmony. Money, health, good looks, a beautiful baby . . . and now all this fuss
about having to express one's own personality. Yes; Lita's attitude was just as
confusing as Dexter's. Was Dexter trying to express his own personality too? If
only they would all talk things out with her—help her to understand, instead of
moving about her in the obscurity, like so many burglars with dark lanterns! This
image jerked her attention back to the Cedarledge estimates, and wearily she
adjusted her eye-glasses and took up her pencil. . .

Her maid rapped. "What dress, please, madam?" To be sure—they were
dining that evening with the Walter Rivingtons. It was the first time they had
invited Pauline since her divorce from Wyant; Mrs. Rivington's was the only

house left in which the waning traditions of old New York still obstinately held out, and divorce was regarded as a social disadvantage. But they had taken Manford's advice successfully in a difficult case, and were too punctilious not to reward him in the one way he would care about. The Rivingtons were the last step of the Manford ladder.

"The silver moiré, and my pearls." That would be distinguished and exclusive-looking. Pauline was thankful Dexter had definitely promised to go with her—he was getting so restive nowadays about what he had taken to calling her dull dinners. . .

The telephone again—this time Dexter's voice. Pauline listened apprehensively, wondering if it would do to speak to him now about Amalasuntha's extraordinary announcement, or whether it might be more tactful to wait. He was so likely to be nervous and irritable at the end of the day. Yes; it was in his eleventh-hour voice that he was speaking.

"Pauline—look here; I shall be kept at the office rather late. Please put off dinner, will you? I'd like a quiet evening alone with you—"

"A quiet. . . But, Dexter, we're dining at the Rivingtons'. Shall I telephone to say you may be late?"

"The Rivingtons?" His voice became remote and utterly indifferent. "No; telephone we won't come. Chuck them. . . I want a talk with you alone . . . can't we dine together quietly at home?" He repeated the phrases slowly, as if he thought she had not understood him.

Chuck the Rivingtons? It seemed like being asked to stand up in church and deny her God. She sat speechless and let the fatal words go on vibrating on the wire.

"Don't you hear me, Pauline? Why don't you answer? Is there something wrong with the line?"

"No, Dexter. There's nothing wrong with the line."

"Well, then. . . You can explain to them . . . say anything you like."

Through the dressing-room door she saw the maid laying out the silver moiré, the chinchilla cloak, the pearls. . .

Explain to the Rivingtons!

"Very well, dear. What time shall I order dinner here?" she questioned heroically.

She heard him ring off, and sat again staring into the fog, which his words had only made more impenetrable.

XV

Manford, the day after his daughter had caught sight of him at the Housetop, started out early for one of his long tramps around the Park. He was not due at his office till ten, and he wanted first to walk himself tired.

For some years after his marriage he had kept a horse in town, and taken his morning constitutional in the saddle; but the daily canter over the same bridle paths was too much like the circuit of his wife's flower-garden. He took to his feet to make it last longer, and when there was no time to walk had in a masseur who prepared him, in the same way as everybody else, for the long hours of sedentary hurry known as "business." The New York routine had closed in on him, and he sometimes felt that, for intrinsic interest, there was little to choose between Pauline's hurry and his own. They seemed, all of them—lawyers, bankers, brokers, railway-directors and the rest—to be cheating their inner emptiness with activities as futile as those of the women they went home to.

It was all wrong—something about it was fundamentally wrong. They all had these colossal plans for acquiring power, and then, when it was acquired, what came of it but bigger houses, more food, more motors, more pearls, and a more self-righteous philanthropy?

The philanthropy was what he most hated: all these expensive plans for moral forcible feeding, for compelling everybody to be cleaner, stronger, healthier and happier than they would have been by the unaided light of Nature. The longing to get away into a world where men and women sinned and begot, lived and died, as they chose, without the perpetual intervention of optimistic millionaires, had become so strong that he sometimes felt the chain of habit would snap with his first jerk.

That was what had secretly drawn him to Jim's wife. She was the one person in his group to whom its catchwords meant absolutely nothing. The others, whatever their private omissions or indulgences, dressed up their selfish cravings in the same wordy altruism. It used to be one's duty to one's neighbour; now it had become one's duty to one's self. Duty, duty—always duty! But when you spoke of duty to Lita she just widened her eyes and said: "Is that out of the Marriage Service? 'Love, honour and obey'— such a funny combination! Who do you suppose invented it? I believe it must have been Pauline." One could never fix her attention on any subject beyond her own immediate satisfaction, and that animal sincerity seemed to Manford her greatest charm. Too great a charm . . . a terrible danger. He saw it now. He thought he had gone to her for relaxation, change—and he had just managed to pull himself up on the edge of a precipice. But for the sickening scene of the other evening, when he had shown her the photograph, he might, old fool that he was, have let himself slip into sentiment; and God knows where that tumble would have landed him. Now a passionate pity had replaced his fatuous emotion, the baleful siren was only a misguided child, and he was to help and save her for Jim's sake and her own.

It was queer that such a mood of calm lucidity had come out of the fury of hate with which he rushed from her house. If it had not, he would have gone mad—smashed something, done something irretrievable. And instead here he was, calmly contemplating his own folly and hers! He must go on seeing her, of course; there was more reason than ever for seeing her; but there would be no danger in it now, only help for her—and perhaps healing for him. To this new mood he clung as to an inviolable refuge. The turmoil and torment of the last months could never reach him again: he had found a way out, an escape. The relief of being quiet, of avoiding a conflict, of settling everything without effusion of blood, stole over him like the spell of the drug-taker's syringe. Poor little Lita . . . never again to be adored (thank heaven), but, oh, so much the more to be helped and pitied. . .

This deceptive serenity had come to him during his call on Mrs. Landish—come from her very insensibility to any of the standards he lived by. He had gone there—he saw it now—moved by the cruel masculine desire to know the worst about a fallen idol. What he called the determination to "face things"—what was it but the savage longing to accumulate all the evidence against poor Lita? Give up the Mahatma investigation? Never! All the more reason now for going on with it; for exposing the whole blackguardly business, opening poor Jim's eyes to his wife's past (better now than later), and helping him to get on his feet again, start fresh, and recover his faith in life and happiness. For of course poor Jim would be the chief sufferer. . . Damn the woman! She wanted to get rid of Jim, did she? Well, here was her chance—only it would be the other way round. The tables would be turned on her. She'd see—! This in his first blind outbreak of rage; but by the time he reached Mrs. Landish's door the old legal shrewdness had come to his rescue, and he had understood that a public scandal was unnecessary, and therefore to be avoided. Easy enough to get rid of Lita without that. With such evidence as he would soon possess they could make any conditions they chose. Jim would keep the boy, and the whole thing be settled quietly—but on their terms, not hers! She would be only too thankful to clear out bag and baggage— clean out of all their lives. Faugh—to think he had delegated his own Nona; to look after her . . . the thought sickened him.

And then, in the end, it had all come out so differently. He needed his hard tramp around the Park to see just why.

It was Mrs. Landish's own attitude—her silly rambling irresponsibility, so like an elderly parody of Lita's youthful carelessness. Mrs. Landish had met Manford's stern interrogations by the vague reply that he mustn't ever come to HER for dates and figures and statistics: that facts meant nothing to her, that the only thing she cared for was Inspiration, Genius, the Divine Fire, or whatever he chose to call it. Perhaps she'd done wrong, but she had sacrificed everything, all her life, to her worship of genius. She was always hunting for it everywhere, and it was because, from the first, she had felt a touch of it in Lita that she had been so devoted to the child. Didn't Manford feel it in Lita too? Of course she, Mrs. Landish, had dreamed of another sort of marriage for her niece . . . Oh, but Manford mustn't misunderstand! Jim was perfect—TOO perfect. That was the trouble. Manford surely guessed the meaning of that "too"? Such absolute reliability, such complete devotion, were sometimes more of a strain to the artistic temperament than scenes and infidelities. And Lita was first and foremost an artist, born to live in the world of art—in quite other values—a fourth-dimensional world, as it were. It wasn't fair to judge her in her present surroundings, ideal as they were in one way—a way that unfortunately didn't happen to be hers! Mrs. Landish persisted in assuming Manford's complete comprehension . . . "If Jim could only be made to understand as you do; to see that ordinary standards don't apply to these rare natures. . . Why, has the child told you what Klawhammer has offered her to turn ONE FILM for him, before even having seen her dance, just on the strength of what Jack Staley and Ardwin had told him?"

Ah—there it was! The truth was out. Mrs. Landish, always in debt, and always full of crazy schemes for wasting more money, had seen a gold mine in the exploitation of her niece's gifts. The divorce, instead of frightening her, delighted her. Manford smiled as he thought how little she would be moved by Pauline's threat to cut off the young couple. Pauline sometimes forgot that, even in her own family, her authority was not absolute. She could certainly not compete financially with Hollywood, and Mrs. Landish's eyes were on Hollywood.

"Dear Mr. Manford—but you look shocked! Absolutely shocked! Does the screen really frighten you? How funny!" Mrs. Landish, drawing her rambling eyebrows together, seemed trying to picture the inner darkness of such a state. "But surely you know the smartest people are going in for it? Why, the Marchesa di San Fedele was showing me the other day a photograph of that beautiful son of hers—one of those really GREEK beings in bathing tights—and telling me that Klawhammer, who had seen it, had authorized her to cable him to come out to Hollywood on trial, all expenses paid. It seems they can almost always recognize the eurythmic people at a glance. Funny, wouldn't it be, if Michelangelo and Lita turned out to be the future Valentino and—"

He didn't remember the rest of the rigmarole. He could only recall shouting out, with futile vehemence: "My wife and I will do everything to prevent a divorce—" and leaving his astonished hostess on a threat of which he knew the uselessness as well as she did.

That was the air in which Lita had grown up, those were the gods of Viking Court! Yet Manford had stormed instead of pitying, been furious instead of tolerant, risked disaster for Lita and Jim instead of taking calm control of the situation. The vision of Lita Wyant and Michelangelo as future film stars, "featured" jointly on every hoarding from Maine to California, had sent the blood to his head. Through a mist of rage he had seen the monstrous pictures and conjectured the loathsome letter-press. And no one would do more than look and laugh! At the thought, he felt the destructive ire of the man who finds his private desires pitted against the tendencies of his age. Well, they would see, that was all: he would show them!

The resolve to act brought relief to his straining imagination. Once again he felt himself seated at his office desk, all his professional authority between him and his helpless interlocutors, and impressive words and skilful arguments ordering themselves automatically in his mind. After all, he was the head of his family—in some degree even of Wyant's family.

XVI

Pauline's nervousness had gradually subsided. About the Rivingtons— why, after all, it wasn't such a bad idea to show them that, with a man of Manford's importance, one must take one's chance of getting him, and make the best of it if he failed one at the last. "Professional engagement; oh, yes, entirely unexpected; extremely important; so dreadfully sorry, but you know lawyers are not their own masters. . ." It had been rather pleasant to say that to a flustered Mrs. Rivington, stammering: "Oh, but COULDN'T he . . . ? But we'll wait . . . we'll dine at half-past nine. . ." Pleasant also to add: "He must reserve his whole evening, I'm afraid," and then hang up, and lean back at leisure, while Mrs. Rivington (how Pauline pictured it!) dashed down in her dressing-gown and crimping pins to re-arrange a table to which as much thought had been given as if a feudal aristocracy were to sit at it.

To Pauline the fact that Manford wanted to be alone with her made even such renunciations easy. How many years had passed since he had expressed such a wish? And did she owe his tardy return to the Mahatma and reduced hips, or the Inspirational Healer and renewed optimism? If only a woman could guess what inclined a man's heart to her, what withdrew it! Pauline, if she had had the standardizing of life, would have begun with human hearts, and had them turned out in series, all alike, rather than let them come into being haphazard, cranky amateurish things that you couldn't count on, or start up again if anything went wrong. . .

Just a touch of rouge? Well, perhaps her maid was right. She DID look rather pale and drawn. Mrs. Herman Toy put it on with a trowel . . . apparently that was what men liked. . . Pauline shed a faint bloom on her cheeks and ran her clever fingers through her prettily waved hair, wondering again, as she did so, if it wouldn't be better to bob it. Then the mauve tea-gown, the Chinese amethysts, and those silver sandals that made her feet so slender. She looked at herself with a sigh of pleasure. Dinner was to be served in the boudoir.

Manford was very late; it was ten o'clock before coffee and liqueurs were put on the low stand by the fire, and the little dinner-table was noiselessly removed. The fire glowed invitingly, and he sank into the armchair his wife pushed forward with a sound like a murmur of content.

"Such a day—" he said, passing his hand across his forehead as if to brush away a tangle of legal problems.

"You do too much, Dexter; you really do. I know how wonderfully young you are for your age, but still—." She broke off, dimly perceiving that, in spite of the flattering exordium, this allusion to his age was not quite welcome.

"Nothing to do with age," he growled. "Everybody who does anything at all does too much." (Did he mean to imply that she did nothing?)

"The nervous strain—" she began, once more wondering if this were not the moment to slip in a word of Alvah Loft. But though Manford had wished to be with her he had apparently no desire to listen to her. It was all her own fault, she felt. If only she had known how to reveal the secret tremors that were rippling through her! There were women not half as clever and tactful—not younger, either, nor even as good-looking—who would have known at once what to say, or how to spell the mute syllables of soul-telegraphy. If her husband had wanted facts—a good confidential talk about the new burglar-alarm, or a clear and careful analysis of the engine- house bills, or the heating system for the swimming pool—she could have found just the confidential and tender accent for such topics. Intimacy, to her, meant the tireless discussion of facts, not necessarily of a domestic order, but definite and palpable facts. For her part she was ready for anything, from Birth Control to neo- impressionism: she flattered herself that few women had a wider range. In confidential moments she preferred the homelier themes, and would have enjoyed best of all being tender and gay about the coal cellar, or reticent and brave about the leak in the boiler; but she was ready to deal with anything as long as it was a fact, something with substance and outline, as to which one could have an opinion and a line of conduct. What paralyzed her was the sense that, apart from his profession, her husband didn't care for facts, and that nothing was less likely to rouse his interest than burglar- alarm wiring, or the last new thing in electric ranges. Obviously, one must take men as they were, wilful, moody and mysterious; but she would have given the world to be told (since for all her application she had never discovered) what those other women said who could talk to a man about nothing.

Manford lit a cigar and stared into the fire. "It's about that fool Amalasuntha," he began at length, addressing his words to the logs.

The name jerked Pauline back to reality. Here was a fact—hard, knobby and uncomfortable! And she had actually forgotten it in the confused pleasure of their tête-à-tête! So he had only come home to talk to her about Amalasuntha. She tried to keep the flatness out of her: "Yes, dear?"

He continued, still fixed on the fire: "You may not know that we've had a narrow escape."

"A narrow escape?"

"That damned Michelangelo—his mother was importing him this very week. The cable had gone. If I hadn't put a stop to it we'd have been saddled with him for life."

Pauline's breath failed her. She listened with straining ears.

"You haven't seen her, then—she hasn't told you?" Manford continued. "She was getting him out on her own responsibility to turn a film for Klawhammer. Simply that! By the mercy of heaven I headed her off—but we hadn't a minute to lose."

In her bewilderment at this outburst, and at what it revealed, Pauline continued to sit speechless. "Michelangelo—Klawhammer? I didn't know! But wouldn't it have been the best solution, perhaps?"

"Solution—of what? Don't you think one member of the family on the screen's enough at a time? Or would it have looked prettier to see him and Lita featured together on every hoarding in the country? My God—I thought I'd done the right thing in acting for you . . . there was no time to consult you . . .

but if YOU don't care, why should I? He's none of MY family . . . and she isn't either, for that matter."

He had swung round from the hearth, and faced her for the first time, his brows contracted, the veins swelling on his temples, his hands grasping his knees as if to constrain himself not to start up in righteous indignation. He was evidently deeply disturbed, yet his anger, she felt, was only the unconscious mask of another emotion—an emotion she could not divine. His vehemence, and the sense of moving in complete obscurity, had an intimidating effect on her.

"I don't quite understand, Dexter. Amalasuntha was here today. She said nothing about films, or Klawhammer; but she did say that you'd made it unnecessary for Michelangelo to come to America."

"Didn't she say how?"

"She said something about—paying his debts."

Manford stood up and went to lean against the mantelpiece. He looked down on his wife, who in her turn kept her eyes on the embers.

"Well—you didn't suppose I made that offer till I saw we were up against it, did you?"

His voice rose again angrily, but a cautious glance at his face showed her that its tormented lines were damp with perspiration. Her immediate thought was that he must be ill, that she ought to take his temperature—she always responded by first-aid impulses to any contact with human distress. But no, after all, it was not that: he was unhappy, that was it, he was desperately unhappy. But why? Was it because he feared he had exceeded his rights in pledging her to such an extent, in acting for her when there was no time to consult her? Apparently the idea of the discord between Lita and Jim, and Lita's thirst for scenic notoriety, had shocked him deeply—much more, in reality, than they had Pauline. If so, his impulse had been a natural one, and eminently in keeping with those Wyant traditions with which (at suitable moments) she continued to identify herself. Yes: she began to understand his thinking it would be odious to her to see the names of her son's wife and this worthless Italian cousin emblazoned over every Picture Palace in the land. She felt moved by his regard for her feelings. After all, as he said, Lita and Michelangelo were no relations of his; he could easily have washed his hands of the whole affair.

"I'm sure what you've done must be right, Dexter; you know I always trust your judgment. Only—I wish you'd explain. . ."

"Explain what?" Her mild reply seemed to provoke a new wave of exasperation. "The only way to stop his coming was to pay his debts. They're very heavy. I had no right to commit you; I acknowledge it."

She took a deep breath, the figure of Michelangelo's liabilities blazing out before her as on a giant blackboard. Then: "You had every right, Dexter," she said. "I'm glad you did it."

He stood silent, his head bent, twisting between his fingers the cigar he had forgotten to relight. It was as if he had been startled out of speech by the promptness of her acquiescence, and would have found it easier to go on arguing and justifying himself.

"That's—very handsome of you, Pauline," he said at length.

"Oh, no—why? You did it out of regard for me, I know. Only— perhaps you won't mind our talking things over a little. About ways and means . . ." she added, seeing his forehead gloom again.

"Ways and means—oh, certainly. But please understand that I don't expect you to shoulder the whole sum. I've had two big fees lately; I've already arranged—"

She interrupted him quickly. "It's not your affair, Dexter. You're awfully generous, always; but I couldn't think of letting you—"

"It IS my affair; it's all of our affair. I don't want this nasty notoriety any more than you do . . . and Jim's happiness wrecked into the bargain. . ."

"You're awfully generous," she repeated.

"It's first of all a question of helping Jim and Lita. If that young ass came over here with a contract from Klawhammer in his pocket there'd be no holding her. And once that gang get hold of a woman. . ." He spoke with a kind of breathless irritation, as though it were incredible that Pauline should still not understand.

"It's very fine of you, dear," she could only murmur.

A pause followed, during which, for the first time, she could assemble her thoughts and try to take in the situation. Dexter had bought off Michelangelo to keep one more disturbing element out of the family complication; perhaps also to relieve himself of the bother of having on his hands, at close quarters, an idle and mischief-making young man. That was comprehensible. But if his first object had been the securing of Jim's peace of mind, might not the same end have been achieved, more satisfactorily to every one but Michelangelo, by his uniting with Pauline to increase Jim's allowance, and thus giving Lita the amusement and distraction of having a lot more money to spend? Even at such a moment, Pauline's practical sense of values made it hard for her to accept the idea of putting so many good thousands into the pockets of Michelangelo's creditors. She was naturally generous; but no matter how she disposed of her fortune, she could never forget that it had been money—and how much money it had been—before it became something else. For her it was never transmuted, but only exchanged.

"You're not satisfied—you don't think I did right?" Manford began again.

"I don't say that, Dexter. I'm only wondering—. Supposing we'd given the money to Jim instead? Lita could have done her house over . . . or built a bungalow in Florida . . . or bought jewels with it. . . She's so easily amused."

"Easily amused!" He broke into a hard laugh. "Why, that amount of money wouldn't amuse her for a week!" His face took on a look of grim introspection. "She wants the universe—or her idea of it. A woman with an offer from Klawhammer dangling in front of her! Mrs. Landish told me the figure—those people could buy us all out and not know it."

Pauline's heart sank. Apparently he knew things about Lita of which she was still ignorant. "I hadn't heard the offer had actually been made. But if it has, and she wants to accept, how can we stop her?"

Manford had thrown himself down into his armchair. He got up again, relit his cigar, and walked across the room and back before answering. "I don't know that we can. And I don't know how we can. But I want to try. . . I want TIME to try. . . Don't you see, Pauline? The child—we mustn't be hard on her. Her beginnings were damnable. . . Perhaps you know—yes? That cursed Mahatma place?" Pauline winced, and looked away from him. He had seen the photograph, then! And heaven knows what more he had discovered in the course of his investigations for the Lindons. . . A sudden light glared out at her. It was for Jim's sake and Lita's that he had dropped the case—sacrificed his convictions, his sense of the duty of exposing a social evil! She faltered: "I do know . . . a little. . ."

"Well, a little's enough. Swine—! And that's the rotten atmosphere she was brought up in. But she's not bad, Pauline . . . there's something still to be done with her . . . give me time . . . time. . ." He stopped abruptly, as if the "me" had slipped out by mistake. "We must all stand shoulder to shoulder to put up this fight for her," he corrected himself with a touch of forensic emphasis.

"Of course, dear, of course," Pauline murmured.

"When we get her to ourselves at Cedarledge, you and Nona and I. . . It's just as well Jim's going off, by the way. He's got her nerves on edge; Jim's a trifle dense at times, you know. . . And, above all, this whole business, Klawhammer and all, must be kept from him. We'll all hold our tongues till the thing blows over, eh?"

"Of course," she again assented. "But supposing Lita asks to speak to me?"

"Well, let her speak—listen to what she has to say. . ." He stopped, and then added, in a rough unsteady voice: "Only don't be hard on her. You won't, will you? No matter what rot she talks. The child's never had half a chance."

"How could you think I should, Dexter?"

"No; no; I don't." He stood up, and sent a slow unseeing gaze about the room. The gaze took in his wife, and rested on her long enough to make her feel that she was no more to him—mauve tea- gown, Chinese amethysts, touch of rouge and silver sandals—than a sheet of glass through which he was staring: staring at what? She had never before felt so inexistent.

"Well—I'm dog-tired—down and out," he said with one of his sudden jerks, shaking his shoulders and turning toward the door. He did not remember to say goodnight to her: how should he have, when she was no longer there for him?

After the door had closed, Pauline in her turn looked slowly about the room. It was as if she were taking stock of the havoc wrought by an earthquake; but nothing about her showed any sign of disorder except the armchair her husband had pushed back, the rug his movement had displaced.

With instinctive precision she straightened the rug, and rolled the armchair back into its proper corner. Then she went up to a mirror and attentively scrutinized herself. The light was unbecoming, perhaps . . . the shade of the adjacent wall-candle had slipped out of place. She readjusted it . . . yes, that was better! But of course, at nearly midnight—and after such a day!—a woman was bound to look a little drawn. Automatically her lips shaped the familiar: "Pauline, don't worry: there's nothing in the world to worry about." But the rouge had vanished from the lips, their thin line looked blue and arid. She turned from the unpleasing sight, putting out one light after another on the way to her dressing-room.

As she bent to extinguish the last lamp its light struck a tall framed photograph: Lita's latest portrait. Lita had the gift of posing—the lines she fell into always had an unconscious eloquence. And that little round face, as sleek as the inside of a shell; the slanting eyes, the budding mouth . . . men, no doubt, would think it all enchanting.

Pauline, with slow steps, went on into the big shining dressing- room, and to the bathroom beyond, all ablaze with white tiling and silvered taps and tubes. It was the hour of her evening uplift exercises, the final relaxing of body and soul before she slept. Sternly she addressed herself to relaxation.

XVII

What was the sense of it all?

Nona, sitting up in bed two days after her nocturnal visit to the Housetop, swept the interval with a desolate eye. She had made her great, her final, refusal. She had sacrificed herself, sacrificed Heuston, to the stupid ideal of an obstinate woman who managed to impress people by dressing up her egotism in formulas of philanthropy and piety. Because Aggie was forever going to church, and bossing the committees of Old Women's Homes and Rest-cures for Consumptives, she was allowed a license of cruelty which would have damned the frivolous.

Destroying two lives to preserve her own ideal of purity! It was like the horrible ailing old men in history books, who used to bathe in human blood to restore their vitality. Every one agreed that there was nothing such a clever sensitive fellow as Stanley Heuston mightn't have made of his life if he'd married a different kind of woman. As it was, he had just drifted: tried the law, dabbled in literary reviewing, taken a turn at municipal politics, another at scientific farming, and dropped one experiment after another to sink, at thirty-five, into a disillusioned idler who killed time with cards and drink and motor-speeding. She didn't believe he ever opened a book nowadays: he was living on the dwindling capital of his early enthusiasms. But, as for what people called his "fastness," she knew it was merely the inevitable opposition to Aggie's virtues. And it wasn't as if there had been children. Nona always ached for the bewildered progeny suddenly bundled from one home to another when their parents embarked on a new conjugal experiment; she could never have bought her happiness by a massacre of innocents. But to be sacrificed to a sterile union—as sterile spiritually as physically—to miss youth and love because of Agnes Heuston's notion of her duty to the elderly clergyman she called God!

That woman he said he was going off with. . . Nona had pretended she didn't know, had opened incredulous eyes at the announcement. But of course she knew; everybody knew; it was Cleo Merrick. She had been "after him" for the last two years, she hadn't a rag of reputation to lose, and would jump at the idea of a few jolly weeks with a man like Heuston, even if he got away from her afterward. But he wouldn't—of course he never would! Poor Stan—Cleo Merrick's noise, her cheek, her vulgarity: how warm and life-giving they would seem as a change from the frigidarium he called home! She would hold him by her very cheapness: her recklessness would seem like generosity, her glitter like heat. Ah—how Nona could have shown him the difference! She shut her eyes and felt his lips on her lids; and her lids became lips. Wherever he touched her, a mouth blossomed. . . Did he know that? Had he never guessed?

She jumped out of bed, ran into her dressing-room, began to bathe and dress with feverish haste. She wouldn't telephone him—Aggie had long ears. She wouldn't send a "special delivery"—Aggie had sharp eyes. She would just summon him by a telegram: a safe anonymous telegram. She would dash out of the house and get it off herself, without even waiting for her cup of coffee to be brought.

"Come and see me any time today. I was too stupid the other night." Yes; he would understand that. She needn't even sign it. . .

On the threshold of her room, the telegram crumpled in her hand, the telephone bell arrested her. Stanley, surely; he must have felt the same need that she had! She fumbled uncertainly with the receiver; the tears were running down her cheeks. She had waited too long; she had exacted the impossible of herself. "Yes—yes? It's you, darling?" She laughed it out through her weeping.

"What's that? It's Jim. That you, Nona?" a quiet voice came back. When had Jim's voice ever been anything but quiet?

"Oh, Jim, dear!" She gulped down tears and laughter. "Yes—what is it? How awfully early you are!"

"Hope I didn't wake you? Can I drop in on my way down town?"

"Of course. When? How soon?"

"Now. In two minutes. I've got to be at the office before nine."

"All right. In two minutes. Come straight up."

She hung up the receiver, and thrust the telegram aside. No time to rush out with it now. She would see Jim first, and send off her message when he left. Now that her decision was taken she felt tranquil and able to wait. But anxiety about Jim rose and swelled in her again. She reproached herself for having given him so little thought for the last two days. Since her parting from Stan on the doorstep in the rainy night everything but her fate and his had grown remote and almost indifferent to her. Well; it was natural enough—only perhaps she had better not be so glib about Aggie Heuston's selfishness! Of course everybody who was in love was selfish; and Aggie, according to her lights, was in love. Her love was bleak and cramped, like everything about her; a sort of fleshless bony affair, like the repulsive plates in anatomical manuals. But in reality those barren arms were stretched toward Stanley, though she imagined they were lifted to God. . . What a hideous mystery life was! And yet Pauline and her friends persisted in regarding it as a Sunday school picnic, with lemonade and sponge cake as its supreme rewards. . .

Here was Jim at her sitting-room door. Nona held out her arms, and slanted a glance at him as he bent his cheek to her kiss. Was the cheek rather sallower than usual? Well, that didn't mean much: he and she were always a yellow pair when they were worried!

"What's up, old man? No—this armchair's more comfortable. Had your coffee?"

He let her change the armchair, but declined the coffee. He had breakfasted before starting, he said—but she knew Lita's household, and didn't believe him.

"Anything wrong with Exhibit A?"

"Wrong? No. That is. . ." She had put the question at random, in the vague hope of gaining time before Lita's name was introduced; and now she had the sense of having unwittingly touched on another problem.

"That is—well, he's nervous and fidgety again: you've noticed?"

"I've noticed."

"Imagining things—. What a complicated world our ancestors lived in, didn't they?"

"Well, I don't know. Mother's world always seems to me alarmingly simple."

He considered. "Yes—that's pioneering and motor-building, I suppose. It's the old New York blood that's so clogged with taboos. Poor father always wants me to behave like a Knight of the Round Table."

Nona lifted her eyebrows with an effort of memory. "How did they behave?"

"They were always hitting some other fellow over the head."

She felt a little catch in her throat. "Who—particularly—does he want you to hit over the head?"

"Oh, we haven't got as far as that yet. It's just the general principle. Anybody who looks too hard at Lita."

"You WOULD have to be hitting about! Everybody looks hard at Lita. How in the world can she help it?"

"That's what I tell him. But he says I haven't got the feelings of a gentleman. Guts, he means, I suppose." He leaned back, crossing his arms wearily behind his back, his sallow face with heavy-lidded eyes tilted to the ceiling. "Do you suppose Lita feels that too?" he suddenly flung at his sister.

"That you ought to break people's heads for her? She'd be the first to laugh at you!"

"So I told him. But he says women despise a man who isn't jealous."

Nona sat silent, instinctively turning her eyes from his troubled face. "Why should you be jealous?" she asked at length.

He shifted his position, stretched his arms along his knees, and brought his eyes down to a level with hers. There was something pathetic, she thought, in such youthful blueness blurred with uncomprehended pain.

"I suppose it's never got much to do with reasons," he said, very low.

"No; that's why it's so silly—and ungenerous."

"It doesn't matter what it is. She doesn't care a hang if I'm jealous or if I'm not. She doesn't care anything about me. I've simply ceased to exist for her."

"Well, then you can't be in her way."

"It seems I am, though. Because I DO exist, for the world; and as the boy's father. And the mere idea gets on her nerves."

Nona laughed a little bitterly. "She wants a good deal of elbow- room, doesn't she? And how does she propose to eliminate you?"

"Oh, that's easy. Divorce."

There was a silence between the two. This was how it sounded—that simple reasonable request—on the lips of the other partner, the partner who still had a stake in the affair! Lately she seemed to have forgotten that side of the question; but how hideously it grimaced at her now, behind the lines of this boyish face wrung with a man's misery!

"Old Jim—it hurts such a lot?"

He jerked away from her outstretched hand. "Hurt? A fellow can stand being hurt. It can't hurt more than feeling her chained to me. But if she goes— what does she go to?"

Ah—that was it! Through the scorch and cloud of his own suffering he had seen it, it was the centre of his pain. Nona glanced down absently at her slim young hands—so helpless and inexperienced looking. All these tangled cross-threads of life, inextricably and fatally interwoven; how were a girl's hands to unravel them?

"I suppose she's talked to you—told you her ideas?" he asked.

Nona nodded.

"Well, what's to be done: can you tell me?"

"She mustn't go—we mustn't let her."

"But if she stays—stays hating me?"

"Oh, Jim, not HATING—!"

"You know well enough that she gets to hate anything that doesn't amuse her."

"But there's the baby. The baby still amuses her."

He looked at her, surprised. "Ah, that's what father says: he calls the baby, poor old chap, my hostage. What rot! As if I'd take her baby from her—and just because she cares for it. If I don't know how to keep her, I don't see that I've got any right to keep her child."

That was the new idea of marriage, the view of Nona's contemporaries; it had been her own a few hours since. Now, seeing it in operation, she wondered if it still were. It was one thing to theorize on the detachability of human beings, another to watch them torn apart by the bleeding roots. This botanist who had recently discovered that plants were susceptible to pain, and that transplanting was a major operation—might he not, if he turned his attention to modern men and women, find the same thing to be still true of a few of them?

"Oh Jim, how I wish you didn't care so!" The words slipped out unawares: they were the last she had meant to speak aloud.

Her brother turned to her; the ghost of his old smile drew up his lip. "Good old girl!" he mocked her—then his face dropped into his hands, and he sat huddled against the armchair, his shaken shoulder-blades warding off her touch.

It didn't last more than a minute; but it was the real, the only answer. He DID care so; nothing could alter it. She looked on stupidly, admitted for the first time to this world-old anguish rooted under all the restless moods of man.

Jim got up, shook back his rumpled hair, and reached for a cigarette. "That's THAT. And now, my child, what can I do? What I'd honestly like, if she wants her freedom, is to give it to her, and yet be able to go on looking after her. But I don't see how that can be worked out. Father says it's madness. He says I'm a morbid coward and talk like the people in the Russian novels. He wants to speak to her himself—"

"Oh, no! He and she don't talk the same language. . ."

Jim paused, pulling absently at his cigarette, and measuring the room with uncertain steps. "That's what I feel. But there's YOUR father; he's been so awfully good to us; and his ideas are less archaic. . ."

Nona had turned away and was looking unseeingly out of the window. She moved back hastily. "No!"

He looked surprised. "You think he wouldn't understand either?"

"I don't mean that. . . But, after all, it's not his job. . . Have you spoken to mother?"

"Mother? Oh, she always thinks everything's all right. She'd give me a cheque, and tell me to buy Lita a new motor or to let her do over the drawing-room."

Nona pondered this answer, which was no more than the echo of her own thoughts. "All the same, Jim: mother's mother. She's always been awfully good to both of us, and you can't let this go on without her knowing, without consulting her. She has a right to your confidence—she has a right to hear what Lita has to say."

He remained silent, as if indifferent. His mother's glittering optimism was a hard surface for grief and failure to fling themselves on. "What's the use?" he grumbled.

"Let me consult her, then: at least let me see how she takes it."

He threw away his cigarette and looked at his watch. "I've got to run; it's nearly nine." He laid a hand on his sister's shoulder. "Whatever you like, old girl. But don't imagine it's going to be any use."

She put her arms about him, and he submitted to her kiss. "Give me time," she said, not knowing what else to answer.

After he had gone she sat motionless, weighed down with half-comprehended misery. This business of living—how right she had been to feel, in her ignorance, what a tortured tangle it was! Where, for instance, did one's own self end and one's neighbour's begin? And how tell the locked tendrils apart in the delicate process of disentanglement? Her precocious half-knowledge of the human dilemma was combined with a youthful belief that the duration of pain was proportioned to its intensity. And at that moment she would have hated any one who had tried to persuade her of the contrary. The only honourable thing about suffering was that it should not abdicate before indifference.

She got up, and her glance fell on the telegram which she had pushed aside when her brother entered. She still had her hat on, her feet were turned toward the door. But the door seemed to open into a gray unpeopled world suddenly shorn of its magic. She moved back into the room and tore up the telegram.

XVIII

"Lita? But of course I'll talk to Lita—" Mrs. Manford, resting one elbow on her littered desk, smiled up encouragingly at her daughter. On the desk lay the final version of the Birth Control speech, mastered and canalized by the skilful Maisie. The result was so pleasing that Pauline would have liked to read it aloud to Nona, had the latter not worn her look of concentrated care. It was a pity, Pauline thought, that Nona should let herself go at her age to these moods of anxiety and discouragement.

Pauline herself, fortified by her morning exercises, and by a "double treatment" ($50) from Alvah Loft, had soared once more above her own perplexities. She had not had time for a word alone with her husband since their strange talk of the previous evening; but already the doubts and uncertainties produced by that talk had been dispelled. Of course Dexter had been moody and irritable: wasn't her family always piling up one worry on him after another? He had always loved Jim as much as he did Nona; and now this menace to Jim's happiness, and the unpleasantness about Lita, combined with Amalasuntha's barefaced demands, and the threatened arrival of the troublesome Michelangelo—such a weight of domestic problems was enough to unnerve a man already overburdened with professional cares.

"But of course I'll talk to Lita, dear; I always meant to. The silly goose! I've waited only because your father—"

Nona's heavy eyebrows ran together like Manford's. "Father?"

"Oh, he's helping us so splendidly about it. And he asked me to wait; to do nothing in a hurry. . ."

Nona seemed to turn this over. "All the same—I think you ought to hear what Lita has to say. She's trying to persuade Jim to let her divorce him; and he thinks he ought to, if he can't make her happy."

"But he MUST make her happy! I'll talk to Jim too," cried Pauline with a gay determination.

"I'd try Lita first, mother. Ask her to postpone her decision. If we can get her to come to Cedarledge for a few weeks' rest—"

"Yes; that's what your father says."

"But I don't think father ought to give up his fishing to join us. Haven't you noticed how tired he looks? He ought to get away from all of us for a few weeks. Why shouldn't you and I look after Lita?"

Pauline's enthusiasm drooped. It was really no business of Nona's to give her mother advice about the management of her father. These modern girls— pity Nona didn't marry, and try managing a husband of her own!

"Your father loves Cedarledge. It's quite his own idea to go there. He thinks Easter in the country with us all will be more restful than California. I haven't influenced him in the least to give up his fishing."

"Oh, I didn't suppose you had." Nona seemed to lose interest in the discussion, and her mother took advantage of the fact to add, with a gentle side-glance at her watch: "Is there anything else, dear? Because I've got to go over my Birth Control speech, and at eleven there's a delegation from—"

Nona's eyes had followed her glance to the scattered pages on the desk. "Are you really going to preside at that Birth Control dinner, mother?"

"Preside? Why not? I happen to be chairman," Pauline answered with a faint touch of acerbity.

"I know. Only—the other day you were preaching unlimited families. Don't the two speeches come rather close together? You might expose yourself to some newspaper chaff if any one put you in parallel columns."

Pauline felt herself turning pale. Her lips tightened, and for a moment she was conscious of a sort of blur in her brain. This girl . . . it was preposterous that she shouldn't understand! And always wanting reasons and explanations at a moment's notice! To be subjected, under one's own roof, to such a perpetual inquisition. . . There was nothing she disliked so much as questions to which she had not had time to prepare the answers.

"I don't think you always grasp things, Nona." The words were feeble, but they were the first that came.

"I'm afraid I don't, mother."

"Then, perhaps—I just suggest it—you oughtn't to be quite so ready to criticize. You seem to imagine there is a contradiction in my belonging to these two groups of . . . of thought. . ."

"They do seem to contradict each other."

"Not in reality. The principles are different, of course; but, you see, they are meant to apply to—to different categories of people. It's all a little difficult to explain to any one as young as you are . . . a girl naturally can't be expected to know. . ."

"Oh, what we girls don't know, mother!"

"Well, dear, I've always approved of outspokenness on such matters. The real nastiness is in covering things up. But all the same, age and experience DO teach one. . . You children mustn't hope to get at all your elders' reasons. . ." That sounded firm yet friendly, and as she spoke she felt herself on safer ground. "I wish there were time to go into it all with you now; but if I'm to keep up with today's engagements, and crowd in a talk with Lita besides— Maisie! Will you call up Mrs. Jim?"

Maisie answered from the other room: "The delegation of the League For Discovering Genius is waiting downstairs, Mrs. Manford—"

"Oh, to be sure! This is rather an important movement, Nona; a new thing. I do believe there's something helpful to be done for genius. They're just organizing their first drive: I heard of it through that wonderful Mrs. Swoffer. You wouldn't care to come down and see the delegation with me? No . . . I sometimes think you'd be happier if you interested yourself a little more in other people . . . in all the big humanitarian movements that make one so proud to be an American. Don't you think it's glorious to belong to the only country where everybody is absolutely free, and yet we're all made to do exactly what is best for us? I say that somewhere in my speech. . . Well, I promise to have my talk with Lita before dinner; whatever happens, I'll squeeze her in. And you and Jim needn't be afraid of my saying anything to set her against us. Your father has impressed that on me already. After all, I've always preached the respect of every one's personality; only Lita must begin by respecting Jim's."

Fresh from a stimulating encounter with Mrs. Swoffer and the encouragers of genius, Pauline was able to face with a smiling composure her meeting with her daughter-in-law. Every contact with the humanitarian movements distinguishing her native country from the selfish laissez faire and cynical indifference of Europe filled her with a new optimism, and shed a reassuring light on all her private cares. America really seemed to have an immediate answer for everything, from the treatment of the mentally deficient to the elucidation of the profoundest religious mysteries. In such an atmosphere of universal simplification, how could one's personal problems not be solved? "The great thing is to believe that they WILL be," as Mrs. Swoffer said, à propos of the finding of funds for the new League For Discovering Genius. The remark was so stimulating to Pauline that she immediately drew a large cheque, and accepted the chairmanship of the committee; and it was on the favouring breeze of the League's applause that she sailed, at the tea-hour, into Lita's boudoir.

"It seems simpler just to ask her for a cup of tea—as if I were dropping in to see the baby," Pauline had reflected; and as Lita was not yet at home, there was time to turn her pretext into a reality. Upstairs, in the blue and silver nursery, her sharp eye detected many small negligences under the artistic surface: soiled towels lying about, a half-empty glass of milk with a drowned fly in it, dead and decaying flowers in the æsthetic flowerpots, and not a single ventilator open in the upper window-panes. She made a mental note of these items, but resolved not to touch on them in her talk with Lita. At Cedarledge, where the nurse would be under her own eye, nursery hygiene could be more tactfully imparted. .

.

The black boudoir was still empty when Pauline returned to it, but she was armed with patience, and sat down to wait. The armchairs were much too low to be comfortable and she hated the semi- obscurity of the veiled lamps. How could one possibly occupy one's time in a pitch-dark room with seats that one had to sprawl in as if they were deck-chairs? She thought the room so ugly and dreary that she could hardly blame Lita for wanting to do it over. "I'll give her a cheque for it at once," she reflected indulgently. "All young people begin by making mistakes of this kind." She remembered with a little shiver the set of imitation tapestry armchairs that she had insisted on buying for her drawing-room when she had married Wyant. Perhaps it would be a good move to greet Lita with the offer of the cheque. . .

Somehow Lita's appearance, when she at length arrived, made the idea seem less happy. Lita had a way of looking as if she didn't much care what one did to please her; for a young woman who spent so much money she made very little effort to cajole it out of her benefactors. "Hullo," she said; "I didn't know you were here. Am I late, I wonder?"

Pauline greeted her with a light kiss. "How can you ever tell if you are? I don't believe there's a clock in the house."

"Yes, there is; in the nursery," said Lita.

"Well, my dear, that one's stopped," rejoined her mother-in-law, smiling.

"You've been seeing the boy? Oh, then you haven't missed me," Lita smiled back as she loosened her furs and tossed off her hat. She ran her hands through her goldfish-coloured hair, and flung herself down on a pile of cushions. "Tea's coming sooner or later, I suppose. Unless—a cocktail? No? Wouldn't you be more comfortable on the floor?" she suggested to her mother-in-law.

Every whalebone in Pauline's perfectly fitting elastic girdle contracted apprehensively. "Thank you; I'm very well here." She assumed as willowy an attitude as the treacherous seat permitted, and added: "I'm so glad to have the chance of a little talk. In this rushing life we all tend to lose sight of each other, don't we? But I hear about you so constantly from Nona that I feel we're very close even when we don't meet. Nona's devoted to you—we all are."

"That's awfully sweet of you," said Lita with her air of radiant indifference.

"Well, my dear, we hope you reciprocate," Pauline sparkled, stretching a maternal hand to the young shoulder at her knee.

Lita slanted her head backward with a slight laugh. Mrs. Manford had never thought her pretty, but today the mere freshness of her parted lips, their rosy lining, the unspoilt curves of her cheek and long white throat, stung the older woman to reluctant admiration.

"Am I expected to be devoted to you ALL?" Lita questioned.

"No, dear; only to Jim."

"Oh—" said Jim's wife, her smile contracting to a faint grimace.

Pauline leaned forward earnestly. "I won't pretend not to know something of what's been happening. I came here today to talk things over with you, quietly and affectionately—like an older sister. Try not to think of me as a mother-in-law!"

Lita's slim eyebrows went up ironically. "Oh, I'm not afraid of mothers-in-law; they're not as permanent as they used to be."

Pauline took a quick breath; she caught the impertinence under the banter, but she called her famous tact to the rescue.

"I'm glad you're not afraid of me, because I want you to tell me perfectly frankly what it is that's bothering you . . . you and Jim. . ."

"Nothing is bothering me particularly; but I suppose I'm bothering Jim," said Lita lightly.

"You're doing more than that, dear; you're making him desperately unhappy. This talk of wanting to separate—"

Lita rose on her elbow among the cushions, and levelled her eyes on Mrs. Manford. They looked as clear and shallow as the most expensive topazes.

"Separations are idiotic. What I want is a hundred per cent New York divorce. And he could let me have it just as easily. . ."

"Lita! You don't know how wretched it makes me to hear you say such things."

"Does it? Sorry! But it's Jim's own fault. Heaps of other girls would jump at him if he was free. And if I'm bored, what's the use of trying to keep me? What on earth can we do about it, either of us? You can't take out an insurance against boredom."

"But why should you be bored? With everything on earth. . ." Pauline waved a hand at the circumjacent luxuries.

"Well; that's it, I suppose. Always the same old everything!"

The mother-in-law softened her voice to murmur temptingly: "Of course, if it's this house you're tired of. . . Nona told me something about your wanting to redecorate some of the rooms; and I can understand, for instance, that this one. . ."

"Oh, this is the only one I don't utterly loathe. But I'm not divorcing Jim on account of the house," Lita answered, with a faint smile which seemed perverse to Pauline.

"Then what is the reason? I don't understand."

"I'm not much good at reasons. I want a new deal, that's all."

Pauline struggled against her rising indignation. To sit and hear this chit of a Cliffe girl speak of husband and home as if it were a matter of course to discard them like last year's fashions! But she was determined not to allow her feelings to master her. "If you had only yourself to think of, what should you do?" she asked.

"Do? Be myself, I suppose! I can't be, here. I'm a sort of all- round fake. I—"

"We none of us want you to be that—Jim least of all. He wants you to feel perfectly free to express your personality."

"Here—in this house?" Her contemptuous gesture seemed to tumble it down like a pack of cards. "And looking at him across the dinner-table every night of my life?"

Pauline paused; then she said gently: "And can you face giving up your baby?"

"Baby? Why should I? You don't suppose I'd ever give up my baby?"

"Then you mean to ask Jim to give up his wife and child, and to assume all the blame as well?"

"Oh, dear, no. Where's the blame? I don't see any! All I want is a new deal," repeated Lita doggedly.

"My dear, I'm sure you don't know what you're saying. Your husband has the misfortune to be passionately in love with you. The divorce you talk of so lightly would nearly kill him. Even if he doesn't interest you any longer, he did once. Oughtn't you to take that into account?"

Lita seemed to ponder. Then she said: "But oughtn't he to take into account that he doesn't interest me any longer?"

Pauline made a final effort at self-control. "Yes, dear; if it's really so. But if he goes away for a time. . . You know he's to have a long holiday soon, and my husband has arranged to have him go down with Mr. Wyant to the island. All I ask is that you shouldn't decide anything till he comes back. See how you feel about him when he's been away for two or three weeks. Perhaps you've been too much together—perhaps New York has got too much on both your nerves. At any rate, do let him go off on his holiday without the heartbreak of feeling it's good-bye. . . My husband begs you to do this. You know he loves Jim as if he were his son—"

Lita was still leaning on her elbow. "Well—isn't he?" she said in her cool silvery voice, with innocently widened eyes.

For an instant the significance of the retort escaped Pauline. When it reached her she felt as humiliated as if she had been caught concealing a guilty secret. She opened her lips, but no sound came from them. She sat wordless, torn between the desire to box her daughter-in-law's ears, and to rush in tears from the house.

"Lita . . ." she gasped . . . "this insult. . ."

Lita sat up, her eyes full of a slightly humorous compunction. "Oh, no! An insult! Why? I've always thought it would be so wonderful to have a love-child. I supposed that was why you both worshipped Jim. And now he isn't even that!" She shrugged her slim shoulders, and held her hands out penitently. "I AM sorry to have said the wrong thing—honestly I am! But it just shows we can never understand each other. For me the real wickedness is to go on living with a man you don't love. And now I've offended you by supposing you once felt in the same way yourself. . ."

Pauline slowly rose to her feet: she felt stiff and shrunken. "You haven't offended me—I'm not going to allow myself to be offended. I'd rather think we don't understand each other, as you say. But surely it's not too late to try. I don't want to discuss things with you; I don't want to nag or argue; I only want you to wait, to come with the baby to Cedarledge, and spend a few quiet weeks with us. Nona will be there, and my husband . . . there'll be no reproaches, no questions . . . but we'll do our best to make you happy. . ."

Lita, with her funny twisted smile, moved toward her mother-in-law. "Why, you're actually crying! I don't believe you do that often, do you?" She bent forward and put a light kiss on Pauline's shrinking cheek. "All right—I'll come to Cedarledge. I AM dead-beat and fed-up, and I daresay it'll do me a lot of good to lie up for a while. . ."

Pauline, for a moment, made no answer: she merely laid her lips on the girl's cheek, a little timidly, as if it had been made of something excessively thin and brittle.

"We shall all be very glad," she said.

On the doorstep, in the motor, she continued to move in the resonance of the outrageous question: "WELL—ISN'T HE?" The violence of her recoil left her wondering what use there was in trying to patch up a bond founded on such a notion of marriage. Would not Jim, as his wife so lightly suggested, run more chance of happiness if he could choose again? Surely there must still be some decent right-minded girls brought up in the old way . . . like Aggie Heuston, say! But Pauline's imagination shivered away from that too. . . Perhaps, after all, her own principles were really obsolete to her children. Only, what was to take their place? Human nature had not changed as fast as social usage, and if Jim's wife left him nothing could prevent his suffering in the same old way.

It was all very baffling and disturbing, and Pauline did not feel as sure as she usually did that the question could be disposed of by ignoring it. Still, on the drive home her thoughts cleared as she reflected that she had gained her main point—for the time, at any rate. Manford had enjoined her not to estrange or frighten Lita, and the two women had parted with a kiss. Manford had insisted that Lita should be induced to take no final decision till after her stay at Cedarledge; and to this also she had acquiesced. Pauline, on looking back, began to be struck by the promptness of Lita's surrender, and correspondingly impressed by her own skill in manoeuvring. There WAS something, after all, in these exercises of the will, these smiling resolves to ignore or dominate whatever was obstructive or unpleasant! She had gained with an almost startling ease the point which Jim and Manford and Nona had vainly struggled for. And perhaps Lita's horrid insinuation had not been a voluntary impertinence, but merely the unconscious avowal of new standards. The young people nowadays, for all their long words and scientific realism, were really more like children than ever. . .

In Pauline's boudoir, Nona, curled up on the hearth, her chin in her hands, raised her head at her mother's approach. To Pauline the knowledge that she was awaited, and that she brought with her the secret of defeat or victory, gave back the healing sense of authority.

"It's all right, darling," she announced; "just a little summer shower; I always told you there was nothing to worry about." And she added with a smile: "You see, Nona, some people DO still listen when your old mother talks to them."

XIX

If only Aggie Heuston had changed those sour-apple curtains in the front drawing-room, Nona thought—if she had substituted deep upholstered armchairs for the hostile gilt seats, and put books in the marqueterie cabinets in place of blue china dogs and Dresden shepherdesses, everything in three lives might have been different. . .

But Aggie had probably never noticed the colour of the curtains or the angularity of the furniture. She had certainly never missed the books. She had accepted the house as it came to her from her parents, who in turn had taken it over, in all its dreary frivolity, from their father and mother. It embodied the New York luxury of the 'seventies in every ponderous detail, from the huge cabbage roses of the Aubusson carpet to the triple layer of curtains designed to protect the aristocracy of the brown-stone age from the plebeian intrusion of light and air.

"Funny," Nona thought again—"that all this ugliness should prick me like nettles, and matter no more to Aggie than if it were in the next street. She's a saint, I know. But what I want to find is a saint who hates ugly furniture, and yet lives among it with a smile. What's the merit, if you never see it?" She addressed herself to a closer inspection of one of the cabinets, in which Aggie's filial piety had preserved her mother's velvet and silver spectacle-case, and her father's ivory opera-glasses, in combination with an alabaster Leaning Tower and a miniature copy of Carlo Dolci's Magdalen.

Queer dead rubbish—but queerer still that, at that moment and in that house, Nona's uncanny detachment should permit her to smile at it! Where indeed—she wondered again—did one's own personality end, and that of others, of people, landscapes, chairs or spectacle- cases, begin? Ever since she had received, the night before, Aggie's stiff and agonized little note, which might have been composed by a child with a tooth-ache, Nona had been apprehensively asking herself if her personality didn't even include certain shreds and fibres of Aggie. It was all such an inextricable tangle. . .

Here she came. Nona heard the dry click of her steps on the stairs and across the polished bareness of the hall. She had written: "If you could make it perfectly convenient to call—" Aggie's nearest approach to a friendly summons! And as she opened the door, and advanced over the cabbage roses, Nona saw that her narrow face, with the eyes too close together, and the large pale pink mouth with straight edges, was sharpened by a new distress.

"It's very kind of you to come, Nona—" she began in her clear painstaking voice.

"Oh, nonsense, Aggie! Do drop all that. Of course I know what it's about."

Aggie turned noticeably paler; but her training as a hostess prevailing over her emotion, she pushed forward a gilt chair. "Do sit down." She placed herself in an adjoining sofa corner. Overhead, Aggie's grandmother, in a voluted gilt frame, held a Brussels lace handkerchief in her hand, and leaned one ruffled elbow on a velvet table-cover fringed with knobby tassels.

"You say you know—" Aggie began.

"Of course."

"Stanley—he's told you?"

Nona's nerves were beginning to jump and squirm like a bundle of young vipers. Was she going to be able to stand much more of these paralyzing preliminaries?

"Oh, yes: he's told me."

Aggie dropped her lids and stared down at her narrow white hands. Then a premonitory twitch ran along her lips and drew her forehead into little wrinkles of perplexity.

"I don't want you to think I've any cause of complaint against Stanley— none whatever. There has never been a single unkind word. . . We've always lived together on the most perfect terms. . ."

Feeling that some form of response was required of her, Nona emitted a vague murmur.

"Only now—he's—he's left me," Aggie concluded, the words wrung out of her in laboured syllables. She raised one hand and smoothed back a flat strand of hair which had strayed across her forehead.

Nona was silent. She sat with her eyes fixed on that small twitching mask— real face it could hardly be called, since it had probably never before been suffered to express any emotion that was radically and peculiarly Aggie's.

"You knew that too?" Aggie continued, in a studiously objective tone.

Nona made a sign of assent.

"He has nothing to reproach me with—nothing whatever. He expressly told me so."

"Yes; I know. That's the worst of it."

"The worst of it?"

"Why, if he had, you might have had a good row that would have cleared the air."

Suddenly Nona felt Aggie's eyes fixed on her with a hungry penetrating stare. "Did you and he use to have good rows, as you call it?"

"Oh, by the hour—whenever we met!" Nona, for the life of her, could not subdue the mocking triumph in her voice.

Aggie's lips narrowed. "You've been very great friends, I know; he's often told me so. But if you were always quarrelling how could you continue to respect each other?"

"I don't know that we did. At any rate, there was no time to think about it; because there was always the making-up, you see."

"The making-up?"

"Aggie," Nona burst out abruptly, "have you never known what it was to have a man give you a jolly good hug, and feel full enough of happiness to scent a whole garden with it?"

Aggie lifted her lids on a glance which was almost one of terror. The image Nona had used seemed to convey nothing to her, but the question evidently struck her with a deadly force.

"A man—what man?"

Nona laughed. "Well, for the sake of argument—Stanley!"

"I can't imagine why you ask such queer questions, Nona. How could we make up when we never quarrelled?"

"Is it queer to ask you if you ever loved your husband?"

"It's queer of you to ask it," said the wife simply. Nona's swift retort died unspoken, and she felt one of her slow secret blushes creeping up to the roots of her hair.

"I'm sorry, Aggie. I'm horribly nervous—and I suppose you are. Hadn't we better start fresh? What was it you wanted to see me about?"

Aggie was silent for a moment, as if gathering up all her strength; then she answered: "To tell you that if he wants to marry you I shan't oppose a divorce any longer."

"Aggie!"

The two sat silent, opposite each other, as if they had reached a point beyond which words could not carry their communion. Nona's mind, racing forward, touched the extreme limit of human bliss, and then crawled back from it bowed and broken-winged.

"But ONLY on that condition," Aggie began again, with deliberate emphasis.

"On condition—that he marries me?"

Aggie made a motion of assent. "I have a right to impose my conditions. And what I want is"—she faltered suddenly—"what I want is that you should save him from Cleo Merrick. . ." Her level voice broke and two tears forced their way through her lashes and fell slowly down her cheeks.

"Save him from Cleo Merrick?" Nona fancied she heard herself laugh. Her thoughts seemed to drag after her words as if she were labouring up hill through a ploughed field. "Isn't it rather late in the day to make that attempt? You say he's already gone off with her."

"He's joined her somewhere—I don't know where. He wrote from his club before leaving. But I know they don't sail till the day after tomorrow; and you must get him back, Nona, you must save him. It's too awful. He can't marry her; she has a husband somewhere who refuses to divorce her."

"Like you and Stanley!"

Aggie drew back as if she had been struck. "Oh, no, no!" She looked despairingly at Nona. "When I tell you I don't refuse now. . ."

"Well, perhaps Cleo Merrick's husband may not, either."

"It's different. He's a Catholic, and his church won't let him divorce. And it can't be annulled. Stanley's just going to live with her . . . openly . . . and she'll go everywhere with him . . . exactly as if they were husband and wife . . . and everybody will know that they're not."

Nona sat silent, considering with set lips and ironic mind the picture thus pitilessly evoked. "Well, if she loves him. . ."

"Loves him? A woman like that!"

"She's been willing to make a sacrifice for him, at any rate. That's where she has a pull over both of us."

"But don't you see how awful it is for them to be living together in that way?"

"I see it's the best thing that could happen to Stanley to have found a woman plucky enough to give him the thing he wanted—the thing you and I both refused him."

She saw Aggie's lifeless cheek redden. "I don't know what you mean by . . . refusing. . ."

"I mean his happiness—that's all! You refused to divorce him, didn't you? And I refused to do—what Cleo Merrick's doing. And here we both are, sitting on the ruins; and that's the end of it, as far as you and I are concerned."

"But it's not the end—it's not too late. I tell you it's not too late! He'll leave her even now if you ask him to . . . I know he will!"

Nona stood up with a dry laugh. "Thank you, Aggie. Perhaps he would—only we shall never find out."

"Never find out? When I keep telling you—"

"Because even if I've been a coward that's no reason why I should be a cad." Nona was buttoning her coat and clasping her fur about her neck with quick precise movements, as if wrapping herself close against the treacherous sweetness that was beginning to creep into her veins. Suddenly she felt she could not remain a moment longer in that stifling room, face to face with that stifling misery.

"The better woman's got him—let her keep him," she said.

She put out her hand, and for a moment Aggie's cold damp fingers lay in hers. Then they were pulled away, and Aggie caught Nona by the sleeve. "But Nona, listen! I don't understand you. Isn't it what you've always wanted?"

"Oh, more than anything in life!" the girl cried, turning breathlessly away.

The outer door swung shut on her, and on the steps she stood still and looked back at the ruins on which she had pictured herself sitting with Aggie Heuston.

"I do believe," she murmured to herself, "I know most of the new ways of being rotten; I only wish I was sure I knew the best new way of being decent. . ."

BOOK III

XX

At the gates of Cedarledge Pauline lifted her head from a last hurried study of the letters and papers Maisie Bruss had thrust into the motor.

The departure from town had been tumultuous. Up to the last minute there had been the usual rush and trepidation, Maisie hanging on the footboard, Powder and the maid hurrying down with final messages and recommendations.

"Here's another batch of bills passed by the architect, Mrs. Manford. And he asks if you'd mind—"

"Yes, yes; draw another cheque for five thousand, Maisie, and send it to me with the others to be signed."

"And the estimates for the new orchid-house. The contractor says building-materials are going up again next week, and he can't guarantee, unless you telephone at once—"

"Has madame the jewel-box? I put it under the rug myself, with madame's motor-bag."

"Thank you, Cécile. Yes, it's here."

"And is the Maison Herminie to deliver the green and gold teagown here or—"

"Here are the proofs of the Birth Control speech, Mrs. Manford. If you could just glance over them in the motor, and let me have them back tonight—"

"The Marchesa, madam, has called up to ask if you and Mr. Manford can receive her at Cedarledge for the next week-end—"

"No, Powder; say no. I'm dreadfully sorry. . ."

"Very good, madam. I understand it was to bring a favourable answer from the Cardinal—"

"Oh; very well. I'll see. I'll telephone from Cedarledge."

"Please, madam, Mr. Wyant's just telephoned—"

"Mr. Wyant, Powder?"

"Mr. Arthur Wyant, madam. To ask—"

"But Mr. Wyant and Mr. James were to have started for Georgia last night."

"Yes, madam; but Mr. James was detained by business, and now Mr. Arthur Wyant asks if you'll please ring up before they leave tonight."

"Very well. (What can have happened, Nona? You don't know?) Say I've started for Cedarledge, Powder; I'll ring up from there. Yes; that's all."

"Mrs. Manford, wait! Here are two more telegrams, and a special—"

"Take care, Maisie; you'll slip and break your leg. . ."

"Yes; but Mrs. Manford! The special is from Mrs. Swoffer. She says the committee have just discovered a new genius, and they're calling an emergency meeting for tomorrow afternoon at three, and couldn't you possibly—"

"No, no, Maisie—I can't! Say I've LEFT—"

The waves of agitation were slow in subsiding. A glimpse, down a side street, of the Marchesa's cheap boarding-house-hotel, revived them; and so did the flash past the inscrutable "Dawnside," aloof on its height above the Hudson. But as the motor slid over the wide suburban Boulevards, and out into the budding country, with the roar and menace of the city fading harmlessly away on the horizon, Pauline's serenity gradually stole back.

Nona, at her side, sat silent; and the mother was grateful for that silence. She had noticed that the girl had looked pale and drawn for the last fortnight; but that was just another proof of how much they all needed the quiet of Cedarledge.

"You don't know why Jim and his father have put off starting, Nona?"

"No idea, mother. Probably business of Jim's, as Powder said."

"Do you know why his father wants to telephone me?"

"Not a bit. Probably it's not important. I'll call up this evening."

"Oh, if you would, dear! I'm really tired."

There was a pause, and then Nona questioned: "Have you noticed Maisie, mother? She's pretty tired too."

"Yes; poor Maisie! Preparing Cedarledge has been rather a rush for her, I'm afraid—"

"It's not only that. She's just been told that her mother has a cancer."

"Oh, poor child! How dreadful! She never said a word to me—"

"No, she wouldn't."

"But, Nona, have you told her to see Disterman AT ONCE? Perhaps an immediate operation . . . you must call her up as soon as we arrive. Tell her, of course, that I'll bear all the expenses—"

After that they both relapsed into silence.

These domestic tragedies happened now and then. One would have given the world to avert them; but when one couldn't one was always ready to foot the bill. . . Pauline wished that she had known . . . had had time to say a kindly word to poor Maisie. . . Perhaps she would have to give her a week off; or at least a couple of days, while she settled her mother in the hospital. At least, if Disterman advised an operation. . .

It was dreadful, how rushed one always was. Pauline would have liked to go and see poor Mrs. Bruss herself. But there were Dexter and Lita and the baby all arriving the day after tomorrow, and only just time to put the last touches to Cedarledge before they came. And Pauline herself was desperately tired, though she had taken a "triple treatment" from Alvah Loft ($100) that very morning.

She always meant to be kind to every one dependent on her; it was only time that lacked—always time! Dependents and all, they were swept away with her in the same ceaseless rush. When now and then one of them dropped by the way she was sorry, and sent back first aid, and did all she could; but the rush never stopped; it couldn't stop; when one did a kindness one could only fling it at its object and whirl by.

The blessèd peace of the country! Pauline drew a deep breath of content. Never before had she approached Cedarledge with so complete a sense of possessorship. The place was really of her own making, for though the house had been built and the grounds laid out years before she had acquired the property, she had stamped her will and her wealth on every feature. Pauline was persuaded that she was fond of the country—but what she was really fond of was doing things to the country, and owning, with this object, as many acres of it as possible. And so it had come about that every year the Cedarledge estate had pushed the encircling landscape farther back, and substituted for its miles of golden-rod and birch and maple more acres of glossy lawn, and more specimen limes and oaks and cut-leaved beeches, domed over more and more windings of expensive shrubbery.

From the farthest gate it was now a drive of two miles to the house, and Pauline found even this too short for her minutely detailed appreciation of what lay between her and her threshold. In the village, the glint of the gilt weathercock on the new half- timbered engine-house; under a rich slope of pasture-land the recently enlarged dairy-farm; then woods of hemlock and dogwood; acres of rhododendron, azalea and mountain laurel acclimatized about a hidden lake; a glimpse of Japanese water-gardens fringed with cherry bloom and catkins; open lawns, spreading trees, the long brick house-front and its terraces, and through a sculptured archway the Dutch garden with dwarf topiary work and endless files of bulbs about the commander's baton of a stately sundial.

To Pauline each tree, shrub, water-course, herbaceous border, meant not only itself, but the surveying of grades, transporting of soil, tunnelling for drainage, conducting of water, the business correspondence and paying of bills, which had preceded its existence; and she would have cared for it far less—perhaps not at all—had it sprung into being unassisted, like the random shadbushes and wild cherry trees beyond the gates.

The faint spring loveliness reached her somehow, in long washes of pale green, and the blurred mauve of budding vegetation; but her eyes could not linger on any particular beauty without its dissolving into soil, manure, nurserymen's catalogues, and bills again—bills. It had all cost a terrible lot of money; but she was proud of that too—to her it was part of the beauty, part of the exquisite order and suitability which reigned as much in the simulated wildness of the rhododendron glen as in the geometrical lines of the Dutch garden.

"Seventy-five thousand bulbs this year!" she thought, as the motor swept by the sculptured gateway, just giving and withdrawing a flash of turf sheeted with amber and lilac, in a setting of twisted and scalloped evergreens.

Twenty-five thousand more bulbs than last year . . . that was how she liked it to be. It was exhilarating to spend more money each year, to be always enlarging and improving, in small ways as well as great, to face unexpected demands with promptness and energy, beat down exorbitant charges, struggle through difficult moments, and come out at the end of the year tired but victorious, with improvements made, bills paid, and a reassuring balance in the bank. To Pauline that was "life."

And how her expenditure at Cedarledge was justifying itself! Her husband, drawn by its fresh loveliness, had voluntarily given up his annual trip to

California, the excitement of tarpon-fishing, the independence of bachelorhood—all to spend a quiet month in the country with his wife and children. Pauline felt that even the twenty-five thousand additional bulbs had had a part in shaping his decision. And what would he say when he saw the new bathrooms, assisted at the village fire-drill, and plunged into the artificially warmed waters of the new swimming pool? A mist of happiness rose to her eyes as she looked out on the spring-misted landscape.

Nona had not followed her mother into the house. Her dogs at her heels, she plunged down hill to the woods and lake. She knew nothing of what Cedarledge had cost, but little of the labour of its making. It was simply the world of her childhood, and she could see it from no other angle, nor imagine it as ever having been different. To her it had always worn the same enchantment, stretched to the same remote distances. At nineteen it was almost the last illusion she had left.

In the path by the lake she felt herself drawn back under the old spell. Those budding branches, the smell of black peaty soil quivering with life, the woodlands faintly starred with dogwood, all were the setting of childish adventures, old games with Jim, Indian camps on the willow-fringed island, and innocent descents among the rhododendrons to boat or bathe by moonlight.

The old skiff had escaped Mrs. Manford's annual "doing-up" and still leaked through the same rusty seams. Pushing out upon the lake, Nona leaned on the oars and let the great mockery of the spring dilate her heart. . .

Manford questioned: "All right, eh? Warm enough? Not going too fast? The air's still sharp up here in the hills;" and Lita settled down beside him into one of the deep silences that enfolded her as softly as her furs. By turning his head a little he could just see the tip of her nose and the curve of her upper lip between hat-brim and silver fox; and the sense of her, so close and so still, sunk in that warm animal hush which he always found so restful, dispelled his last uneasiness, and made her presence at his side seem as safe and natural as his own daughter's.

"Just as well you sent the boy by train, though—I foresaw I'd get off too late to suit the young gentleman's hours."

She curled down more deeply at his side, with a contented laugh.

Manford, intent on the steering wheel, restrained the impulse to lay a hand over hers, and kept his profile steadily turned to her. It was wonderful, how successfully his plan was working out . . . how reasonable she'd been about it in the end. Poor child! No doubt she would always be reasonable with people who knew how to treat her. And he flattered himself that he did. It hadn't been easy, just at first—but now he'd struck the right note and meant to hold it. Not paternal, exactly: she would have been the first to laugh at anything as old-fashioned as that. Heavy fathers had gone out with the rest of the tremolo effects. No; but elder brotherly. That was it. The same free and friendly relation which existed, say, between Jim and Nona. Why, he had actually tried chaffing Lita, and she hadn't minded—he had made fun of that ridiculous Ardwin, and she had just laughed and shrugged. That little shrug—when her white shoulder, as the dress slipped from it, seemed to be pushing up into a wing! There was something birdlike and floating in all her motions. . . Poor child, poor little girl. . . He really felt like her elder brother; and his looking-glass told him that he didn't look much too old for the part. . .

The sense of having just grazed something dark and lurid, which had threatened to submerge them, gave him an added feeling of security, a holiday feeling, as if life stretched before him as safe and open as his coming fortnight at Cedarledge. How glad he was that he had given up his tarpon-fishing, managed to pack Jim and Wyant off to Georgia, and secured this peaceful interval in which to look about him and take stock of things before the grind began again!

The day before yesterday—just after Pauline's departure—it had seemed as if all their plans would be wrecked by one of Wyant's fits of crankiness. Wyant always enjoyed changing his mind after every one else's was made up; and at the last moment he had telephoned to say that he wasn't well enough to go south. He had rung up Pauline first, and being told that she had left had communicated with Jim; and Jim, distracted, had appealed to Manford. It was one of his father's usual attacks of "nervousness"; cousin Eleanor had seen it coming, and tried to cut down the whiskies-and- sodas; finally Jim begged Manford to drop in and reason with his predecessor.

These visits always produced a profound impression on Wyant; Manford himself, for all his professional acuteness, couldn't quite measure the degree or guess the nature of the effect, but he felt his power, and preserved it by seeing Wyant as seldom as possible. This time, however, it seemed as if things might not go as smoothly as usual. Wyant, who looked gaunt and excited, tried to carry off the encounter with the jauntiness he always assumed in Manford's presence. "My dear fellow! Sit down, do. Cigar? Always delighted to see my successor. Any little hints I can give about the management of the concern—"

It was his usual note, but exaggerated, overemphasized, lacking the Wyant touch—and he had gone on: "Though why the man who has failed should offer advice to the man who has succeeded, I don't know. Well, in this case it's about Jim. . . Yes, you're as fond of Jim as I am, I know. . . Still, he's MY son, eh? Well, I'm not satisfied that it's a good thing to take him away from his wife at this particular moment. Know I'm old-fashioned, of course . . . all the musty old traditions have been superseded. You and your set have seen to that— introduced the breezy code of the prairies. . . But my son's my son; he wasn't brought up in the new way, and, damn it all, Manford, you understand; well, no—I suppose there are some things you never WILL understand, no matter how devilish clever you are, and how many millions you've made."

The apple-cart had been near upsetting; but if Manford didn't understand poor Wyant's social code he did know how to keep his temper when it was worth while, and how to talk to a weak overexcited man who had been drinking too hard, and who took no exercise.

"Worried about Jim, eh? Yes—I don't wonder. I am too. Fact is, Jim's worked himself to a standstill, and I feel partly responsible for it, for I put him onto that job at the bank, and he's been doing it too well—overdoing it. That's the whole trouble, and that's why I feel responsible to you all for getting him away as soon as possible, and letting him have a complete holiday. . . Jim's young—a fortnight off will straighten him out. But you're the only person who can get him away from his wife and baby, and wherever Lita is there'll be jazz and nonsense, and bills and bothers; that's why his mother and I have offered to take the lady on for a while, and give him his chance. As man to man, Wyant, I think we two ought to stand together and see this thing through. If we do, I guarantee everything will come out right. Do you good too—being off like that with your boy, in a good climate, loafing on the beach and watching Jim recuperate. Wish I could run down and join you—and I don't say I won't make a dash for it, just for a week-end, if I can break away from the family. A-1 fishing at the island—and I know you used to be a great fisherman. As for Lita, she'll be safe enough with Pauline and Nona."

The trick was done.

But why think of it as a trick, when at the time he had meant every word he spoke? Jim WAS dead-beat—DID need a change—and yet could only have been got away on the pretext of having to take his father south. Queer, how in some inner fold of one's conscience a collection of truths could suddenly seem to look like a tissue of lies! . . . Lord, but what morbid rubbish! Manford was on his honour to make the whole thing turn out as true as it sounded, and he was going to. And there was an end of it. And here was Cedarledge. The drive hadn't lasted a minute. . .

How lovely the place looked in the twilight, a haze of tender tints melting into shadow, the long dark house-front already gemmed with orange panes!

"You'll like it, won't you, Lita?" A purr of content at his elbow.

If only Pauline would have the sense to leave him alone, let him enjoy it all in Lita's lazy inarticulate way, not cram him with statistics and achievements, with expenditures and results. He was so tired of her perpetual stock-taking, her perpetual rendering of accounts and reckoning up of interest. He admired it all, of course—he admired Pauline herself more than ever. But he longed to let himself sink into the spring sweetness as a man might sink on a woman's breast, and just feel her quiet hands in his hair.

"There's the dogwood! Look! Never seen it in bloom here before, have you? It's one of our sights." He had counted a good deal on the effect of the dogwood. "Well, here we are—Jove, but it's good to be here! Why, child, I believe you've been asleep. . ." He lifted her, still half-drowsing, from the motor—

And now, the illuminated threshold, Powder, the footmen, the inevitable stack of letters—and Pauline.

But outside the spring dusk was secretly weaving its velvet spell. He said to himself: "Shouldn't wonder if I slept ten hours at a stretch tonight."

XXI

The last day before her husband's arrival had been exhausting to Pauline; but she could not deny that the results were worth the effort. When had she ever before heard Dexter say on such a full note of satisfaction: "Jove, but it's good to be back! What have you done to make the place look so jolly?", or seen his smiling glance travel so observantly about the big hall with its lamps and flowers and blazing hearth? "Well, Lita, this is better than town, eh? You didn't know what a good place Cedarledge could be! Don't rush off upstairs—they're bringing the baby down. Come over to the fire and warm up; it's nipping here in the hills. Hullo, Nona, you quiet mouse—didn't even see you, curled up there in your corner. . ."

Yes; the arrival had been perfect. Even Lita's kiss had seemed spontaneous. And Dexter had praised everything, noticed all the improvements; had voluntarily announced that he meant to inspect the new heating system and the model chicken hatchery the next morning. "Wonderful, what a way you have of making things a hundred per cent better when they seemed all right before! I suppose even the eggs at breakfast tomorrow will be twice their normal size."

One such comment paid his wife for all she had done, and roused her inventive faculty to fresh endeavour. Wasn't there something else she could devise to provoke his praise? And the beauty of it was that it all looked as if it had been done so easily. The casual observer would never have suspected that the simple life at Cedarledge gave its smiling organizer more trouble than a season of New York balls.

That also was part of Pauline's satisfaction. She even succeeded in persuading herself, as she passed through the hall with its piled-up golf clubs and tennis rackets, its motor coats and capes and scarves stacked on the long table, and the muddy terriers comfortably rolled up on chintz-cushioned settles, that it was really all as primitive and impromptu as it looked, and that she herself had always shared her husband's passion for stamping about in the mud in tweed and homespun.

"One of these days," she thought, "we'll give up New York altogether, and live here all the year round, like an old-fashioned couple, and Dexter can farm while I run the poultry-yard and dairy." Instantly her practical imagination outlined the plan of an up-to-date chicken-farm on a big scale, and calculated the revenues to be drawn from really scientific methods of cheese and butter-making. Spring broilers, she knew, were in ever-increasing demand, and there was a great call in restaurants and hotels for the little foreign-looking cream-cheeses in silver paper. . .

"The Marchesa has rung up again, madam," Powder reminded her, the second morning at breakfast. Everybody came down to breakfast at Cedarledge; it was part of the simple life. But it generally ended in Pauline's throning alone behind the tea-urn, for her husband and daughter revelled in unpunctuality when they were on a holiday, and Lita's inability to appear before luncheon was tacitly taken for granted.

"The Marchesa?" Pauline was roused from the placid enjoyment of her new-laid egg and dewy butter. Why was it that one could never completely protect one's self against bores and bothers? They had done everything they could for Amalasuntha, and were now discovering that gratitude may take more troublesome forms than neglect.

"The Marchesa would like to consult you about the date of the Cardinal's reception."

Ah, then it was a fact—it was really settled! A glow of satisfaction swept away Pauline's indifference, and her sense of fairness obliged her to admit that, for such a service, Amalasuntha had a right to a Sunday at Cedarledge. "It will bore her to death to spend two days here alone with the family; but she will like to be invited, and in the course of time she'll imagine it was a big house-party," Pauline reflected.

"Very well, Powder. Please telephone that I shall expect the Marchesa next Saturday."

That gave them, at any rate, the inside of a week to themselves. After six days alone with his women-kind perhaps even Dexter would not be sorry for a little society; and if so, Pauline, with the Marchesa as a bait, could easily drum up a country-neighbour dinner. The Toys, she happened to remember, were to be at the Greystock Country Club over Easter. She smiled at the thought that this might have made Dexter decide to give up California for Cedarledge. She was not afraid of Mrs. Toy any longer, and even recognized that her presence in the neighbourhood might be useful. Pauline could never wholly believe—at least not for many hours together—that people could be happy in the country without all sorts of social alleviations; and six days of quiet seemed to her measurable only in terms of prehistoric eras. When had her mind ever had such a perspective to range over? Knowing it could be shortened at will she sighed contentedly, and decided to devote the morning to the study of a new refrigerating system she had recently seen advertised.

Dexter had not yet made his tour of inspection with her; but that was hardly surprising. The first morning he had slept late, and lounged about on the terrace in the balmy sunshine. In the afternoon they had all motored to Greystock for a round of golf; and today, on coming down to breakfast, Pauline had learned with surprise that her husband, Nona and Lita were already off for an early canter, leaving word that they would breakfast on the road. She did not know whether to marvel most at Lita's having been coaxed out of bed before breakfast, or at Dexter's taking to the saddle after so many years. Certainly the Cedarledge air was wonderfully bracing and rejuvenating; she herself was feeling its effects. And though she would have liked to show her husband all the improvements she felt no impatience, but only a quiet satisfaction in the success of her plans. If they could give Jim back a contented Lita the object of their holiday would be attained; and in a glow of optimism she sat down at her writing- table and dashed off a joyful letter to her son.

"Dexter is wonderful; he has already coaxed Lita out for a ride before breakfast. . . Isn't that a triumph? When you get back you won't know her. . . I shouldn't have a worry left if I didn't think Nona is looking too pale and drawn. I shall persuade her to take a course of Inspirational treatment as soon as we get back to town. By the way," her pen ran on, "have you heard the news about Stan Heuston? People say he's gone to Europe with that dreadful Merrick woman, and that now Aggie will really have to divorce him. . . Nona, who has always been such a friend of Stan's, has of course heard the report, but doesn't seem to know any more than the rest of us. . ."

Nothing amused Arthur Wyant more than to be supplied with such tit- bits of scandal before they became common property. Pauline couldn't help feeling that father and son must find the evenings long in their island bungalow; and in the overflow of her own satisfaction she wanted to do what she could to cheer them.

In spite of her manifold occupations the day seemed long. She had visited the baby, seen the cook, consulted with Powder about the working of the new burglar-alarm, gone over the gardens, catalogues in hand, with the head-gardener, walked down to the dairy and the poultry yard to say that Mr. Manford would certainly inspect them both the next day, and called up Maisie Bruss to ask news of her mother, and tell her to prepare a careful list for the reception to the Cardinal; yet an astonishing amount of time still remained. It was delightful to be in the country, to study the working-out of her improvements, and do her daily exercises with windows open on the fresh hill breezes; but already her real self was projected forward into complicated plans for the Cardinal's entertainment. She wondered if it would not be wise to run up to town the next morning and consult Amalasuntha; and reluctantly decided that a talk on the telephone would do.

The talk was long, and on the whole satisfactory; but if Maisie had been within reach the arrangements for the party would have made more progress. It was most unlucky that the doctors thought Maisie ought to stay with her mother till the latter could get a private room at the hospital. ("A ROOM, of course, Maisie dear; I won't have her in a ward. Not for the world! Just put it down on your account, please. So glad to do it!") She really was glad to do all she could; but it was unfortunate (and no one would feel it more than Maisie) that Mrs. Bruss should have been taken ill just then. To fill the time, Pauline decided to go for a walk with the dogs.

When she returned she found Nona, still in her riding-habit, settled in a sofa-corner in the library, and deep in a book.

"Why, child, where did you drop from? I didn't know you were back."

"The others are not. Lita suddenly took it into her head that it would be fun to motor over to Greenwich and dine at the Country Club, and so father got a motor at Greystock and telephoned for one of the grooms to fetch the horses. It sounded rather jolly, but I was tired, so I came home. It's nearly full moon, and they'll have a glorious run back." Nona smiled up at her mother, as if to say that the moon made all the difference.

"Oh, but that means dancing, and getting home at all hours! And I promised Jim to see that Lita kept quiet, and went to bed early. What's the use of our having persuaded her to come here? Your father ought to have refused to go."

"If he had, there were plenty of people lunching at Greystock who would have taken her on. You know—the cocktail crowd. That's why father sacrificed himself."

Pauline reflected. "I see. Your father always has to sacrifice himself. I suppose there's no use trying to make Lita listen to reason."

"Not unless one humours her a little. Father sees that. We mustn't let her get bored here—she won't stay if we do."

Pauline felt a sudden weariness in all her bones. It was as if the laboriously built-up edifice of the simple life at Cedarledge had already crumbled into dust at a kick of Lita's little foot. The engine-house, the poultry yard, the new burglar-alarm and the heating of the swimming pool—when would Dexter ever have time to inspect and admire them, if he was to waste his precious holiday in scouring the country after Lita?

"Then I suppose you and I dine alone," Pauline said, turning a pinched little smile on her daughter.

XXII

What a time of year it was—the freed earth suddenly breaking into life from every frozen seam! Manford wondered if he had ever before had time to feel the impetuous loveliness of the American spring.

In spite of his drive home in the small hours he had started out early the next morning for a long tramp. Sleep—how could a man sleep with that April moonlight in his veins? The moon that was everywhere—caught in pearly puffs on the shadbush branches, scattered in ivory drifts of wild plum bloom, tipping the grasses of the wayside with pale pencillings, sheeting the recesses of the woodland with pools of icy silver. A freezing burning magic, into which a man plunged, and came out cold and aglow, to find everything about him as unreal and incredible as himself. . .

After the blatant club restaurant, noise, jazz, revolving couples, Japanese lanterns, screaming laughter, tumultuous good-byes, this white silence, the long road unwinding and twisting itself up again, blind faces of shuttered farmhouses, black forests, misty lakes—a cut through a world in sleep, all dumb and moon-bemused. . .

The contrast was beautiful, intolerable. . .

Sleep? He hadn't even gone to bed. Just plunged into a bath, and stretched out on his lounge to see the dawn come. A mysterious sight that, too; the cold fingers of the light remaking a new world, while men slept, unheeding, and imagined they would wake to some familiar yesterday. Fools!

He breakfasted—ravenously—before his wife was down, and swung off with a couple of dogs on a long tramp, he didn't care where.

Even the daylight world seemed unimaginably strange: as if he had never really looked at it before. He walked on slowly for three or four miles, vaguely directing himself toward Greystock. His long tramps as a boy, in his farming days, had given him the habit of deliberate steady walking, and the unwonted movement refreshed rather than tired him—or at least, while it tired his muscles, it seemed to invigorate his brain. Excited? No—just pleasantly stimulated. . .

He stretched himself out under a walnut tree on a sunny slope, lit his pipe and gazed abroad over fields and woods. All the land was hazy with incipient life. The dogs hunted and burrowed, and then came back to doze at his feet with pleasant dreamings. The sun on his face felt warm and human, and gradually life began to settle back into its old ruts—a comfortable routine, diversified by pleasant episodes. Could it ever be more, to a man past fifty?

But after a while a chill sank on his spirit. He began to feel cold and hungry, and set out to walk again.

Presently he found it was half-past eleven—time to be heading for home. Home; and the lunch-table; Pauline; and Nona; and Lita. Oh, God, no—not yet. . . He trudged on, slowly and sullenly, deciding to pick up a mouthful of lunch somewhere by the way.

At a turn of the road he caught sight of a woman's figure strolling across a green slope above him. Strong and erect in her trim golfing skirt, she came down in his direction swinging a club in her hand. Why, sure enough, he was actually on the edge of the Greystock course! The woman was alone, without companions or caddies—going around for a trial spin, or perhaps simply taking a stroll, as he was, drinking in the intoxicating air. . .

"Hul-LO!" she called, and he found himself advancing toward Gladys Toy.

Was this active erect woman in her nut-brown sweater and plaited skirt the same as the bejewelled and redundant beauty of so many wearisome dinners? Something of his old interest—the short-lived fancy of a week or two—revived in him as she swung along, treading firmly but lightly on her broad easy shoes.

"Hul-LO!" he responded. "Didn't know you were here."

"I wasn't. I only came last night. Isn't it glorious?" Even her slow-dripping voice moved faster and had a livelier ring. Decidedly, he admired a well-made woman, a woman with curves and volume—all the more after the stripped skeletons he had dined among the night before. Mrs. Toy had height enough to carry off her pounds, and didn't look ashamed of them, either.

"Glorious? Yes, YOU are!" he said.

"Oh, ME?"

"What else did you mean, then?"

"Don't be silly! How did you get here?"

"On my feet."

"Gracious! From Cedarledge? You must be dead."

"Don't you believe it. I walked over to lunch with you."

"You've just said you didn't know I was here."

"You mustn't believe everything I say."

"All right. Then I won't believe you walked over to lunch with me."

"Will you believe me when I tell you you're awfully beautiful?"

"Yes!" she challenged him.

"And that I want to kiss you?"

She smiled with the eyes of a tired swimmer, and he saw that her slender stock of repartee was exhausted. "Herman'll be here tonight," she said.

"Then let's make the most of today."

"But I've asked some people to lunch at the club."

"Then you'll chuck them, and come off and lunch with me somewhere else."

"Oh, will I—shall I?" She laughed, and he saw her breast rise on her shortened breath. He caught her to him and planted a kiss in the middle of her laughter.

"Now will you?"

She was a rich armful, and he remembered how splendid he had thought plump rosy women in his youth, before money and fashion imposed their artificial standards.

When he re-entered the doors of Cedarledge the cold spring sunset was slanting in through the library windows on the tea-table at which his wife and Nona sat. Of Lita there was no sign; Manford heard with indolent amusement that she was reported to be just getting up. His sentiment about Lita had settled into fatherly indulgence; he no longer thought the epithet inappropriate. But underneath the superficial kindliness he felt for her, as for all the world, he was aware of a fundamental indifference to most things but his own comfort and convenience. Such was the salutary result of fresh air and recovered leisure. How absurd to work one's self into a state of fluster about this or that—money or business or women! Especially women. As he looked back on the last weeks he saw what a fever of fatigue he must have been in to take such an exaggerated view of his own emotions. After three days at Cedarledge serenity had descended on him like a benediction. Gladys Toy's cheeks were as smooth as nectarines; and the keen morning light had shown him that she wasn't in the least made up. He recalled the fact with a certain pleasure, and then dismissed her from his mind—or rather she dropped out of herself. He wasn't in the humour to think long about anybody or anything . . . he revelled in his own laziness and indifference.

"Tea? Yes; and a buttered muffin by all means. Several of them. I'm as hungry as the devil. Went for a long tramp this morning before any of you were up. Mrs. Toy ran across me, and brought me back in her new two-seater. A regular beauty—the car, I mean— you'll have to have one like it, Nona. . . Jove, how good the fire feels . . . and what is it that smells so sweet? Carnations—why, they're giants! We must go over the green-houses tomorrow, Pauline; and all the rest of it. I want to take stock of all your innovations."

At that moment he felt able to face even the tour of inspection, and all the facts and calculations it would evoke. Everything seemed easy now that he had found he could shake off his moonlight obsession by spending a few hours with a pretty woman who didn't mind being kissed. He was to meet Mrs. Toy again the day after tomorrow; and in the interval she would suffice to occupy his mind when he had nothing more interesting to think of.

As he was putting a match to his pipe Lita came into the room with her long glide. Her boy was perched on her shoulder, and she looked like one of Crivelli's enigmatic Madonnas carrying a little red-haired Jesus.

"Gracious! Is this breakfast or tea? I seem to have overslept myself after our joy-ride," she said, addressing a lazy smile to Manford.

She dropped to her knees before the fire and held up the boy to Pauline. "Kiss his granny," she commanded in her faintly derisive voice.

It was very pretty, very cleverly staged; but Manford said to himself that she was too self-conscious, and that her lips were too much painted. Besides, he had always hated women with prominent cheekbones and hollows under them. He settled back comfortably into the afternoon's reminiscences.

XXIII

Decidedly, there was a different time-measure for life in town and in the country.

The dinner for Amalasuntha organized (and the Toys secured for it), there were still two days left in that endless inside of a week which was to have passed so rapidly. Yet everything had gone according to Pauline's wishes. Dexter had really made the promised round of house and grounds, and had extended his inspection to dairy, poultry yard and engine-house. And he had approved of everything—approved almost too promptly and uncritically. Was it because he had not been sufficiently interested to note defects, or at any rate to point them out? The suspicion, which stirred in his wife when she observed that he walked through the cow-stables without making any comment on the defective working of the new ventilating system, became a certainty when, on their return to the house, she suggested their going over the accounts together. "Oh, as long as the architect has o.k.'d them! Besides, it's too late now to do anything, isn't it? And your results are so splendid that I don't see how they could be overpaid. Everything seems to be perfect—"

"Not the ventilating system in the Alderneys' stable, Dexter."

"Oh, well; can't that be arranged? If it can't, put it down to profit and loss. I never enjoyed anything more than my swim this morning in the pool. You've managed to get the water warmed to exactly the right temperature."

He slipped out to join Nona on the putting green below the terrace.

Yes; everything was all right; he was evidently determined that everything should be. It had been the same about Michelangelo's debts. At first he had resisted his wife's suggestion that they should help to pay them off, in order to escape the young man's presence in New York; then he had suddenly promised the Marchesa to settle the whole amount, without so much as a word to Pauline. It was as if he were engrossed in some deep and secret purpose, and resolved to clear away whatever threatened to block his obstinate advance. She had seen him thus absorbed when a "big case" possessed him. But there were no signs now of professional preoccupation; no telephoning, wiring, hurried arrivals of junior members or confidential clerks. He seemed to have shaken off "the office" with all his other cares. There was something about his serene good humour that obscurely frightened her.

Once she might have ascribed it to an interest—an exaggerated interest—in his step-son's wife. That idea had already crossed Pauline's mind: she remembered its cold brush on the evening when her husband had come home unexpectedly to see her, and had talked so earnestly and sensibly about bringing Lita and her boy to Cedarledge. The mere flit of a doubt—no more; and even then Pauline had felt its preposterousness, and banished it in disgust and fear.

Now she smiled at the fear. Her husband's manner to Lita was perfect—easy, good humoured but slightly ironic. At the time of Jim's marriage Dexter had had that same smile. He had thought the bride silly and pretentious, he had even questioned her good looks. And now the first week at Cedarledge showed that, if his attitude had grown kindlier, it was for Jim's sake, not Lita's. Nona and Lita were together all day long; when Manford joined them he treated both in the same way, as a man treats two indulged and amusing daughters.

What was he thinking of, then? Gladys Toy again, perhaps? Pauline had imagined that was over. Even if it were not, it no longer worried her. Dexter had had similar "flare-ups" before, and they hadn't lasted. Besides, Pauline had gradually acquired a certain wifely philosophy, and was prepared to be more lenient to her second husband than to the first. As wives grew older they had to realize that husbands didn't always keep pace with them. . .

Not that she felt herself too old for Manford's love; all her early illusions had rushed back to her the night he had made her give up the Rivington dinner. But her dream had not survived that evening. She had understood then that he meant they should be "only friends"; that was all the future was to hold for her. Well; for a grandmother it ought to be enough. She had no patience with the silly old women who expected "that sort of nonsense" to last. Still, she meant, on her return to town, to consult a new Russian who had invented a radium treatment which absolutely wiped out wrinkles. He called himself a Scientific Initiate . . . the name fascinated her.

From these perplexities she was luckily distracted by the urgent business of the Cardinal's reception. Even without Maisie she could do a good deal of preparatory writing and telephoning; but she was mortified to find how much her handwriting had suffered from the long habit of dictation. She never wrote a note in her own hand nowadays—except to distinguished foreigners, since Amalasuntha had explained that they thought typed communications ill-bred. And her unpractised script was so stiff and yet slovenly that she decided she must have her hands "treated" as she did her other unemployed muscles. But how find time for this new and indispensable cure? Her spirits rose with the invigorating sense of being once more in a hurry.

Nona sat on the south terrace in the sun. The Cedarledge experiment had lasted eight days now, and she had to own that it had turned out better than she would have thought possible.

Lita was giving them wonderfully little trouble. After the first flight to Greenwich she had shown no desire for cabarets and night- clubs, but had plunged into the alternative excitement of violent outdoor sports; relapsing, after hours of hard exercise, into a dreamy lassitude unruffled by outward events. She never spoke of her husband, and Nona did not know if Jim's frequent—too frequent— letters, were answered, or even read. Lita smiled vaguely when he was mentioned, and merely remarked, when her mother-in-law once risked an allusion to the future: "I thought we were here to be cured of plans." And Pauline effaced her blunder with a smile.

Nona herself felt more and more like one of the trench-watchers pictured in the war-time papers. There she sat in the darkness on her narrow perch, her eyes glued to the observation-slit which looked out over seeming emptiness. She had often wondered what those men thought about during the endless hours of watching, the days and weeks when nothing happened, when no faintest shadow of a skulking enemy crossed their span of no-man's land. What kept them from falling asleep, or from losing themselves in waking dreams, and failing to give warning when the attack impended? She could imagine a man led out to be shot in the Flanders mud because, at such a moment, he had believed himself to be dozing on a daisy bank at home. . .

Since her talk with Aggie Heuston a sort of curare had entered into her veins. She was sharply aware of everything that was going on about her, but she felt unable to rouse herself. Even if anything that mattered ever did happen again, she questioned if she would be able to shake off the weight of her indifference. Was it really ten days now since that talk with Aggie? And had everything of which she had then been warned fulfilled itself without her lifting a finger? She dimly remembered having acted in what seemed a mood of heroic self-denial; now she felt only as if she had been numb. What was the use of fine motives if, once the ardour fallen, even they left one in the lurch?

She thought: "I feel like the oldest person in the world, and yet with the longest life ahead of me . . ." and a shiver of loneliness ran over her.

Should she go and hunt up the others? What difference would that make? She might offer to write notes for her mother, who was upstairs plunged in her visiting-list; or look in on Lita, who was probably asleep after her hard gallop of the morning; or find her father, and suggest going for a walk. She had not seen her father since lunch; but she seemed to remember that he had ordered his new Buick brought round. Off again—he was as restless as the others. All of them were restless nowadays. Had he taken Lita with him, perhaps? Well—why not? Wasn't he here to look after Lita? A sudden twitch of curiosity drew Nona to her feet, and sent her slowly upstairs to her sister-in-law's room. Why did she have to drag one foot after the other, as if some hidden influence held her back, signalled a mute warning not to go? What nonsense! Better make a clean breast of it to herself once for all, and admit—

"I beg pardon, Miss." It was the ubiquitous Powder at her heels. "If you're going up to Mrs. Manford's sitting-room would you kindly tell her that Mr. Manford has telephoned he won't be back from Greystock till late, and she's please not to wait dinner?" Powder looked a little as if he would rather not give that particular message himself.

"Greystock? Oh, all right. I'll tell her."

Golf again—golf and Gladys Toy. Nona gave her clinging preoccupations a last shake. This was really a lesson to her! To be imagining horrible morbid things about her father while he was engaged in a perfectly normal elderly man's flirtation with a stupid woman he would forget as soon as he got back to town! A real Easter holiday diversion. "After all, he gave up his tarpon- fishing to come here, and Gladys isn't a bad substitute—as far as weight goes. But a good deal less exciting as sport." A dreary gleam of amusement crossed her mind.

Softly she pushed open the door of one of the perfectly appointed spare-rooms: a room so studiously equipped with every practical convenience—from the smoothly-hung window-ventilators to the jointed dressing-table lights, from the little portable telephone, and the bed-table with folding legs, to the tall threefold mirror which lost no curve of the beauty it reflected—that even Lita's careless ways seemed subdued to the prevailing order.

Lita was on the lounge, one long arm drooping, the other folded behind her in the immemorial attitude of sleeping beauty. Sleep lay on her lightly, as it does on those who summon it at will. It was her habitual escape from the boredom between thrills, and in such intervals of existence as she was now traversing she plunged back into it after every bout of outdoor activity.

Nona tiptoed forward and looked down on her. Who said that sleep revealed people's true natures? It only made them the more enigmatic by the added veil of its own mystery. Lita's head was nested in the angle of a thin arm, her lids rounded heavily above the sharp cheek-bones just swept by their golden fringe, the pale bow of the mouth relaxed, the slight steel-strong body half shown in the parting of a flowered dressing-gown. Thus exposed, with gaze extinct and loosened muscles, she seemed a mere bundle of contradictory whims tied together by a frail thread of beauty. The hand of the downward arm hung open, palm up. In its little hollow lay the fate of three lives. What would she do with them? How could one conceive of her knowing, or planning, or imagining— conceive of her in any sort of durable human relations to any one or anything?

Her eyes opened and a languid curiosity floated up through them.

"That you? I must have fallen asleep. I was trying to count up the number of months we've been here, and numbers always make me go to sleep."

Nona laughed and sat down at the foot of the lounge. "Dear me— just as I thought you were beginning to be happy!"

"Well, isn't this what you call being happy—in the country?"

"Lying on your back, and wondering how many months there are in a week?"

"A week? Is it only a week? How on earth can you be sure, when one day's so exactly like another?"

"Tomorrow won't be. There's the blow-out for Amalasuntha, and dancing afterward. Mother's idea of the simple life."

"Well, all your mother's ideas ARE simple." Lita yawned, her pale pink mouth drooping like a faded flower. "Besides, it's ages till tomorrow. Where's your father? He was going to take me for a spin in the new Buick."

"He's broken his promise, then. Deserted us all and sneaked off to Greystock on his lone."

A faint redness rose to Lita's cheek-bones. "Greystock and Gladys Toy? Is that HIS idea of the simple life? About on a par with your mother's. . . Did you ever notice the Toy ankles?"

Nona smiled. "They're not unnoticeable. But you forget that father's getting to be an old gentleman. . . Fathers mustn't be choosers. . ."

Lita made a slight grimace. "Oh, he could do better than that. There's old Cosby, who looks heaps older—didn't he want to marry you? . . . Nona, you darling, let's take the Ford and run over to Greenwich for dinner. Would your mother so very much mind? Does she want us here the whole blessed time?"

"I'll go and ask her. But on a Friday night the Country Club will be as dead as the moon. Only a few old ladies playing bridge."

"Well, then we'll have the floor to ourselves. I want a good practice, and it's a ripping floor. We can dance with the waiters. It'll be fun to shock the old ladies. I noticed one of the waiters the other day—must be an Italian—built rather like Tommy Ardwin. . . I'm sure he dances. . ."

That was all life meant to Lita—would ever mean. Good floors to practise new dance-steps on, men—any men—to dance with and be flattered by, women—any women—to stare and envy one, dull people to startle, stupid people to shock—but never any one, Nona questioned, whom one wanted neither to startle nor shock, neither to be envied nor flattered by, but just to lose one's self in for good and all? Lita lose herself—? Why, all she wanted was to keep on finding herself, immeasurably magnified, in every pair of eyes she met!

And here were Nona and her father and mother fighting to preserve this brittle plaything for Jim, when somewhere in the world there might be a real human woman for him. . . What was the sense of it all?

XXIV

The Marchesa di San Fedele's ideas about the country were perfectly simple; in fact she had only one. She regarded it as a place in which there was more time to play bridge than in town. Thank God for that!—and the rest one simply bore with. . . Of course there was the obligatory going the rounds with host or hostess: gardens, glass, dairy, chicken-hatchery, and heaven knew what besides (stables, thank goodness, were out of fashion—even if people rode they no longer, unless they kept hounds, dragged one between those dreary rows of box stalls, or made one admire the lustrous steel and leather of the harness room, or the monograms stencilled in blue and red on the coach-house floor).

The Marchesa's life had always been made up of doing things as dull as going over model dairies in order to get the chance, or the money, to do others as thrilling to her as dancing was to Lita. It was part of the game: one had to pay for what one got: the thing was to try and get a great deal more than the strict equivalent.

"Not that I don't marvel at your results, Pauline; we all do. But they make me feel so useless and incapable. All this wonderful creation—baths and swimming-pools and hatcheries and fire-engines, and everything so perfect, indoors and out! Sometimes I'm glad you've never been to our poor old San Fedele. But of course bathrooms will have to be put in at San Fedele if Michelangelo finds an American bride when he comes over. . ."

Pauline laid down the pen she had taken up to record the exact terms in which she was to address the Cardinal's secretary. ("A PERSONAL note, dear; yes, in your own writing; they don't yet understand your new American ways at the Vatican. . .")

"When Michelangelo comes over?" Pauline echoed.

The Marchesa's face was sharper than a knife. "It's my little surprise. I didn't mean you or Dexter to know till the contract was signed. . ."

"What contract?"

"My boy's to do Cæsar Borgia in the new film. Klawhammer cabled a definite offer the day you left for the country. And of course I insisted on Michelangelo's sailing instantly, though he'd planned to spend the spring in Paris and was rather cross at having to give it up. But as I told him, now is the moment to secure a lovely American bride. We all know what your rich papas-in-law over here always ask: 'What debts? What prospects? What other women?' The woman matter can generally be arranged. The debts ARE, in this case— thanks to your generosity. But the prospects—what were THEY, I ask you? Months of green mould at San Fedele for a fortnight's splash in Rome . . . oh, I don't disguise it! And what American bride would accept THAT? The San Fedele pearls, yes—but where is the San Fedele plumbing? But now, my dear, Michelangelo presents himself as an equal . . . superior, I might say, if I weren't afraid of being partial. Cæsar Borgia in a Klawhammer film— no one knows how many millions it may mean! And of course Michelangelo is the very type. . .
."

"To do me the favour to transmit to his Eminence. . . Yes; this really is a surprise, Amalasuntha." Inwardly Pauline was saying: "After all, why not? If his own mother doesn't mind seeing him all over the place on film posters. And perhaps now he may pay us back— in common decency he'll have to!"

She saw no serious reason for displeasure, once she had dropped her carefully cultivated Wyant attitude. "If only it doesn't upset Lita again, and make her restless!" But they really couldn't hope to keep all Lita's friends and relations off the screen.

"Arthur was amazed—and awfully pleased, after the first recoil. Dear Arthur, you know, always recoils at first," the Marchesa continued, with her shrewd deprecating smile, which insinuated that Pauline of course wouldn't. (It was odd, Pauline reflected; the Marchesa always looked like a peasant when she was talking business.)

"Arthur? You've already written to him about it?"

"No, dear. I ran across him yesterday in town. You didn't know Arthur'd come back? I thought he said he'd telephoned to Nona, or somebody. A touch of gout—got fidgety because he couldn't see his doctor. But he looked remarkably well, I thought—so handsome still, in his élancé Wyant way; only a little too flushed, perhaps. Yes . . . poor Eleanor. . . Oh, no; he said Jim was still on the island. Perfectly contented fishing. Jim's the only person I know who's always perfectly contented . . . such a lesson. . ." The Marchesa's sigh seemed to add: "Very restful—but how I should despise him if he were my Michelangelo!"

Pauline could hear—oh, how distinctly!—all that her former husband would have to say about Michelangelo's projects. They would be food for an afternoon's irony. But that did not greatly trouble her—nor did Wyant's unexpected return. He was always miserable out of reach of his doctor. And the fact that Jim hadn't come back proved that there was nothing seriously wrong. Pauline thought: "I'll write to Jim again, and tell him how perfect Dexter has been about Lita and the baby, and that will convince him there's no need to hurry back."

Complacency returned to her. How should it not, with the list for the Cardinal's reception nearly complete, and the telephonic assurance of the Bishop of New York and the Chief Rabbi that both these dignitaries would be present? Socially also, though the season was over, the occasion promised to be brilliant. Lots of people were coming back just to see how a Cardinal was received. Even the Rivingtons were coming—she had it from the Bishop. Yes, the Rivingtons had certainly been more cordial since she and Manford had thrown them over at the last minute. That was the way to treat people who thought themselves so awfully superior. What wouldn't the Rivingtons have given to capture the Cardinal? But he was sailing for Italy the day after Pauline's reception—that was the beauty of it! No one else could possibly have him. Amalasuntha had stage-managed the whole business very cleverly. She had even overcome the Cardinal's scruples when he heard that Mrs. Manford was chairman of the Birth Control committee. . . And tonight, at the dinner, how pleasant everybody's congratulations would be! Pauline gloried in her achievement for Manford's sake. Despite his assurance to the contrary she could never imagine, for more than a moment at a time, that such successes were really indifferent to him.

Lita appeared in the drawing-room after almost everybody had arrived. She was always among the last; and in the country, as she said, there was no way of knowing what time it was. Even at Cedarledge, where all the clocks agreed to a second, one could never believe them, and always suspected they must have stopped together, twelve hours before.

"Besides, what's the use of knowing what time it is in the country? Time for WHAT?"

She came in quietly, almost unnoticeably, with the feathered gait that was half-way between drifting and floating; and at once, in spite of the twenty people assembled, had the shining parquet and all the mirrors to herself. That was her way: that knack of clearing the floor no matter how quietly she entered. And tonight—!

Well; perhaps, Manford thought, all the other women WERE a little overdressed. Women always had a tendency to overdress when they dined with the Manfords; to wear too many jewels, and put on clothes that glistened. Even at Cedarledge Pauline's parties had a New York atmosphere. And Lita, in her straight white slip, slim and unadorned as a Primitive angel, with that close coif of goldfish-coloured hair, and not a spangle, a jewel, a pearl even, made the other women's clothes look like upholstery.

Manford, by the hearth, slightly bored in anticipation, yet bound to admit that, like all his wife's shows, it was effectively done— Manford received the shock of that quiet entrance, that shimmer widening into light, and then turned to Mrs. Herman Toy. Full noon there; the usual Rubensy redundance flushed by golfing in a high wind, by a last cocktail before dressing, by the hurried wriggle into one of those elastic sheaths the women—the redundant women— wore. Well; he liked ripeness in a fruit to be eaten as soon as plucked. And Gladys' corn-yellow hair was almost as springy and full of coloured shadows as the other's red. But the voice, the dress, the jewels, the blatant jewels! A Cartier show-case spilt over a strawberry mousse. . . And the quick possessive look, so clumsily done—brazen, yet half-abashed! When a woman's first business was to make up her mind which it was to be. . . Chances were the man didn't care, as long as her ogling didn't make him ridiculous. . . Why couldn't some women always be in golf clothes— if any? Gala get-up wasn't in everybody's line. . . There was Lita speaking to Gladys now—with auburn eyebrows lifted just a thread. The contrast—! And Gladys purpler and more self- conscious—God, why did she have her clothes so tight? And that drawing-room drawl! Why couldn't she just sing out: "Hul-LO!" as she did in the open?

The Marchesa—how many times more was he to hear Pauline say: "Amalasuntha on your right, dear." Oh, to get away to a world where nobody gave dinners, and there were no Marchesas on one's right! He knew by heart the very look of the little cheese soufflés, light as cherubs' feathers, that were being handed around before the soup on silver-gilt dishes with coats-of-arms. Everything at Cedarledge was silver-gilt. Pauline, as usual, had managed to transplant the party to New York, when all he wanted was to be quiet, smoke his pipe, and ride or tramp with Nona and Lita. Why couldn't she see it? Her vigilant eye sought his—was it for approval or admonition? What was she saying? "The Cardinal? Oh, yes. It's all settled. So sweet of him! Of course you must all promise to come. But I've got another little surprise for you after dinner. No; not a word beforehand; not if you were to put me on the rack." What on earth did she mean?

"A surprise? Is this a surprise party?" It was Amalasuntha now. "Then I must produce mine. But I daresay Pauline's told you. About Michelangelo and Klawhammer. . . Cæsar Borgia . . . such a sum that I don't dare to mention it—you'd think I was mixing up the figures. But I've got them down in black and white. Of course, as the producers say, Michelangelo's so supremely the type—it's more than they ever could have hoped for." What was the woman raving about? "He sails tomorrow," she said. Sailing again— was that damned Michelangelo always sailing? Hadn't his debts been paid on the express condition—? But no; there's been nothing, as the Marchesa called it, "in black and white." The transaction had been based on the implicit understanding that nothing but dire necessity would induce Michelangelo to waste his charms on New York. Dire necessity—or the chance to put himself permanently beyond it! A fortune from a Klawhammer film. As Amalasuntha said, it was incalculable. . .

"It's the type, you see: between ourselves, there's always been a rumour of Borgia blood on the San Fedele side. A naughty ancestress! Perhaps you've noticed the likeness? You remember that wonderful profile portrait of Cæsar Borgia in black velvet? What gallery IS it in? Oh, I know—it came out in 'Vogue'!" Amalasuntha visibly bridled at her proficiency. She was aware that envious people said the Italians knew nothing of their own artistic inheritance. "I remember being so struck by it at the time—I said to Venturino: 'But it's the image of our boy!' Though Michelangelo will have to grow a beard, which makes him furious. . . But then the millions!"

Manford, looking up, caught a double gaze bent in his direction. Gladys Toy's vast blue eyes had always been like searchlights; but tonight they seemed actually to be writing her private history over his head, like an advertising aeroplane. The fool! But was the other look also meant for him? That half-shaded glint of Lita's— was it not rather attached to the Marchesa, strung like a telephone wire to her lips? Klawhammer . . . Michelangelo . . . a Borgia film. . . Those listening eyes missed not a syllable. . .

"The offers those fellows make—right and left—nobody takes much account of them. Wait till I see your contract, as you call it. . . If you really think it's a job for a gentleman," Manford growled.

"But, my friend, gentlemen can't be choosers! Who are the real working-class today? Our old aristocracies, alas! And besides, is it ever degrading to create a work of art? I thought in America you made so much of creativeness—constructiveness—what do you call it? Is it less creative to turn a film than to manufacture bathtubs? Can there be a nobler mission than to teach history to the millions by means of beautiful pictures? . . . Yes! I see Lita listening, and I know she agrees with me. . . Lita! What a Lucrezia for his Cæsar! But why look shocked, dear Dexter? Of course you know that Lucrezia Borgia has been entirely rehabilitated? I saw that also in 'Vogue.' She was a perfectly pure woman—and her hair was exactly the colour of Lita's."

They were finishing coffee in the drawing-room, the doors standing open into the tall library where the men always smoked—the library which (as Stanley

Heuston had once remarked) Pauline's incorruptible honesty had actually caused her to fill with books.

"Oh, what IS it? Not a fire? . . . A chimney in the house? . . . But it's actually here. . . Not a . . ."

The women, a-flutter at the sudden siren-shriek, the hooting, rushing and clattering up the drive, surged across the parquet, flowed with startled little cries out into the hall, and saw the unsurprisable Powder signalling to two perfectly matched footmen to throw open the double doors.

"A fire? The engine . . . the . . . oh, it's a FIRE-DRILL! . . . A PARADE! How realistic! How lovely of you! What a beauty the engine is!" Pauline stood smiling, watch in hand, as the hook-and- ladder motor clattered up the drive and ranged itself behind the engine. The big lantern over the front door illuminated fresh scarlet paint and super-polished brasses, the firemen's agitated helmets and perspiring faces, the flashing hoods of the lamps.

"Just five minutes to the second! Wonderful!" She was shaking hands with each member of the amateur brigade in turn. "I can't tell you how I congratulate you—every one of you! Such an achievement . . . you really manoeuvre like professionals. No one would have believed it was the first time! Dexter, will you tell them a hot supper has been prepared downstairs!" To the guests she was explaining in a triumphant undertone: "I wanted to give them the chance to show off their new toy . . . Yes, I believe it's absolutely the most perfected thing in fire-engines. Dexter and I thought it was time the village was properly equipped. It's really more on account of the farmers—such a sense of safety for the neighbourhood. . . Oh, Mr. Motts, I think you're simply wonderful, all of you. Mr. Manford and my daughter are going to show you the way to supper. . . Yes, yes, you MUST! Just a sandwich and something hot."

She dominated them all, grave and glittering as a goddess of Velocity. "She enjoys it as much as other women do love-making," Manford muttered to himself.

XXV

Manford didn't know what first gave him the sense that Lita had slipped out among the departing guests; slipped out, and not come back. When the idea occurred to him it was already lodged in his mind, hard and definite as a verified fact. She had vanished from among them into the darkness.

But only a moment ago; there was still time to dash round to the shed in the service court, where motors were sometimes left for the night, and where he had dropped his Buick just in time to rush in and dress for dinner. He would have no trouble in overtaking her.

The Buick was gone.

Hatless and coatless in the soft night air, he rushed down the drive on its track. No moon tonight, but a deceptive velvet mildness, such as sometimes comes in spring before the wind hauls round to a frosty quarter. He hurried on, out of the open gate, along the road toward the village; and there, at the turn of the New York turnpike—just the road he had expected her to take—stood his Buick, a figure stooping over it in the lamp-glare. A furious stab of jealousy shot through him—"There's a man with her; who?" But the man was only his own overcoat, which he had left on the seat of the car when he dashed home for dinner, and which was now drawn over Lita's shoulders. It was she who stood in the night, bent over the mysteries of the car's insides.

She looked up and called out: "Oh, look here—give me a hand, will you? The thing's stuck." Manford moved around within lamp-range, and she stared a moment, her little face springing out at him uncannily from the darkness. Then she broke into a laugh. "You?"

"Were you asking a total stranger to repair your motor? Rather risky, on a country road in the middle of the night."

She shrugged and smiled. "Not as risky as doing it myself. The chances are that even a total stranger would know more about the inside of this car than I do."

"Lita, you're mad! Damn the car. What are you doing here anyhow?"

She paused, one hand on the bonnet, while with the other she pushed back a tossed lock from her round forehead. "Running away," she said simply.

Manford took a quick breath. The thing was, he admonished himself, to take this lightly, as nearly as possible in her own key—above all to avoid protesting and exclaiming. But his heart was beating like a trip-hammer. She was more of a fool than he had thought.

"Running away from that dinner? I don't blame you. But it's over. Still, if you want to wash out the memory of it, get into the motor and we'll go for a good spin—like that one when we came back from Greenwich."

Her lips parted in a faint smile. "Oh, but that ended up at Cedarledge."

"Well—?"

"Bless you; I'm not going back."

"Where ARE you going?"

"To New York first—after that I don't know. . . Perhaps my aunt's. . . Perhaps Hollywood. . ."

The rage in him exploded. "Perhaps Dawnside—eh? Own up!"

She laughed and shrugged again. "Own up? Why not? Anywhere where I can dance and laugh and be hopelessly low-lived and irresponsible."

"And get that blackguard crew about you again, all those—. Lita! Listen to me. Listen. You've got to."

"Got to?" She rounded on him in a quick flare of anger. "I wonder who you think you're talking to? I'm not Gladys Toy."

The unexpectedness of the challenge struck him dumb. For challenge it was, unmistakably. He felt a rush of mingled strength and fear— fear at this inconceivable thing, and the strength her self- betrayal gave him. He returned with equal violence: "No—you're not. You're something so utterly different. . ."

"Oh," she burst in, "don't tell me I'm too sacred, and all that. I'm fed up with the sanctities—that's the trouble with me. Just own up you like 'em artificially fattened. Why, that woman's ankles are half a yard round. Can't you SEE it? Or is that really the way you admire 'em? I thought you wanted to be with me. . . I thought that was why you were here. . . Do you suppose I'd have come all this way just to be taught to love fresh air and family life? The hypocrisy—!"

Her little face was flashing on him furiously, red lips parted on a glitter of bright teeth. "She must have a sausage-machine, to cram her into that tube she had on tonight. No human maid could do it. . . 'Utterly different'? I should hope so! I'd like to see HER get a job with Klawhammer—unless he means to do a 'Barnum,' and wants a Fat Woman . . . I . . ."

"LITA!"

"You're STUPID . . . you're stupider than anything on God's earth!"

"Lita—" He put his hand over hers. Let the whole world crash, after this. . .

Pauline sat in her upstairs sitting-room, full of that sense of repose which comes of duties performed and rewards laid up. How could it be otherwise, at the close of a day so rich in moral satisfactions? She scanned it again, from the vantage of her midnight vigil in the sleeping house, and saw that all was well in the little world she had created.

Yes; all was well, from the fire-drill which had given a rather languishing dinner its requisite wind-up of excitement to the arrangements for the Cardinal's reception, Amalasuntha's skilful turning of that Birth Control obstacle, and the fact that Jim was philosophically remaining in the south in spite of his father's unexpected return. The only shadow on the horizon was Michelangelo's—Dexter would certainly be angry about that. But she was not going to let Michelangelo darken her holiday, when everything else in life was so smooth and sunshiny.

She remembered her resolve to write to Jim, and took up her pen with a smile.

"I can guess what heavenly weather you must be having from the delicious taste of spring we're having here. The baby is out in the sunshine all day: he's gained nearly a pound, and is getting almost as brown as if it were summer. Lita looks ever so much better too, though she'd never forgive my suggesting that she had put on even an ounce. But I don't believe she has, for she and Nona and Dexter are riding or golfing or racing over the country from morning to night like a pack of children. You can't think how jolly and hungry and sleepy they all are when they get home for tea. It was a wonderful invention of Dexter's to bring Lita and the baby here while you were having your holiday, and you'll agree that it has worked miracles when you see them.

"Amalasuntha tells me your father is back. I expected to hear that he had got restless away from his own quarters; but she says he's looking very well. Nona will go in and see him next week, and report. Meanwhile I'm so glad you're staying on and making the most of your holiday. Do get all the rest and sunshine you can, and trust your treasures a little longer to your loving old

"MOTHER."

There—that would certainly reassure him. It had reassured her merely to write it: given her the feeling, to which she always secretly inclined, that a thing was so if one said it was, and doubly so if one wrote it down.

She sealed the letter, pushed back her chair, and glanced at the little clock on her writing-table. A quarter to two! She had a right to feel sleepy, and even to curtail her relaxing exercises. The country stillness was so deep and soothing that she hardly needed them. . .

She opened the window, and stood drinking in the hush. The spring night was full of an underlying rustle and murmur that was a part of the silence. But suddenly a sharp sound broke on her—the sound of a motor coming up the drive. In the stillness she caught it a long way off, probably just after the car turned in at the gate. The sound was so unnatural, breaking in on the deep nocturnal dumbness of dim trees and starlit sky, that she drew back startled. She was not a nervous woman, but she thought irritably of a servants' escapade—something that the chauffeur would have to be spoken to about the next day. Queer, though—the motor did not turn off toward the garage. Standing in the window she followed its continued approach; then heard it slow down and stop—somewhere near the service court, she conjectured.

Could it be that Lita and Nona had been off on one of their crazy trips since the guests had left? She must really protest at such imprudence. . . She felt angry, nervous, uncertain. It was uncanny, hearing that invisible motor come so near the house and stop. . . She hesitated a moment, and then crossed to her own room, opened the door of the little anteroom beyond, and stood listening at her husband's bedroom door. It was ajar, all dark within. She hesitated to speak, half fearing to wake him; but at length she said in a low voice: "Dexter—."

No answer. She pronounced his name again, a little louder, and then cautiously crossed the threshold and switched on the light. The room was empty, the bed undisturbed. It was evident that Manford had not been up to his room since their guests had left. It was he, then, who had come back in the motor. . . She extinguished the light and turned back into her own room. On her dressing-table stood the little telephone which communicated with the servants' quarters, with Maisie Bruss's office, and with Nona's room. She stood wavering before the instrument. Why shouldn't she call up Nona, and ask—? Ask what? If the girls had been off on a lark they would be sure to tell her in the morning. And if it was Dexter alone, then—

She turned from the telephone, and slowly began to undress. Presently she heard steps in the hall, then in the anteroom; then her husband moving softly about in his own room, and the unmistakable sounds of his undressing. . . She drew a long breath, as if trying to free her lungs of some vague oppression. . . It was Dexter—well, yes, only Dexter . . . and he hadn't cared to leave the motor at the garage at that hour. . . Naturally. . . How glad she was that she hadn't rung up Nona! Suppose her doing so had startled Lita or the baby. . .

After all, perhaps she'd better do her relaxing exercises. She felt suddenly staring wide awake. But she was glad she'd written that reassuring letter to Jim—she was glad, because it was TRUE. . .

XXVI

When Nona told her mother that she wanted to go to town the next day to see Mrs. Bruss and Maisie, Mrs. Manford said: "It's only what I expected of you, darling," and added after a moment: "Do you think I ought—?"

"No, of course not. It would simply worry Maisie."

Nona knew it was the answer that her mother awaited. She knew that nothing frightened and disorganized Pauline as much as direct contact with physical or moral suffering—especially physical. Her whole life (if one chose to look at it from a certain angle) had been a long uninterrupted struggle against the encroachment of every form of pain. The first step, always, was to conjure it, bribe it away, by every possible expenditure—except of one's self. Cheques, surgeons, nurses, private rooms in hospitals, X-rays, radium, whatever was most costly and up-to-date in the dreadful art of healing—that was her first and strongest line of protection; behind it came such lesser works as rest-cures, change of air, a seaside holiday, a whole new set of teeth, pink silk bed-spreads, lace cushions, stacks of picture papers, and hot-house grapes and long-stemmed roses from Cedarledge. Behind these again were the final, the verbal defenses, made of such phrases as: "If I thought I could do the least good"—"If I didn't feel it might simply upset her"—"SOME doctors still consider it contagious"—with the inevitable summing-up: "The fewer people she sees the better. . ."

Nona knew that this attitude was not caused by lack of physical courage. Had Pauline been a pioneer's wife, and seen her family stricken down by disease in the wilderness, she would have nursed them fearlessly; but all her life she had been used to buying off suffering with money, or denying its existence with words, and her moral muscles had become so atrophied that only some great shock would restore their natural strength. . .

"Great shock! People like mother never have great shocks," Nona mused, looking at the dauntless profile, the crisply waving hair, reflected in the toilet-mirror. "Unless I were to give her one . . ." she added with an inward smile.

Mrs. Manford restored her powder-puff to its crystal box. "Do you know, darling, I believe I'll go to town with you tomorrow. It was very brave of Maisie to make the effort of coming here the other day, but of course, I didn't like to burden her with too many details at such a time (when's the operation—tomorrow?), and there are things I could perfectly well attend to myself, without bothering her; without her even knowing. Yes; I'll motor up with you early."

"She'll always delegate her anxieties," Nona mused, not unenviously, as Cécile slipped Mrs. Manford's spangled teagown over her firm white shoulders. Pauline turned a tender smile on her daughter. "It's so like you, Nona, to want to be with Maisie for the operation—so FINE, dear."

Voice and smile were full of praise; yet behind the praise (Nona also knew) lurked the unformulated apprehension: "All this running after sick people and unhappy people—is it going to turn into a vocation?" Nothing could have been more distasteful to Mrs. Manford than the idea that her only daughter should be not only good, but MERELY good: like poor Aggie Heuston, say. . . Nona could hear her mother murmuring: "I can't imagine where on earth she got it from," as if alluding to some physical defect unaccountable in the offspring of two superbly sound progenitors.

They started early, for forty-eight hours of accumulated leisure had reinforced Pauline's natural activity. Amalasuntha, mysteriously smiling and head-shaking over the incommunicable figures of Klawhammer's offer, had bustled back to town early on Monday, leaving the family to themselves—and a certain feeling of flatness had ensued. Dexter, his wife thought, seemed secretly irritated, but determined to conceal his irritation from her. It was about Michelangelo, no doubt. Lita was silent and sleepy. No one seemed to have anything particular to do. Even in town Mondays were always insipid. But in the afternoon Manford "took Lita off their hands," as his wife put it, by carrying her away for the long- deferred spin in the Buick; and Pauline plunged back restfully into visiting-lists and other domestic preoccupations. She certainly had nothing to worry about, and much to rejoice in, yet she felt languid and vaguely apprehensive. She began to wonder if Alvah Loft's treatment were of the lasting sort, or if it lost its efficacy, like an uncorked drug. Perhaps the Scientific Initiate she had been told about would have a new panacea for the mind as well as for the epiderm. She would telephone and make an appointment; it always stimulated her to look forward to seeing a new healer. As Mrs. Swoffer said, one ought never to neglect a spiritual opportunity; and one never knew on whom the Spirit might have alighted. Mrs. Swoffer's conversation was always soothing and yet invigorating, and Pauline determined to see her too. And there was Arthur— poor Exhibit A!—on Jim's account it would be kind to look him up if there were time; unless Nona could manage that too, in the intervals of solacing Maisie. It was so depressing—and so useless—to sit in a hospital parlour, looking at old numbers of picture papers, while those awful white-sleeved rites went on in the secret sanctuary of tiles and nickel-plating. It would do Nona good to have an excuse for slipping away.

Pauline's list of things-to-be-done had risen like a spring tide as soon as she decided to go to town for the day. There was hair- waving, manicuring, dressmaking—her dress for the Cardinal's reception. How was she ever to get through half the engagements on her list? And of course she must call at the hospital with a big basket of grapes and flowers. . .

On the steps of the hospital Nona paused and looked about her. The operation was over—everything had "gone beautifully," as beautifully as it almost always does on these occasions. Maisie had been immensely grateful for her coming, and as surprised as if an angel from the seventh heaven had alighted to help her through. The two girls had sat together, making jerky attempts at talk, till the nurse came and said: "All right—she's back in bed again"; and then Maisie, after a burst of relieving tears, had tiptoed off to sit in a corner of her mother's darkened room and await the first sign of returning consciousness. There was nothing more for Nona to do, and she went out into the April freshness with the sense of relief that the healthy feel when they escape back to life after a glimpse of death.

On the hospital steps she ran into Arthur Wyant.

"Exhibit, dear! What are you doing here?"

"Coming to inquire for poor Mrs. Bruss. I heard from Amalasuntha. . ."

"That's kind of you. Maisie'll be so pleased."

She gave him the surgeon's report, saw that his card was entrusted to the right hands, and turned back into the street with him. He looked better than when he had left for the south; his leg was less stiff, and he carried his tall carefully dressed figure with a rigid jauntiness. But his face seemed sharper yet higher in colour. Fever or cocktails? She wondered. It was lucky that their meeting would save her going to the other end of the town to see him.

"Just like you, Exhibit, to remember poor Maisie. . ."

He raised ironic eyebrows. "Is inquiring about ill people obsolete? I see you still keep up the tradition."

"Oh, I've been seeing it through with Maisie. Some one had to."

"Exactly. And your mother held aloof, but financed the whole business?"

"Splendidly. She always does."

He frowned, and stood hesitating, and tapping his long boot-tip with his stick. "I rather want to have a talk with your mother."

"With mother?" Nona was on the point of saying: "She's in town today—" then, remembering Pauline's crowded list, she checked the impulse.

"Won't I do as a proxy? I was going to suggest your carrying me off to lunch."

"No, my dear, you won't—as a proxy. But I'll carry you off to lunch."

The choice of a restaurant would have been laborious—for Wyant, when taken out of his rut, became a mass of manias, prejudices and inhibitions—but Nona luckily remembered a new Bachelor Girls' Club ("The Singleton") which she had lately joined, and packed him into a taxi still protesting.

They found a quiet corner in a sociable low-studded dining-room, and she leaned back, listening to his disconnected monologue and smoking one cigarette after another in the nervous inability to eat.

The ten days on the island? Oh, glorious, of course—hot sunshine— a good baking for his old joints. Awfully kind of her father to invite him . . . he'd appreciated it immensely . . . was going to write a line of thanks. . . Jim, too, had appreciated his father's being included. . . Only, no, really; he couldn't stay; in the circumstances he couldn't. . .

"What circumstances, Exhibit? Getting the morning papers twenty- four hours late?"

Wyant frowned, looked at her sharply, and then laughed an uneasy wrinkled laugh. "Impertinent chit!"

"Own up, now; you were bored stiff. Communion with Nature was too much for you. You couldn't stick it. Few can."

"I don't say I'm as passive as Jim."

"Jim's just loving it down there, isn't he? I'm so glad you persuaded him to stay."

Wyant frowned again, and stared past her at some invisible antagonist. "It was about the only thing I COULD persuade him to do."

Nona's hand hung back from the lighting of another cigarette. "What else did you try to?"

"What else? Why to ACT, damn it . . . take a line . . . face things . . . face the music." He stopped in a splutter of metaphors, and dipped his bristling moustache toward his coffee.

"What things?"

"Why: is he going to keep his wife, or isn't he?"

"He thinks that's for Lita to decide."

"For Lita to decide! A pretext for his damned sentimental inertness. A MAN—my son! God, what's happened to the young men? Sit by and see . . . see. . . Nona, couldn't I manage to have a talk with your mother?"

"You're having one with me. Isn't that enough for the moment?"

He gave another vague laugh, and took a light from her extended cigarette. She knew that, though he found her mother's visits oppressive, he kept a careful record of their number, and dimly resented any appearance of being "crowded out" by Pauline's other engagements. "I suppose she comes up to town sometimes, doesn't she?"

"Sometimes—but in such a rush! And we'll be back soon now. She's got to get ready for the Cardinal's reception."

"Great doings, I hear. Amalasuntha dropped in on me yesterday. She says Lita's all agog again since that rotten Michelangelo's got a film contract, and your father's in an awful state about it. Is he?"

"The family are not used yet to figuring on the posters. Of course it's only a question of time."

"I don't mean in a state about Michelangelo, but about Lita."

"Father's been a perfect brick about Lita."

"Oh, he has, has he? Very magnanimous.—Thanks; no—no cigar. . . Of course, if anybody's got to be a brick about Lita, I don't see why it's not her husband's job; but then I suppose you'll tell me. . ."

"Yes; I shall; please consider yourself told, won't you? Because I've got to get back to the hospital."

"The modern husband's job is a purely passive one, eh? That's your idea too? If you go to him and say: 'How about that damned scoundrel and your wife'—"

"What damned scoundrel?"

"Oh, I don't say . . . anybody in particular . . . and he answers: 'Well, what am I going to do about it?' and you say: 'Well, and your honour, man; what about your honour?' and he says: 'What's my honour got to do with it if my wife's sick of me?' and you say: 'God! But THE OTHER MAN . . . aren't you going to break his bones for him?' and he sits and looks at you and says: 'Get up a prize-fight for her?'. . . God! I give it up. My own son! We don't speak the same language, that's all."

He leaned back, his long legs stretched under the table, his tall shambling body disjointed with the effort at a military tautness, a kind of muscular demonstration of what his son's moral attitude ought to be.

"Damn it—there was a good deal to be said for duelling."

"And to whom do you want Jim to send his seconds? Michelangelo or Klawhammer?"

He stared, and echoed her laugh. "Ha! Ha! That's good. Klawhammer! Dirty Jew . . . the kind we used to horsewhip. . . Well, I don't understand the new code."

"Why do you want to, Exhibit? Come along. You've got me to look after in the meantime. If you want to be chivalrous, tuck me under your arm and see me back to the hospital."

"A prize-fight—get up a prize-fight for her! God—I should understand even that better than lying on the beach smoking a pipe and saying: 'What can a fellow do about it?' DO!"

Act—act—act! How funny it was, Nona reflected, as she remounted the hospital steps: the people who talked most of acting seldom did more than talk. Her father, for instance, so resolute and purposeful, never discoursed about action, but quietly went about what had to be done. Whereas poor Exhibit, perpetually inconsequent and hesitating, was never tired of formulating the most truculent plans of action for others. "Poor Exhibit indeed— incorrigible amateur!" she thought, understanding how such wordy dilettantism must have bewildered and irritated the young and energetic Pauline, fresh from the buzzing motor works at Exploit.

Nona felt a sudden exasperation against Wyant for trying to poison Jim's holiday by absurd insinuations and silly swagger. It was lucky that he had got bored and come back, leaving the poor boy to bask on the sands with his pipe and his philosophy. After all, it was to be supposed that Jim knew what he wanted, and how to take care of it, now he had it.

"At all events," Nona concluded, "I'm glad he didn't get hold of mother and bother her with his foolish talk." She shot up in the lift to the white carbolic-breathing passage where, with a heavy whiff of ether, Mrs. Bruss's door opened to receive her.

XXVII

The restorative effect of a day away from the country was visible in Pauline's face and manner when she dawned on the breakfast-table the next morning. The mere tone in which she murmured: "How lovely it is to get back!" showed how lovely it had been to get away—and she lingered over the new-laid eggs, the golden cream, all the country freshnesses and succulences, with the sense of having richly earned them by a long day spent in arduous and agreeable labours.

"When there are tiresome things to be done the great thing is to do them at once," she announced to Nona across the whole-wheat toast and scrambled eggs. "I simply hated to leave all this loveliness yesterday; but how much more I'm going to enjoy it today because I did!"

Her day in town had in truth been exceptionally satisfactory. All had gone well, from her encounter, at Amalasuntha's, with one of the Cardinal's secretaries, to the belated glimpse of Maisie Bruss, haggard but hopeful on the hospital steps, receiving the hamper of fruit and flowers with grateful exclamations, and assurances that the surgeon was "perfectly satisfied," and that there was "no reason why the dreadful thing should ever reappear." In a wave of sympathetic emotion Pauline had leaned from the motor to kiss her and say: "Your mother must have a good rest at Atlantic City as soon as she can be moved—I'll arrange it. Sea air is such a tonic . . ." and Maisie had thanked and wept again. . . It was pleasant to be able, in a few words, to make any one so happy. . .

She had found Mrs. Swoffer too; found her in a super-terrestrial mood, beaming through inspired eye-glasses, and pouring out new torrents of stimulation.

Yes: Alvah Loft was a great man, Mrs. Swoffer said. She, for her part, had never denied it for a moment. How could Pauline have imagined that her faith in Alvah Loft had failed her? No—but there were periods of spiritual aridity which the brightest souls had to traverse, and she had lately had reason to suspect, from her own experience and from Pauline's, that perhaps Alvah Loft was at present engaged in such a desert. Certainly to charge a hundred dollars for a "triple treatment" (which was only three minutes longer than the plain one), and then produce no more lasting results—well, Mrs. Swoffer preferred not to say anything uncharitable. . . Then again, she sometimes suspected that Alvah Loft's doctrine might be only for beginners. That was what Sacha Gobine, the new Russian Initiate, plainly intimated. Of course there were innumerable degrees in the spiritual life, and it might be that sometimes Alvah Loft's patients got beyond his level—got above it—without his being aware of the fact. Frankly, that was what Gobine thought (from Mrs. Swoffer's report) must have happened in the case of Pauline. "I believe your friend has reached a higher plane"—that was the way the Initiate put it. "She's been at the gate" (he called the Mahatma and Alvah Loft "gatekeepers"), "and now the gate has opened, and she has entered in—entered into . . ." But Mrs. Swoffer said she'd rather not try to quote him because she couldn't put it as beautifully as he did, and she wanted Pauline to hear it in his own mystical language. "It's eternal rejuvenation just to sit and listen to him," she breathed, laying an electric touch on her visitor's hand.

Rejuvenation! The word dashed itself like cool spray against Pauline's strained nerves and parched complexion. She could never hear it without longing to plunge deep into its healing waters. Between manicure and hair-waver she was determined to squeeze in a moment with Gobine.

And the encounter, as she told Nona, had been like "a religious experience"—apparently forgetful of the fact that every other meeting with a new prophet had presented itself to her in identical terms.

"You see, my dear, it's something so entirely new, so completely different . . . so emotional; yes, emotional; that's the word. The Russians, of course, ARE emotional; it's their peculiar quality. Alvah Loft—and you understand that I don't in the least suggest any loss of faith in him; but Alvah Loft has a mind which speaks to the MIND; there is no appeal to the feelings. Whereas in Gobine's teaching there is a mystic strain, a kind of Immediacy, as Mrs. Swoffer calls it. . . Immediacy. . ." Pauline lingered on the term. It captivated her, as any word did when she first heard it used in a new connection. "I don't know how one could define the sensation better. 'Soul-unveiling' is Gobine's expression. . . But he insists on time, on plenty of time. . . He says we are all parching our souls by too much hurry. Of course I always felt that with Alvah Loft. I felt like one of those cash-boxes they shoot along over your head in the department stores. Number one, number two, and so on—always somebody treading on your heels. Whereas Gobine absolutely refuses to be hurried. Sometimes he sees only one patient a day. When I left him he told me he thought he would not see any one else till the next morning. 'I don't want to mingle your soul with any other.' Rather beautiful, wasn't it? And he does give one a wonderful dreamy sense of rest. . ."

She closed her eyes and leaned back, evoking the gaunt bearded face and heavy-lidded eyes of the new prophet, and the moist adhesive palm he had laid in benediction on her forehead. How different from the thick-lipped oily Mahatma, and from the thin dry Alvah Loft, who seemed more like an implement in a laboratory than a human being! "Perhaps one needs them all in turn," Pauline murmured half-aloud, with the self-indulgence of the woman who has never had to do over an out-of-fashion garment.

"One ought to be able to pass on last year's healers to one's poor relations, oughtn't one, mother?" Nona softly mocked; but her mother disarmed her with an unresentful smile.

"Darling! I know you don't understand these things yet—only, child, I do want you to be a little on your guard against becoming BITTER, won't you? There—you don't mind your old mother's just suggesting it?"

Really Nona worried her at times—or would, if Gobine hadn't shed over her this perfumed veil of Peace. Yes—Peace: that was what she had always needed. Perfect confidence that everything would always come right in the end. Of course the other healers had taught that too; some people might say that Gobine's evangel was only the Mahatma's doctrine of the Higher Harmony. But the resemblance was merely superficial, as the Scientific Initiate had been careful to explain to her. Her previous guides had not been Initiates, and had no scientific training; they could only guess, whereas he KNEW. That was the meaning of Immediacy: direct contact with the Soul of the Invisible. How clear and beautiful he made it all! How all the little daily problems shrivelled up and vanished like a puff of smoke to eyes cleared by that initiation! And he had seen at once that Pauline was one of the few who COULD be initiated; who were worthy to be drawn out of the senseless modern rush and taken in Beyond the Veil. She closed her eyes again, and felt herself there with him. . . "Of course he treats hardly anybody," Mrs. Swoffer had assured her; "not one in a hundred. He says he'd rather starve than waste his time on the unmystical. (He saw at once that you were mystical.) Because he takes time—he must have it. . . Days, weeks, if necessary. Our crowded engagements mean nothing to him. He won't have a clock in the house. And he doesn't care whether he's paid or not; he says he's paid in soul-growth. Marvellous, isn't it?"

Marvellous indeed! And how different from Alvah Loft's Taylorized treatments, his rapidly rising scale of charges, and the unbroken stream of patients succeeding each other under his bony touch! And how one came back from communion with the Invisible longing to help others, to draw all one's dear ones with one Beyond the Veil. Pauline had gone to town with an unavowed burden on her mind. Jim, Lita, her husband, that blundering Amalasuntha, that everlasting Michelangelo; and Nona, too—Nona, who looked thinner and more drawn every day, and whose tongue seemed to grow sharper and more derisive; who seemed—at barely twenty—to be turning from a gay mocking girl into a pinched fault-finding old maid. . .

All these things had weighed on Pauline more than she cared to acknowledge; but now she felt strong enough to lift them, or rather they had become as light as air. "If only you Americans would persuade yourselves of the utter unimportance of the Actual—of the total non-existence of the Real." That was what Gobine had said, and the words had thrilled her like a revelation. Her eyes continued to rest with an absent smile on her daughter's ironic face, but what she was really thinking of was: "How on earth can I possibly induce him to come to the Cardinal's reception?"

That was one of the things that Nona would never understand her caring about. She would credit—didn't Pauline know!—her mother with the fatuous ambition to use her united celebrities for a social "draw," as a selfish child might gather all its toys into one heap; she would never see how important it was to bring together the representatives of the conflicting creeds, the bearers of the multiple messages, in the hope of drawing from their contact the flash of revelation for which the whole creation groaned. "If only the Cardinal could have a quiet talk with Gobine," Pauline thought; and, immediately dramatizing the possibility, saw herself steering his Eminence toward the innermost recess of her long suite of drawing-rooms, where the Scientific Initiate, shaggy but inspired, would suddenly stand before the Prince of the Church while she guarded the threshold from intruders. What new life it might put into the ossified Roman dogmas if the Cardinal could be made to understand that beautiful new doctrine of Immediacy! But how could she ever persuade Gobine to kiss the ring?

"And Mrs. Bruss—any news? I thought Maisie seemed really hopeful."

"Yes; the night wasn't bad. The doctors think she'll go on all right—for the present."

Pauline frowned; it was distasteful to have the suggestion of suffering and decay obtruded upon her beatific mood. She was living in a world where such things were not, and it seemed cruel— and unnecessary—to suggest to her that perhaps all Mrs. Bruss had already endured might not avail to spare her future misery.

"I'm sure we ought to try to resist looking ahead, and creating imaginary suffering for ourselves or others. Why should the doctors say 'for the present'? They can't possibly tell if the disease will ever come back."

"No; but they know it generally does."

"Can't you see, Nona, that that's just what MAKES it? Being prepared to suffer is really the way to create suffering. And creating suffering is creating sin, because sin and suffering are really one. We ought to refuse ourselves to pain. All the great Healers have taught us that."

Nona lifted her eyebrows in the slightly disturbing way she had. "Did Christ?"

Pauline felt her colour rise. This habit of irrelevant and rather impertinent retort was growing on Nona. The idea of stirring up the troublesome mysteries of Christian dogma at the breakfast- table! Pauline had no intention of attacking any religion. But Nona was really getting as querulous as a teething child. Perhaps that was what she was, morally; perhaps some new experience was forcing its way through the tender flesh of her soul. The suggestion was disturbing to all Pauline's theories; yet confronted with her daughter's face and voice she could only take refuge in the idea that Nona, unable to attain the Higher Harmony, was struggling in a crepuscular wretchedness from which she refused to be freed.

"If you'd only come to Gobine with me, dear, these problems would never trouble you any more."

"They don't now—not an atom. What troubles me is the plain human tangle, as it remains after we've done our best to straighten it out. Look at Mrs. Bruss!"

"But the doctors say there's every chance—"

"Did you ever know them not to, after a first operation for cancer?"

"Of course, Nona, if you take sorrow and suffering for granted—"

"I don't, mother; but, apparently, Somebody does, judging from their diffusion and persistency, as the natural history books say."

Pauline felt her smooth brows gather in an unwelcome frown. The child had succeeded in spoiling her breakfast and in unsettling the happy equilibrium which she had imparted to her world. She didn't know what ailed Nona, unless she was fretting over Stan Heuston's disgraceful behaviour; but if so, it was better that she should learn in time what he was, and face her disillusionment. She might actually have ended by falling in love with him, Pauline reflected, and that would have been very disagreeable on account of Aggie. "What she needs is to marry," Pauline said to herself, struggling back to serenity.

She glanced at her watch, wondered if it were worth while to wait any longer for her husband, and decided to instruct Powder to keep his breakfast hot, and produce fresh coffee and rice-cakes when he rang.

Dexter, the day before, had taken Lita off on another long excursion. They had turned up so late that dinner had to be postponed for them, and had been so silent and remote all the evening that Pauline had ventured a jest on the soporific effects of country air, and suggested that every one should go to bed early. This morning, though it was past ten o'clock, neither of the two had appeared; and Nona declared herself ignorant of their plans for the day.

"It's a mercy Lita is so satisfied here," Pauline sighed, resigning herself to another dull day at the thought of the miracle Manford was accomplishing. She had felt rather nervous when Amalasuntha had appeared with her incredible film stories, and her braggings about the irresistible Michelangelo; but Lita did not seem to have been unsettled by them.

"Jim will have a good deal to be grateful for when he gets home," Pauline smiled to her daughter. "I do hope he'll appreciate what your father has done. His staying on the island seems to show that he does. By the way," she added, with another smile, "I didn't tell you, did I, that I ran across Arthur yesterday?"

Nona hesitated a moment. "So did I."

"Oh, did you? He didn't mention it. He looks better, don't you think so? But I found him excited and restless—almost as if another attack of gout were coming on. He was annoyed because I wouldn't go and see him then and there, though it was after six, and I should have had to dine in town."

"It's just as well you didn't, after such a tiring day."

"He was so persistent—you know how he is at times. He insisted that he must have a talk with me, though he wouldn't tell me about what."

"I don't believe he knows. As you say, he's always nervous when he has an attack coming on."

"But he seemed so hurt at my refusing. He wanted me to promise to go back today. And when I told him I couldn't he said that if I didn't he'd come out here."

Nona gave an impatient shrug. "How absurd! But of course he won't. I don't exactly see dear old Exhibit walking up to the front door of Cedarledge."

Pauline's colour rose again; she too had pictured the same possibility, only to reject it. Wyant had always refused to cross her threshold in New York, though she lived in a house bought after her second marriage; surely he would be still more reluctant to enter Cedarledge, where he and she had spent their early life together, and their son had been born. There were certain things, as he was always saying, that a man didn't do: that was all.

Nona was still pondering. "I wouldn't go to town to see him, mother; why should you? He was excited, and rather cross, yesterday, but he really hadn't anything to say. He just wanted to hear himself talk. As long as we're here he'll never come, and when this mood passes off he won't even remember what it was about. If you like I'll write and tell him that you'll see him as soon as we get back."

"Thank you, dear. I wish you would."

How sensible the child could be when she chose! Her answer chimed exactly with her mother's secret inclination, and the latter, rising from the breakfast-table, decided to slip away to a final revision of the Cardinal's list. It was pleasant, for once, to have time to give so important a matter all the attention it deserved.

XXVIII

When Nona came down the next morning it was raining—a cold blustery rain, lashing the branches about and driving the startled spring back into its secret recesses.

It was the first rain since their arrival at Cedarledge, and it seemed to thrust them back also—back into the wintry world of town, of dripping streets, early lamplight and crowded places of amusement.

Mrs. Manford had already breakfasted and left the dining-room, but her husband's plate was still untouched. He came in as Nona was finishing, and after an absent-minded nod and smile dropped silently into his place. He sat opposite the tall rain-striped windows, and as he stared out into the grayness it seemed as if some of it, penetrating into the room in spite of the red sparkle of the fire, had tinged his face and hair. Lately Nona had been struck by his ruddiness, and the vigour of the dark waves crisping about his yellow-brown temples; but now he had turned sallow and autumnal. "What people call looking one's age, I suppose—as if we didn't have a dozen or a hundred ages, all of us!"

Her father had withdrawn his stare from the outer world and turned it toward the morning paper on the book-stand beside his plate. With lids lowered and fixed lips he looked strangely different again—rather like his own memorial bust in bronze. She shivered a little. . .

"Father! Your coffee's getting cold."

He pushed aside the paper, glanced at the letters piled by his plate, and lifted his eyes to Nona's. The twinkle she always woke seemed to struggle up to her from a long way off.

"I missed my early tramp and don't feel particularly enthusiastic about breakfast."

"It's not enthusiastic weather."

"No." He had grown absent-minded again. "Pity; when we've so few days left."

"It may clear, though."

What stupid things they were saying! Much either he or she cared about the weather, when they were in the country and had the prospect of a good tramp or a hard gallop together. Not that they had had many such lately; but then she had been busy with her mother, trying to make up for Maisie's absence; and there had been the interruption caused by the week-end party; and he had been helping to keep Lita amused—with success, apparently.

"Yes. . . I shouldn't wonder if it cleared." He frowned out toward the sky again. "Round about midday." He paused, and added: "I thought of running Lita over to Greystock."

She nodded. They would no doubt stay and dine, and Lita would get her dance. Probably Mrs. Manford wouldn't mind, though she was beginning to show signs of wearying of tête-à-tête dinners with her daughter. But they could go over the reception list again; and Pauline could talk about her new Messiah.

Nona glanced down at her own letters. She often forgot to look at them till the day was nearly over, now that she knew the one writing her eyes thirsted for would not be on any of the envelopes. Stanley Heuston had made no sign since they had parted that night on the doorstep. . .

The door opened, and Lita came in. It was the first time since their arrival that she had appeared at breakfast. She faced Manford as she entered, and Nona saw her father's expression change. It was like those funny old portraits in the picture- restorers' windows, with a veil of age and dust removed from one half to show the real surface underneath. Lita's entrance did not make him look either younger or happier; it simply removed from his face the soul-disguising veil which life interposes between a man's daily world and himself. He looked stripped—exposed . . . exposed . . . that was it. Nona glanced at Lita, not to surprise her off her guard, but simply to look away from her father.

Lita's face was what it always was: something so complete and accomplished that one could not imagine its being altered by any interior disturbance.

It was like a delicate porcelain vase, or a smooth heavy flower, that a shifting of light might affect, but nothing from within would alter. She smiled in her round-eyed unseeing way, as a little gold-and-ivory goddess might smile down on her worshippers, and said: "I got up early because there wasn't any need to."

The reason was one completely satisfying to herself, but its effect on her hearers was perhaps disappointing. Nona made no comment, and Manford merely laughed—a vague laugh addressed, one could see, less to her words, which he appeared not to have noticed, than to the mere luminous fact of her presence; the kind of laugh evoked by the sight of a dazzling fringed fish or flower suddenly offered to one's admiration.

"I think the rain will hold off before lunch," he said, communicating the fact impartially to the room.

"Oh, what a pity—I wanted to get my hair thoroughly drenched. It's beginning to uncurl with the long drought," Lita said, her hand wavering uncertainly between the dishes Powder had placed in front of her. "Grape-fruit, I think—though it's so awfully ocean- voyagy. Promise me, Nona—!" She turned to her sister-in-law.

"Promise you what?"

"Not to send me a basket of grape-fruit when I sail."

Manford looked up at her impenetrable porcelain face. His lips half parted on an unspoken word; then he pushed back his chair and got up.

"I'll order the car at eleven," he said, in a tone of aimless severity.

Lita was scooping a spoonful of juice out of the golden bowl of the grape-fruit. She seemed neither to heed nor to hear. Manford laid down his napkin and walked out of the room.

Lita threw back her head to let the liquid slip slowly down between her lips. Her gold-fringed lids fluttered a little, as if the fruit-juice were a kiss.

"When are you sailing?" Nona asked, reaching for the cigarette- lighter.

"Don't know. Next week, I shouldn't wonder."

"For any particular part of the globe?"

Lita's head descended, and she turned her chestnut-coloured eyes softly on her sister-in-law. "Yes; but I can't remember what it's called."

Nona was looking at her in silence. It was simply that she was so beautiful. A vase? No—a lamp now: there WAS a glow from the interior. As if her red corpuscles had turned into millions of fairy lamps. . .

Her glance left Nona's and returned to her plate. "Letters. What a bore! Why on earth don't people telephone?"

She did not often receive letters, her congenital inability to answer them having gradually cooled the zeal of her correspondents; of all, that is, excepting her husband. Almost every day Nona saw one of Jim's gray-blue envelopes on the hall table. That particular colour had come to symbolize to her a state of patient expectancy.

Lita was turning over some impersonal looking bills and advertisements. From beneath them the faithful gray-blue envelope emerged. Nona thought: "If only he wouldn't—!" and her eyes filled.

Lita looked pensively at the post-mark and then laid the envelope down unopened.

"Aren't you going to read your letter?"

She raised her brows. "Jim's? I did—yesterday. One just like it."

"Lita! You're—you're perfectly beastly!"

Lita's languid mouth rounded into a smile. "Not to you, darling. Do you want me to read it?" She slipped a polished finger-tip under the flap.

"Oh, no; no! Don't—not like that!" It made Nona wince. "I wish she HATED Jim—I wish she wanted to kill him! I could bear it better than this," the girl stormed inwardly. She got up and turned toward the door.

"Nona—wait! What's the matter? Don't you really want to hear what he says?" Lita stood up also, her eyes still on the open letter. "He—oh. . ." She turned toward her sister-in-law a face from which the inner glow had vanished.

"What is it? Is he ill? What's wrong?"

"He's coming home. He wants me to go back the day after tomorrow." She stood staring in front of her, her eyes fixed on something invisible to Nona, and beyond her.

"Does he say why?"

"He doesn't say anything but that."

"When did you expect him?"

"I don't know. Not for ages. I never can remember about dates. But I thought he liked it down there. And your father said he'd arranged—"

"Arranged what?" Nona interrupted.

Lita seemed to become aware of her again, and turned on her a smooth inaccessible face. "I don't know: arranged with the bank, I suppose."

"To keep him there?"

"To let him have a good long holiday. You all thought he needed it so awfully, didn't you?"

Nona stood motionless, staring out of the window. She saw her father drive up in the Buick. The rain had diminished to a silver drizzle shot with bursts of sun, and through the open window she heard him call: "It's going to clear after all. We'd better start."

Lita went out of the door, humming a tune.

"Lita!" Nona called out, moved by some impulse to arrest, to warn— she didn't know what. But the door had closed, and Lita was already out of hearing.

All through the day it kept on raining at uncomfortable intervals. Uncomfortable, that is, for Pauline and Nona. Whenever they tried to get out for a walk a deluge descended; then, as soon as they had splashed back to the house with the dripping dogs, the clouds broke and mocked them with a blaze of sunshine. But by that time they were either revising the list again, or had settled down to Mah-jongg in the library.

"Really, I can't go up and change into my walking shoes AGAIN!" Pauline remonstrated to the weather; and a few minutes later the streaming window-panes had justified her.

"April showers," she remarked with a slightly rigid smile. She looked deprecatingly at her daughter. "It was selfish of me to keep you here, dear. You ought to have gone with your father and Lita."

"But there were all those notes to do, mother. And really I'm rather fed-up with Greystock."

Pauline executed a repetition of her smile. "Well, I fancy we shall have them back for tea. No golf this afternoon, I'm afraid," she said, glancing with a certain furtive satisfaction at the increasing downpour.

"No; but Lita may want to stay and dance."

Pauline made no comment, but once more addressed her disciplined attention to the game.

The fire, punctually replenished, continued to crackle and drowse. The warmth drew out the strong scent of the carnations and rose-geraniums, and made the room as languid as a summer garden. Dusk fell from the cloud-laden skies, and in due course the hand which tended the fire drew the curtains on their noiseless rings and lit the lamps. Lastly Powder appeared, heading the processional entrance of the tea-table.

Pauline roused herself from a languishing Mah-jongg to take her expected part in the performance. She and Nona grouped themselves about the hearth, and Pauline lifted the lids of the little covered dishes with a critical air.

"I ordered those muffins your father likes so much," she said, in a tone of unwonted wistfulness. "Perhaps we'd better send them out to be kept hot."

Nona agreed that it would be better; but as she had her hand on the bell the sound of an approaching motor checked her. The dogs woke with a happy growling and bustled out. "There they are after all!" Pauline said.

There was a minute or two of silence, unmarked by the usual yaps of welcome; then a sound like the depositing of wraps and an umbrella; then Powder on the threshold, for once embarrassed and at a loss.

"Mr. Wyant, madam."

"Mr. Wyant?"

"Mr. Arthur Wyant. He seemed to think you were probably expecting him," Powder continued, as if lengthening the communication in order to give her time.

Mrs. Manford, seizing it, rose to the occasion with one of her heroic wing-beats. "Yes—I WAS. Please show him in," she said, without risking a glance at her daughter.

Arthur Wyant came in, tall and stooping in his shabby well-cut clothes, a nervous flush on his cheekbones. He paused, and sent a half-bewildered stare about the room—a look which seemed to say that when he had made up his mind that he must see Pauline he had failed to allow for the familiarity of the setting in which he was to find her.

"You've hardly changed anything here," he said abruptly, in the far- off tone of a man slowly coming back to consciousness.

"How are you, Arthur? I'm sorry you've had such a rainy day for your trip," Mrs. Manford responded, with an easy intonation intended to reach the retreating Powder.

Her former husband took no notice. His eyes continued to travel about the room in the same uncertain searching way.

"Hardly anything," he repeated, still seemingly unaware of any presence in the room but his own. "That Raeburn, though—yes. That used to be in the dining-room, didn't it?" He passed his hand over his forehead, as if to brush away some haze of oblivion, and walked up to the picture.

"Wait a bit. It's in the place where the Sargent of Jim as a youngster used to hang—Jim on his pony. Just over my writing- table, so that I saw it whenever I looked up. . ." He turned to Pauline. "Jolly picture. What have you done with it? Why did you take it away?"

Pauline coloured, but a smile of conciliation rode gallantly over her blush. "I didn't. That is—Dexter wanted it. It's in his room; it's been there for years." She paused, and then added: "You know how devoted Dexter is to Jim."

Wyant had turned abruptly from the contemplation of the Raeburn. The colour in Pauline's cheek was faintly reflected in his own. "Stupid of me . . . of course. . . Fact is, I was rather rattled when I came in, seeing everything so much the same. . . You must excuse my turning up in this way; I had to see you about something important. . . Hullo, Nona—"

"Of course I excuse you, Arthur. Do sit down—here by the fire. You must be cold after your wet journey . . . so unseasonable, after the weather we've been having. Nona will ring for tea," Pauline said, with her accent of indomitable hospitality.

XXIX

Nona, that night, in her mother's doorway, wavered a moment and then turned back. "Well, then—goodnight, mother."

"Goodnight, child."

But Mrs. Manford seemed to waver too. She stood there in her rich dusky draperies, and absently lifted a hand to detach one after the other of her long earrings. It was one of Mrs. Manford's rules never to keep up her maid to undress her.

"Can I unfasten you, mother?"

"Thanks, dear, no; this teagown slips off so easily. You must be tired. . ."

"No; I'm not tired. But you. . ."

"I'm not either." They stood irresolute on the threshold of the warm shadowy room lit only by a waning sparkle from the hearth. Pauline switched on the lamps.

"Come in then, dear." Her strained smile relaxed, and she laid a hand on her daughter's shoulder. "Well, it's over," she said, in the weary yet satisfied tone in which Nona had sometimes heard her pronounce the epitaph of a difficult but successful dinner.

Nona followed her, and Pauline sank down in an armchair near the fire. In the shaded lamplight, with the glint of the fire playing across her face, and her small head erect on still comely shoulders, she had a sweet dignity of aspect which moved her daughter incongruously.

"I'm so thankful you've never bobbed your hair, mother."

Mrs. Manford stared at this irrelevancy; her stare seemed to say that she was resigned to her daughter's verbal leaps, but had long since renounced the attempt to keep up with them.

"You're so handsome just as you are," Nona continued. "I can understand dear old Exhibit's being upset when he saw you here, in the same surroundings, and looking, after all, so much as you must have in his day. . . And when he himself is so changed. . ."

Pauline lowered her lids over the vision. "Yes. Poor Arthur!" Had she ever, for the last fifteen years, pronounced her former husband's name without adding that depreciatory epithet? Somehow pity—an indulgent pity—was always the final feeling he evoked. She leaned back against the cushions, and added: "It was certainly unfortunate, his taking it into his head to come out here. I didn't suppose he would have remembered so clearly how everything looked. . . The Sargent of Jim on the pony. . . Do you think he minded?"

"Its having been moved to father's room? Yes; I think he did."

"But, Nona, he's always been so grateful to your father for what he's done for Jim—and for Lita. He ADMIRES your father. He's often told me so."

"Yes."

"At any rate, once he was here, I couldn't do less than ask him to stay to dine."

"No; you couldn't. Especially as there was no train back till after dinner."

"And, after all, I don't, to this minute, know what he came for!"

Nona lifted her eyes from an absorbed contemplation of the fire. "You don't?"

"Oh, of course, in a vague way, to talk about Jim and Lita. The same old things we've heard so many times. But I quieted him very soon about that. I told him Lita had been perfectly happy here— that the experiment had been a complete success. He seemed surprised that she had given up all her notions about Hollywood and Klawhammer . . . apparently Amalasuntha has been talking a lot of nonsense to him . . . but when I said that Lita had never once spoken of Hollywood, and that she was going home the day after tomorrow to join her husband, it seemed to tranquillize him completely. Didn't he seem to you much quieter when he drove off?"

"Yes; he was certainly quieter. But he seemed to want particularly to see Lita."

Pauline drew a quick breath. "Yes. On the whole I was glad she wasn't here. Lita has never known how to manage Arthur, and her manner is sometimes so irritating. She might have said something that would have upset him again. It was really a relief when your father telephoned that they had decided to dine at Greystock— though I could see that Arthur thought that funny too. His ideas have never progressed an inch; he's always remained as old-fashioned as his mother." She paused a moment, and then went on: "I saw you were a little startled when I asked him if he wouldn't like to spend the night. But I didn't want to appear inhospitable."

"No; not in this house," Nona agreed with her quick smile. "And of course one knew he wouldn't—"

Pauline sighed. "Poor Arthur! He's always so punctilious."

"It wasn't only that. He was suffering horribly."

"About Lita? So foolish! As if he couldn't trust her to us—"

"Not only about Lita. But just from the fact of being here—of having all his old life thrust back on him. He seemed utterly unprepared for it—as if he'd really succeeded in not thinking about it at all for years. And suddenly there it was: like the drowning man's vision. A drowning man—that's what he was like."

Pauline straightened herself slightly, and Nona saw her brows gather in a faint frown. "What dreadful ideas you have! I thought I'd never seen him looking better; and certainly he didn't take too much wine at dinner."

"No; he was careful about that."

"And I was careful too. I managed to give a hint to Powder." Her frown relaxed, and she leaned back with another sigh, this time of appeasement. After all, her look seemed to say, she was not going to let herself be unsettled by Nona's mortuary images, now that the whole business was over, and she had every reason to congratulate herself on her own share in it.

Nona (but it was her habit!) appeared less sure. She hung back a moment, and then said: "I haven't told you yet. On the way down to dinner. . ."

"What, dear?"

"I met him on the upper landing. He asked to see the baby . . . that was natural. . ."

Pauline drew her lips in nervously. She had thought she had all the wires in her hands; and here was one—She agreed with an effort: "Perfectly natural."

"The baby was asleep, looking red and jolly. He stood over the crib a long time. Luckily it wasn't the old nursery."

"Really, Nona! He could hardly expect—"

"No; of course not. Then, just as we were going downstairs, he said: 'Funny, how like Jim the child is growing. Reminds me of that old portrait.' And he jerked out at me: 'Could I see it?'"

"What—the Sargent?"

Nona nodded. "Could I refuse him?"

"I suppose that was natural too."

"So I took him into father's study. He seemed to remember every step of the way. He stood and looked and looked at the picture. He didn't say anything . . . didn't answer when I spoke. . . I saw that it went through and through him."

"Well, Nona, byegones are byegones. But people do bring things upon themselves, sometimes—"

"Oh, I know, mother."

"Some people might think it peculiar, his rambling about the house like that—his coming here at all, with his ideas of delicacy! But I don't blame him; and I don't want you to," Pauline continued firmly. "After all, it's just as well he came. He may have been a little upset at the moment; but I managed to calm him down; and I certainly proved to him that everything's all right, and that Dexter and I can be trusted to know what's best for Lita." She paused, and then added: "Do you know, I'm rather inclined not to mention his visit to your father—or to Lita. Now it's over, why should they be bothered?"

"No reason at all." Nona rose from her crouching attitude by the fire, and stretched her arms above her head. "I'll see that Powder doesn't say anything. And besides, he wouldn't. He always seems to know what needs explaining and what doesn't. He ought to be kept to avert cataclysms, like those fire-extinguishers in the passages. . . Goodnight, mother—I'm beginning to be sleepy."

Yes; it was all over and done with; and Pauline felt that she had a right to congratulate herself. She had not told Nona how "difficult" Wyant had been for the first few minutes, when the girl had slipped out of the library after tea and left them alone. What was the use of going into all that? Pauline had been a little nervous at first—worried, for instance, as to what might happen if Dexter and Lita should walk in while Arthur was in that queer excited state, stamping up and down the library floor, and muttering, half to himself and half to her: "Damn it, am I in my own house or another man's? Can anybody answer me that?"

But they had not walked in, and the phase of excitability had soon been over. Pauline had only had to answer: "You're in MY house, Arthur, where, as Jim's father, you're always welcome. . ." That had put a stop to his ravings, shamed him a little, and so brought him back to his sense of what was due to the occasion, and to his own dignity.

"My dear—you must excuse me. I'm only an intruder here, I know—"

And when she had added: "Never in my house, Arthur. Sit down, please, and tell me what you want to see me about—" why, at that question, quietly and reasonably put, all his bluster had dropped, and he had sat down as she bade him, and begun, in his ordinary tone, to rehearse the old rigmarole about Jim and Lita, and Jim's supineness, and Lita's philanderings, and what would the end of it be, and did she realize that the woman was making a laughing-stock of their son—yes, that they were talking about it at the clubs?

After that she had had no trouble. It had been easy to throw a little gentle ridicule over his apprehensions, and then to reassure him by her report of her own talk with Lita (though she winced even now at its conclusion), and the affirmation that the Cedarledge experiment had been entirely successful. Then, luckily, just as his questions began to be pressing again—as he began to hint at some particular man, she didn't know who—Powder had come in to show him up to one of the spare-rooms to prepare for dinner; and soon after dinner the motor was at the door, and Powder (again acting for Providence) had ventured to suggest, sir, that in view of the slippery state of the roads it would be well to get off as promptly as possible. And Nona had taken over the seeing-off, and with a long sigh of relief Pauline had turned back into the library, where Wyant's empty whisky-and-soda glass and ash-tray stood, so uncannily, on the table by her husband's armchair. Yes; she had been thankful when it was over. . .

And now she was thankful that it had happened. The encounter had fortified her confidence in her own methods and given her a new proof of her power to surmount obstacles by smiling them away. She had literally smiled Arthur out of the house, when some women, in a similar emergency, would have made a scene, or stood on their dignity. Dignity! Hers consisted, more than ever, in believing the best of every one, in persuading herself and others that to impute evil was to create it, and to disbelieve it was to prevent its coming into being. Those were the Scientific Initiate's very words: "We manufacture sorrow as we do all the other toxins." How grateful she was to him for that formula! And how light and happy it made her feel to know that she had borne it in mind, and proved its truth, at so crucial a moment! She looked back with pity at her own past moods of distrust, her wretched impulses of jealousy and suspicion, the moments when even those nearest her had not been proof against her morbid apprehensions. . .

How absurd and far away it all seemed now! Jim was coming back the day after tomorrow. Lita and the baby were going home to him. And the day after that they would all be going back to town; and then the last touches would be put to the ceremonial of the Cardinal's reception. Oh, she and Powder would have their hands full! All of the big silver-gilt service would have to be got out of the safety vaults and gone over. . . Luckily the last reports of Mrs. Bruss's state were favourable, and no doubt Maisie would be back as usual. . . Yes, life was really falling into its usual busy and pleasurable routine. Rest in the country was all very well; but rest, if overdone, became fatiguing. . .

She found herself in bed, the lights turned off, and sleep descending on her softly.

Before it held her, she caught, through misty distances, the sound of her husband's footfall, the opening and shutting of his door, and the muffled noises of his undressing. Well . . . so he was back . . . and Lita . . . silly Lita . . . no harm, really. . . Just as well they hadn't met poor Arthur. . . Everything was all right . . . the Cardinal. . .

XXX

Pauline sat up suddenly in bed. It was as if an invisible hand had touched a spring in her spinal column, and set her upright in the darkness before she was aware of any reason for it.

No doubt she had heard something through her sleep; but what? She listened for a repetition of the sound.

All was silence. She stretched out her hand to an onyx knob on the table by her bed, and instantly the face of a miniature clock was illuminated, and the hour chimed softly; two strokes followed by one. Half-past two—the silentest hour of the night; and in the vernal hush of Cedarledge! Yet certainly there had been a sound— a sharp explosive sound. . . Again! There it was: a revolver shot . . . somewhere in the house. . .

Burglars?

Her feet were in her slippers, her hand on the electric light switch. All the while she continued to listen intently. Dead silence everywhere. . .

But how had burglars got in without starting the alarm? Ah—she remembered! Powder had orders never to set it while any one was out of the house; it was Dexter who should have seen that it was connected when he got back from Greystock with Lita. And naturally he had forgotten to.

Pauline was on her feet, her hair smoothed back under her fillet- shaped cap of silver lace, her "rest-gown" of silvery silk slipped over her night-dress. This emergency garb always lay at her bedside in case of nocturnal alarms, and she was equipped in an instant, and had already reconnected the burglar-alarm, and sounded the general summons for Powder, the footmen, the gardeners and chauffeurs. Her hand played irresolutely over the complicated knobs of the glittering switchboard which filled a panel of her dressing-room; then she pressed the button marked "Engine-house." Why not? There had been a series of bad suburban burglaries lately, and one never knew. . . It was just as well to rouse the neighbourhood. . . Dexter was so careless. Very likely he had left the front door open.

Silence still—profounder than ever. Not a sound since that second shot, if shot it was. Very softly she opened her door and paused in the anteroom between her room and her husband's. "Dexter!" she called.

No answer; no responding flash of light. Men slept so heavily. She opened, lighted—"Dexter!"

The room was empty, her husband's bed unslept in. But then—what? Those sounds of his return? Had she been dreaming when she thought she heard them? Or was it the burglars she had heard, looting his room, a few feet off from where she lay? In spite of her physical courage a shiver ran over her. . .

But if Dexter and Lita were not yet back, whence had the sound of the shot come, and who had fired it? She trembled at the thought of Nona—Nona and the baby! They were alone with the baby's nurse on the farther side of the house. And the house seemed suddenly so immense, so resonant, so empty. . .

In the shadowy corridor outside her room she paused again for a second, straining her ears for a guiding sound; then she sped on, pushing back the swinging door which divided the farther wing from hers, turning on the lights with a flying hand as she ran. . . On the deeply carpeted floors her foot-fall made no sound, and she had the sense of skimming over the ground inaudibly, like something ghostly, disembodied, which had no power to break the hush and make itself heard. . .

Half way down the passage she was startled to see the door of Lita's bedroom open. Sounds at last—sounds low, confused and terrified—issued from it. What kind of sounds? Pauline could not tell; they were rushing together in a vortex in her brain. She heard herself scream "Help!" with the strangled voice of a nightmare, and was comforted to feel the rush of other feet behind her: Powder, the men-servants, the maids. Thank God the system worked! Whatever she was coming to, at least they would be there to help. . .

She reached the door, pushed it—and it unexpectedly resisted. Some one was clinging to it on the inner side, struggling to hold it shut, to prevent her entering. She threw herself against it with all her strength, and saw her husband's arm and hand in the gap. "Dexter!"

"Oh, God." He fell back, and the door with him. Pauline went in.

All the lights were on—the room was a glare. Another man stood shivering and staring in a corner, but Pauline hardly noticed him, for before her on the floor lay Lita's long body, in a loose spangled robe, flung sobbing over another body.

"Nona—Nona!" the mother screamed, rushing forward to where they lay.

She swept past her husband, dragged Lita back, was on her knees on the floor, her child pressed to her, Nona's fallen head against her breast, Nona's blood spattering the silvery folds of the rest-gown, destroying it forever as a symbol of safety and repose.

"Nona—child! What's happened? Are you hurt? Dexter—for pity's sake! Nona, look at me! It's mother, darling, mother—"

Nona's eyes opened with a flutter. Her face was ashen-white, and empty as a baby's. Slowly she met her mother's agonized stare. "All right . . . only winged me." Her gaze wavered about the disordered room, lifting and dropping in a butterfly's bewildered flight. Lita lay huddled on the couch in her spangles, twisted and emptied, like a festal garment flung off by its wearer. Manford stood between, his face a ruin. In the corner stood that other man, shrinking, motionless. Pauline's eyes, following her child's, travelled on to him.

"Arthur!" she gasped out, and felt Nona's feeble pressure on her arm.

"Don't . . . don't. . . It was an accident. Father—an accident! FATHER!"

The door of the room was wide now, and Powder stood there, unnaturally thin and gaunt in his improvised collarless garb, marshalling the gaping footmen, with gardeners, chauffeurs and maids crowding the corridor behind them. It was really marvellous, how Pauline's system had worked.

Manford turned to Arthur Wyant, his stony face white with revenge. Wyant still stood motionless, his arms hanging down, his body emptied of all its strength, a broken word that sounded like "honour" stumbling from his bedraggled lips.

"FATHER!" At Nona's faint cry Manford's arm fell to his side also, and he stood there as powerless and motionless as the other.

"All an accident . . ." breathed from the white lips against Pauline.

Powder had stepped forward. His staccato orders rang back over his shoulder. "Ring up the doctor. Have a car ready. Scour the gardens. . . One of the women here! Madam's maid!"

Manford suddenly roused himself and swung about with dazed eyes on the disheveled group in the doorway. "Damn you, what are you doing here, all of you? Get out—get out, the lot of you! Get out, I say! Can't you hear me?"

Powder bent a respectful but controlling eye on his employer. "Yes, sir; certainly, sir. I only wish to state that the burglar's mode of entrance has already been discovered." Manford met this with an unseeing stare, but the butler continued imperturbably: "Thanks to the rain, sir. He got in through the pantry window; the latch was forced, and there's muddy footprints on my linoleum, sir. A tramp was noticed hanging about this afternoon. I can give evidence—"

He darted swiftly between the two men, bent to the floor, and picked up something which he slipped quickly and secretly into his pocket. A moment later he had cleared his underlings from the threshold, and the door was shut on them and him.

"Dexter," Pauline cried, "help me to lift her to the bed."

Outside, through the watchful hush of the night, a rattle and roar came up the drive. It filled the silence with an unnatural clamour, immense, mysterious and menacing. It was the Cedarledge fire-brigade, arriving double quick in answer to their benefactress's summons.

Pauline, bending over her daughter's face, fancied she caught a wan smile on it. . .

XXXI

Nona Manford's room was full of spring flowers. They had poured in, sent by sympathizing friends, ever since she had been brought back to town from Cedarledge.

That was two weeks ago. It was full spring now, and her windows stood wide to the May sunset slanting across the room, and giving back to the tall branches of blossoming plum and cherry something of their native scent and freshness.

The reminder of Cedarledge would once have doubled their beauty; now it made her shut her eyes sharply, in the inner recoil from all the name brought back.

She was still confined to her room, for the shot which had fractured her arm near the shoulder had also grazed her lung, and her temperature remained obstinately high. Shock, the doctors said, chiefly . . . the appalling sight of a masked burglar in her sister-in-law's bedroom; and being twice fired at—twice!

Lita corroborated the story. She had been asleep when her door was softly opened, and she had started up to see a man in a mask, with a dark lantern. . . Yes; she was almost sure he had a mask; at any rate she couldn't see his face; the police had found the track of muddy feet on the pantry linoleum, and up the back stairs.

Lita had screamed, and Nona had dashed to the rescue; yes, and Mr. Manford—Lita thought Mr. Manford had perhaps got there before Nona. But then again, she wasn't sure. . . The fact was that Lita had been shattered by the night's experience, and her evidence, if not self-contradictory, was at least incoherent.

The only really lucid witnesses were Powder, the butler, and Nona Manford herself. Their statements agreed exactly, or at least dovetailed into each other with perfect precision, the one completing the other. Nona had been first on the scene: she had seen the man in the room—she too thought that he was masked—and he had turned on her and fired. At that moment her father, hearing the shots, had rushed in, half-dressed; and as he did so the burglar fled. Some one professed to have seen him running away through the rain and darkness; but no one had seen his face, and there was no way of identifying him. The only positive proof of his presence—except for the shot—was the discovery by Powder, of those carefully guarded footprints on the pantry floor; and these, of course, might eventually help to trace the criminal. As for the revolver, that also had disappeared; and the bullets, one of which had been found lodged in the door, the other in the panelling of the room, were of ordinary army calibre, and offered no clue. Altogether it was an interesting problem for the police, who were reported to be actively at work on it, though so far without visible results.

Then, after three days of flaming headlines and journalistic conjectures, another sensation crowded out the Cedarledge burglary. The newspaper public, bored with the inability of the police to provide fresh fuel for their curiosity, ceased to speculate on the affair, and interest in it faded out as quickly as it had flared up.

During the last few days Nona's temperature had gradually dropped, and she had been allowed to see visitors; first one in the day, then two or three, then four or five—so that by this time her jaws were beginning to feel a little stiff with the continual rehearsal of her story, embellished (at the visitors' request) with an analysis of her own emotions. She always repeated her narrative in exactly the same terms, and presented the incidents in exactly the same order; by now she had even learned to pause at the precise point where she knew her sympathizing auditors would say: "But, my dear, how perfectly awful—what DID it feel like?"

"Like being shot in the arm."

"Oh, Nona, you're so cynical! But before that—when you SAW THE MAN—weren't you absolutely sick with terror?"

"He didn't give me time to be sick with anything but the pain in my shoulder."

"You'll never get her to confess that she was frightened!"

And so the dialogue went on. Did her listeners notice that she recited her tale with the unvarying precision of a lesson learned by heart? Probably not; if they did, they made no sign. The papers had all been full of the burglary at Cedarledge: a masked burglar—and of the shooting of Miss Manford, and the would-be murderer's escape. The account, blood-curdling and definite, had imposed itself on the public credulity with all the authority of heavy headlines and continual repetition. Within twenty-four hours the Cedarledge burglary was an established fact, and suburban millionaires were doubling the number of their night watchmen, and looking into the newest thing in burglar-alarms. Nona, leaning back wearily on her couch, wondered how soon she would be allowed to travel and get away from it all.

The others were all going to travel. Her mother and father were off that very evening to the Rocky Mountains and Vancouver. From there they were going to Japan and, in the early autumn, to Ceylon and India. Pauline already had letters to all the foremost Native Princes, and was regretting that there was not likely to be a Durbar during their visit. The Manfords did not expect to be back till January or February; Manford's professional labours had become so exhausting that the doctors, fearing his accumulated fatigue might lead to a nervous break-down, had ordered a complete change and prolonged absence from affairs. Pauline hoped that Nona would meet them in Egypt on their way home. A sunny Christmas together in Cairo would be so lovely. . .

Arthur Wyant had gone also—to Canada, it was said, with cousin Eleanor in attendance. Some insinuated that a private inebriate asylum in Maine was the goal of his journey; but no one really knew, and few cared. His remaining cronies, when they heard that he had been ill, and was to travel for a change, shrugged or smiled, and said: "Poor old Arthur—been going it too strong again," and then forgot about him. He had long since lost his place in the scheme of things.

Even Lita and Jim Wyant were on a journey. They had sailed the previous week for Paris, where they would arrive in time for the late spring season, and Lita would see the Grand Prix, the new fashions and the new plays. Jim's holiday had been extended to the end of August: Manford, ever solicitous for his stepson, had arranged the matter with the bank. It was natural, every one agreed, that Jim should have been dreadfully upset by the ghastly episode at Cedarledge, in which his wife might have been a victim as well as Nona; and his intimates knew how much he had worried about his father's growing intemperance. Altogether, both Wyants and Manfords had been subjected to an unusual strain; and when rich people's nerves are out of gear the pleasant remedy of travel is the first prescribed.

Nona turned her head uneasily on the cushions. She felt incurably weary, and unable to rebound to the spring radiance which usually set her blood in motion. Her immobility had begun to wear on her. At first it had been a relief to be quiescent, to be out of things, to be offered up as the passive victim and the accepted evidence of the Cedarledge burglary. But now she was sick to nausea of the part, and envious of the others who could escape by flight—by perpetual evasion.

Not that she really wanted to be one of them; she was not sure that she wanted to go away at all—at least in the body. Spiritual escape was what she craved; but by what means, and whither? Perhaps it could best be attained by staying just where she was, by sticking fast to her few square feet of obligations and responsibilities. But even this idea made no special appeal. Her obligations, her responsibilities—what were they? Negative, at best, like everything else in her life. She had thought that renunciation would mean freedom—would mean at least escape. But today it seemed to mean only a closer self-imprisonment. She was tired, no doubt. . .

There was a tap on the door, and her mother entered. Nona raised her listless eyes curiously. She always looked at her mother with curiosity now: curiosity not so much as to what had changed in her, but as to what had remained the same. And it was extraordinary how Pauline, the old Pauline, was coming to the surface again through the new one, the haggard and stricken apparition of the Cedarledge midnight. . .

"My broken arm saved her," Nona thought, remembering, with a sort of ironical admiration, how that dishevelled spectre had become Pauline Manford again, in command of herself and the situation, as soon as she could seize on its immediate, its practical, sides; could grasp those handles of reality to which she always clung.

Now even that stern and disciplined figure had vanished, giving way, as the days passed and reassurance grew, to the usual, the everyday Pauline, smilingly confident in herself and in the general security of things. Had that dreadful night at Cedarledge ever been a reality to her? If it had, Nona was sure, it had already faded into the realms of fable, since its one visible result had been her daughter's injury, and that was on the way to healing. Everything else connected with it had happened out of sight and under ground, and for that reason was now as if it had never existed for Pauline, who was more than ever resolutely two-dimensional.

Physically, at least, the only difference Nona could detect was that a skilful make-up had filled in the lines which, in spite of all the arts of the face-restorers, were weaving their permanent web about her mother's lips and eyes. Under this delicate mask Pauline's face looked younger and fresher than ever, and as smooth and empty as if she had just been born again—"And she HAS, after all," Nona concluded.

She sat down by the couch, and laid a light hand caressingly on her daughter's.

"Darling! Had your tea? You feel really better, don't you? The doctor says the massage is to begin tomorrow. By the way—" she tossed a handful of newspaper cuttings onto the coverlet—"perhaps some of these things about the reception may amuse you. Maisie's been saving them to show you. Of course most of the foreign names are wrong; but the description of the room is rather good. I believe Tommy Ardwin wrote the article for the 'Looker-on.' Amalasuntha says the Cardinal will like it. It seems he was delighted with the idea of the flash-light photographs. Altogether he was very much pleased."

"Then you ought to be, mother." Nona forced her pale lips into a smile.

"I AM, dear. If I do a thing at all I like to do it well. That's always been my theory, you know: the best or nothing. And I do believe it was a success. But perhaps I'm tiring you—." Pauline stood up irresolutely. She had never been good at bedsides unless she could play some active and masterful part there. Nona was aware that her mother's moments alone with her had become increasingly difficult as her strength had returned, and there was nothing more to be done for her. It was as well that the Manfords were starting on their journey that evening.

"Don't stay, mother; I'm all right, really. It's only that things still tire me a little—"

Pauline lingered, looking down on the girl with an expression of anxiety struggling through her smooth rejuvenation.

"I wish I felt happier about leaving you, darling. I know you're all right, of course; but the idea of your staying in this house all by yourself—"

"It's just what I shall like. And on father's account you ought to get away."

"It's what I feel," Pauline assented, brightening.

"You must be awfully busy with all the last things to be done. I'm as comfortable as possible; I wish you'd just go off and forget about me."

"Well, Maisie IS clamouring for me," Pauline confessed from the threshold.

The door shut, and Nona closed her eyes with a sigh. Tomorrow—tomorrow she would be alone! And in a week, perhaps, she would get back to Cedarledge, and lie on the terrace with the dogs about her, and no one to ask questions, to hint and sympathize, or be discreet and evasive. . .

Yes, in spite of everything, the idea of returning to Cedarledge now seemed more bearable than any other. . .

In a restless attempt to ease her position she stretched her hand out, and it came in contact with the bundle of newspaper cuttings. She shrank back with a little grimace; then she smiled. After the night at Cedarledge every one had supposed—even Maisie and Powder had—that the Cardinal's reception would have to be given up, since, owing to his Eminence's impending departure, it could not be deferred. But it had come off on the appointed day—only the fourth after the burglary—and Pauline had made it a success. The girl really admired her mother for that. Something in her own composition responded to the energy with which the older woman could meet an emergency when there was no way of turning it. The party had been not only brilliant but entertaining. Every one had been there, all the official and ecclesiastical dignitaries, including the Bishop of New York and the Chief Rabbi—yes, even the Scientific Initiate, looking colossal and Siberian in some half- priestly dress that added its note to the general picturesqueness; and yet there had been no crush, no confusion, nothing to detract from the dignity and amenity of the evening. Nona suspected her mother of longing to invite the Mahatma, whose Oriental garb would have been so effective, and who would have been so flattered, poor man! But she had not risked it, and her chief lion, after the great ecclesiastics, had turned out to be Michelangelo, the newly arrived, with the film-glamour enhancing his noble Roman beauty, and his mother at his side, explaining and parading him.

"The pity is that dear Jim and Lita have sailed," the Marchesa declared to all who would give ear. "That's really a great disappointment. I did hope Lita would have been here tonight. She and my Michelangelo would have made such a glorious couple: the Old World and the New. Or as Antony and Cleopatra— only fancy! My boy tells me that Klawhammer is looking for a Cleopatra. But dear Lita will be back before long—." And she mingled her hopes and regrets with Mrs. Percy Landish's.

XXXII

Nona shut her eyes again. Ever since that intolerable night she had ached with the incessant weariness of not being able to sleep, and of trying to hide from those about her how brief her intervals of oblivion had been. During the hours of darkness she seemed to be forever toiling down perspectives of noise and glare, like a wanderer in the labyrinth of an unknown city. Even her snatches of sleep were so crowded with light and noise, so dazzled with the sense of exposure, that she was not conscious of the respite till it was over. It was only by day, alone in her room, that her lids, in closing, sometimes shut things out. . .

Such a respite came to her now; and she started up out of nothingness to find her father at her side. She had not expected to see him alone before they parted. She had fancied that her parents would contrive to postpone their joint farewells till after dinner, just before driving off to their train. For a moment she lay and looked up at Manford without being clearly conscious that he was there, and without knowing what to say if he were.

It appeared that he did not know either. Perhaps he had been led to her side, almost in spite of himself, by a vague craving to be alone with her just once before they parted; or perhaps he had come because he suspected she might think he was afraid to. He sat down without speaking in the chair which Pauline had left.

Dusk had fallen, and Nona was aware of the presence at her side only as a shadowy bulk. After a while her father put out his hand and laid it on hers.

"Why, it's nearly dark," she said. "You'll be off in an hour or so now."

"Yes. Your mother and I are dining early."

She wound her fingers into his, and they sat silent again. She liked to have him near her in this way, but she was glad, for his sake and her own, that the twilight made his face indistinct. She hoped their silence might be unbroken. As long as she neither saw nor heard him there was an unaccountable comfort in feeling him near—as if the living warmth he imparted were something they shared indissolubly.

"In a couple of hours now—" he began, with an attempt at briskness. She was silent, and he went on: "I wanted to be with you alone for a minute like this. I wanted to say—"

"Father—."

He turned suddenly in his chair, and bending down over her pressed his forehead against the coverlet. She freed her hand and passed it through the thin hair on his temples.

"Don't. There's nothing to say."

She felt a tremor of his shoulders as they pressed against her, and the tremor ran through her own body and seemed to loosen the fibres of her heart.

"Old dad."

"Nona."

After that they remained again without speaking till a clock chimed out from somewhere in the shadows. Manford got up. He gave himself one of his impatient shakes, and stooped to kiss his daughter on the forehead.

"I don't believe I'll come up again before we go."

"No."

"It's no use—"

"No."

"I'll look after your mother—do all I can. . . Goodbye, dear."

"Goodbye, father."

He groped for her forehead again, and went out of the room; and she closed her eyes and lay in the darkness, her heart folded like two hands around the thought of him.

"Nona, darling!" There were still the goodbyes to her mother to be gone through. Well, that would be comparatively easy; and in a lighted room too, with Pauline on the threshold, slim, erect and consciously equipped for travel— complete and wonderful! Yes; it would be almost easy.

"Child, it's time; we're off in a few minutes. But I think I've left everything in order. Maisie's downstairs; she has all my directions, and the list of stations to which she's to wire how you are while we're crossing the continent."

"But, mother, I'm all right; it's not a bit necessary—"

"Dear! You can't help my wanting to hear about you."

"No; I know. I only meant you're not to worry."

"Of course I won't worry; I wouldn't LET myself worry. You know how I feel about all that. And besides," added Mrs. Manford victoriously, "what in the world is there to worry about?"

"Nothing," Nona acquiesced with a smile.

Pauline bent down and placed a lingering kiss where Manford's lips had just brushed his daughter's forehead. Pauline played her part better—and made it correspondingly easier for her fellow-actors to play theirs.

"Goodbye, mother dear. Have all sorts of a good time, won't you?"

"It will be a very interesting trip—with a man as clever and cultivated as your father. . . If only you could have come with us! But you'll promise to join us in Egypt?"

"Don't ask me to promise anything yet, mother."

Pauline raised herself to her full height and stood looking down intently at her daughter. Under her smooth new face Nona again seemed to see the flicker of anxiety pass back and forward, like a light moving from window to window in a long-uninhabited house. The glimpse startled the girl and caught her by the heart. Suddenly something within her broke up. Her lips tightened like a child's, and she felt the tears running down her cheeks.

"Nona! You're not crying?" Pauline was kneeling at her side.

"It's nothing, mother—nothing. Go! Please go!"

"Darling—if I could only see you happy one of these days."

"Happy?"

"Well, I mean like other people. Married—" the mother hastily ventured.

Nona had brushed away her tears. She raised her head and looked straight at Pauline.

"Married? Do you suppose being married would make me happy? I wonder why you should! I don't want to marry—there's nobody in the world I would marry." She continued to stare up at her mother with hard unwavering eyes. "Marry! I'd a thousand times rather go into a convent and have done with it," she exclaimed.

"A convent—Nona! Not A CONVENT?"

Pauline had got to her feet and stood before her daughter with distress and amazement breaking through every fissure of her paint. "I never heard anything so horrible," she said.

Deeper than all her eclectic religiosity, deeper than her pride in receiving the Cardinal, deeper than the superficial contradictions and accommodations of a conscience grown elastic from too much use, Nona watched, with a faint smile, the old Puritan terror of gliding priests and incense and idolatry rise to the surface of her mother's face. Perhaps that terror was the only solid fibre left in her.

"I sometimes think you want to break my heart, Nona. To tell me this now! . . . Go into a convent . . ." the mother groaned.

The girl let her head drop back among the cushions.

"Oh, but I mean a convent where nobody believes in anything," she said.

Lightning Source UK Ltd.
Milton Keynes UK
23 September 2009

144068UK00001B/175/P